THE ONLY BOY FOR ME

THE ONLY BOY FOR ME

GIL McNEIL

BLOOMSBURY

First published in Great Britain 2001

Copyright © 2001 by Gil McNeil

Bloomsbury Publishing Plc, 38 Soho Square, London W1D 3HB

The moral right of the author has been asserted

A CIP catalogue record for this book
is available from the British Library

ISBN 0 7475 5482 X (hardback)
10 9 8 7 6 5 4 3 2 1

ISBN 0 7475 5698 9 (export paperback)
10 9 8 7 6 5 4 3 2 1

Typeset by Hewer Text Ltd, Edinburgh
Printed by Clays Ltd, St Ives plc

for Dad, Joe and Max, Mum, Julia and Ruth

Chapter One

Notes from a Small Kitchen

M ONDAY MORNING. ALL MY good intentions of making organic porridge and enjoying a serene breakfast go right out the window when I wake up and discover it's ten twenty. I leap out of bed screaming, and bang my foot on the wardrobe. Limp into the kitchen to find it's four am. Charlie must have been playing with my alarm clock. Again. I stagger back to bed, and reset the clock to avoid having a heart attack next time I look at it.

When I wake up again it's seven fifteen, but it still feels like I need eight hours more sleep and my foot is throbbing. A very ugly half-hour follows where Charlie darkly mutters from underneath his duvet that his human rights are being violated and he must be allowed to sleep. I finally get him downstairs, still in his pyjamas, and offer half an hour of cartoons if he eats his breakfast. He agrees, settles down on the sofa and then promptly refuses to eat.

'Darling, stop being silly, you know you have to eat breakfast, and cereal is good for you. It's a school day and you need a proper breakfast.'

'A proper breakfast has bacon in it, or sausage. Why do we never have sausages for breakfast? James has sausages.'

'I'm sure some mornings James just has cereal.'

1

'No he doesn't. He always has sausages. He has them in his lunchbox too. Why can't I have sausages in my lunchbox? I hate turkey sandwiches. I think it's cruel to turkeys.'

'Well, sausages aren't exactly kind to animals, you know.'

'Yes they are. They make them out of old animals who have come to the end of their natural lifes, but turkeys are young and could have babies and everything. But they get chopped up before they get a chance.'

'Look, just get on with it, or I'm going to get really cross.'

'Being horrible isn't nice you know, Mummy.'

'No, and neither is being very annoying in the mornings. Now hurry up, or we'll be late. You need to eat your cereal. Now.'

'I don't need to eat it, I don't want to eat it, it looks like sick.'

Thankfully a diversion is caused by the new postman, Dave, creeping up the drive looking tentative because last week Charlie ran out to greet him wearing only a pair of pants and a Superman cloak. Dave tried to join in the fun, and asked him if he could fly. Whereupon Charlie shot up the tree in the front garden and began his countdown to blast-off, leaving poor Dave to hurl his post on the ground and run around the bottom of the tree with his arms outstretched, looking desperate. It took me ten minutes to get Charlie out of the tree, by which time he was half frozen. I don't know why the postmen round here insist on operating on a first-name basis, but they do. All part of friendly village life, I suppose. Charlie leaps up and down at the window like a manic clockwork toy until Dave is safely back in his van and reversing at speed. He then eats his cereal having forgotten our earlier battle, and only manages to spill about half a gallon of milk on to the living-room carpet.

We are now on the verge of being really late so I forgo the

pleasure of watching him take fifteen minutes to put on a pair of socks and dress him myself.

'I can do it myself, you know.'

'Yes I know, but we're in a rush, darling, and I like helping you.'

'Yes, but don't tuck my vest in so tight; boys don't have their vests tucked in you know.'

'Of course they do, or they would get cold tummies.'

'No, they don't. James never has his vest tucked in.'

I decide, not for the first time, that I hate James, who is constantly quoted as an expert witness in all domestic disputes. Finally we are heading for the car, with bookbag, lunchbox and swimming kit. While I am trying to lock the back door and not drop his lunchbox, Charlie disappears to see the rabbits, Buzz and Woody, in their hutch in the back garden.

'Hello, how are you this morning?' This is greeted with silence, and the sound of lots of scuffling.

'Mummy, the rabbits are doing sex. If they're both boys, does that mean they're gay?'

I can't cope with this line of conversation so early in the morning.

'Of course not, they're just playing.'

Then I panic about sexual stereotypes and add, 'And anyway, it would be fine if they were gay,' whilst firmly grasping the hood of his anorak and pulling him up the path.

Charlie looks horrified.

'No it would not. I want them to have babies; it would be lovely to have baby rabbits. We could start a farm and anyway I don't want gay rabbits, I want proper ones. Get off my hood, you're strangling me!'

I launch into my very realistic impression of the mad

policeman in *Withnail and I*, repeating 'Get in the car, get in the car' in a high-pitched nasal scream.

Our milkman, Ted, picks the perfect moment, as ever, to arrive, block the drive with his float and start wittering on about being late again with a sarcastic grin on his face. I manage to overcome a strong desire to punch him in the mouth, as, apart from the legal implications, getting milk delivered when you live in the country is no joke. His round covers about three hundred miles and he sometimes doesn't arrive until teatime. I shove Charlie into the car, and smile with what I know is a mad fixed grin. Ted sensibly beats a hasty retreat to his float. We then follow him up the lane at three miles an hour, stopping while he delivers to two houses before we get to a part wide enough to pass him. I then accelerate rather more than I meant to, and Charlie is pressed back into his seat by a G force similar to that usually only experienced by fighter pilots. Half thrilled and half terrified, Charlie begins a lecture on road safety.

'If a hedgehog had been crossing the road it would have stood no chance, hedgehogs can't run, you know. You should be more careful.'

'Hedgehogs don't come out in the daytime, darling. Calm down.'

'An ill hedgehog might be awake; it might have had a nightmare and be going for a walk, you just don't know.'

'I do know, and we didn't run over a hedgehog. Look, we're nearly at school now, so everything's fine.'

It's crucial that we don't begin an argument just as we reach the school gates, or getting him out of the car will be a major challenge.

'I promise I'll drive nice and slowly on the way home, and if I find any hedgehogs recovering from nightmares I'll take them home and give them a drink.'

Charlie is not sure, but leans towards being mollified by this until he remembers bloody *Blue Peter* and their dire warnings about never giving milk to hedgehogs or they blow up. He begins a long list of instructions on what I should do with various kinds of wildlife which I might find wandering along the lanes of Kent in need of help. He's just reached pandas and how vital it is to find a fresh supply of bamboo shoots, when he spots that James is just arriving. The wildlife-in-peril lecture is promptly abandoned and they trot off into school together quite happily.

The school building is over two hundred years old, and two of the teachers, including Charlie's Miss Pike, have been there for so long that they taught some of the parents of the current pupils. It's not exactly cutting edge but there's a lovely relaxed atmosphere which counts for a lot when you're six. I do sometimes worry that Charlie is not receiving the broadest of educations: the school's idea of being multi-ethnic is asking the children to bring in leeks for St David's Day. But one of the main reasons I moved out of London was so that Charlie could go to a little village school like I did, instead of the huge local primary that he was destined for. I went on the Parents' Tour and got lost twice. And the strains of living in London were starting to take their toll. The nightly parking battle was getting too much for me, and I was starting to fantasise about leaving work early so I could park in my road rather than six streets away.

After countless weekends of driving round the villages of Kent seeing a succession of dreary bungalows and chucking sweets at Charlie to try to keep him quiet, we ended up in Marhurst, just outside Whitstable. It's a small house, one of four, down a tiny lane just off the village green, with an apple tree in the front garden. It only grows miniature crab apples, but I didn't know that at the time. The village has a shop and a pub, and is only about half an hour away from Mum and Dad. We've got three bedrooms and a huge playroom for Charlie, for well under half what it would have cost in London. We can now go for walks in the woods rather than trudging through parks dodging joggers and mad cyclists. It's not exactly *Cider with Rosie*, but it's as close as you can get to it and still be able to drive to London. I stand watching the children file into their classrooms, hopping and skipping about, and realise, not for the first time, that I truly cannot imagine anything worse than being a teacher of Mixed Infants. Just as I'm getting back into the car I spot James's mother, Kate, who looks as shattered as I am, and we agree to meet later for coffee.

Get home to face a huge pile of ironing, which I ignore, washing-up ditto. I manage to avoid the temptation of collapsing in front of daytime telly by going upstairs to the spare bedroom which I use as my office, and starting on my accounts. I begin fiddling about with spreadsheets, and manage to press some secret command which turns one spreadsheet into four separate ones all in a new jumbled-up order. I cannot get the bloody thing back to normal, so give up in disgust and go downstairs to eat biscuits. Realise I'm now late for coffee, and race off, repeating my earlier stunt by accelerating with great force and nearly flattening the cat from next door.

I arrive at Kate's cottage to find her in wellington boots in the kitchen bailing out the washing machine which has sloshed gallons of water all over the floor. I help her mop up, and she pours two gin and tonics. I'm secretly rather shocked by this, but completely understand when she points out that the washing machine collapsing is the least of her worries. James is sticking to his sausage-only diet, which means she has to buy hugely expensive organic sausages to avoid him having an intake of God knows what in cheap commercial ones. Her daughter Phoebe has gone vegetarian and wants to pierce her tongue, but as she's only eight Kate is refusing. And her ex-husband Phil has stopped paying maintenance because his girlfriend has just had a baby, and she's used all his credit cards to buy designer baby gear so the bank has frozen his account.

Luckily Kate's parents are fabulously wealthy and keep chucking huge sums of money at her. They hated Phil. But, as Kate points out, this only means that her mother keeps reminding her of what a major mistake she made. She's recently taken to holding dinner parties where all her ghastly County friends bring their unmarried sons to introduce to Kate. The last one was so dull she fell asleep during dinner, and her mother was so furious that she woke her up by dripping hot candle wax on her hand whilst pretending to collect up the coffee cups.

'So, how was lunch with your mother yesterday?'

'Absolutely bloody, if you must know. God, she's really getting worse. She spent half an hour banging on at Phoebe about the dangers of being a vegetarian. She told her she'd get rickets and have bandy legs if she didn't eat beef. But when I told James not to flick carrots at the dogs, she told me to leave him alone and stop being such a terrible bully. And then to cap it all my Aunt Marjorie turned up for tea.'

'Oh God.'

'Yes. She had a lovely time, actually, giving me a long lecture on how terrible one-parent families are. Honestly, I nearly hit her. Bloody old bat, but if you defend yourself you end up sounding like a harpy.'

'I know. When we registered at the doctor's the woman on reception threw a total fit because I left the Father's

Details blank on the form. She gave me a long speech about how Doctor might need to know in an emergency. When I asked what kind of emergency would require contacting a man who's never clapped eyes on Charlie, she got really incensed and began a whole new speech about Young Women Today. She was really starting to enjoy herself when that nice one came out from the back, you know, the one with short grey hair and glasses.'

'Oh yes, she's lovely.'

'Well, she said, "What seems to be the problem?" and Mrs Hitler began going into one again. The waiting-room was full of people listening in, having a marvellous time. I was just about to slap her, and claim I thought she was having some sort of fit, when the nice one said, "That's quite enough, Mavis," and then turned to me and said, "I'm so sorry about that, she's just started on the hormones and I don't think they've got the dosage quite right yet."'

'Oh, how brilliant.'

'Yes, it was rather.'

'But you see what I mean. Nobody goes up to women like my Aunt Marjorie and says, "Look, you loathe your husband and all you really care about is money, so don't have kids, just stick with dogs. At least you can put them in kennels when the novelty wears off instead of sending them to boarding school." My cousin George is a complete basket case because of that bloody woman, but nobody would dare tell her she was a selfish old bag who should never have had children in the first place.'

'No, I don't suppose they would.'

'Fackers.' This is a sign Kate is really agitated. She actually means to say 'fuckers', but it just comes out like this. She also says 'super' a great deal, and 'jolly good'. And if you fall down the stairs and slice the top off your head she

8

is quite likely to say, 'Oh, what bad luck.' But despite her disconcerting tendency to lapse into a caricature out of *Horse and Hound*, she's my best friend in the village. We were thrown together when Charlie and James became friends, ferrying them backwards and forwards for tea, and agreeing what our line was on vital questions like bedtime – because if James is allowed to stay up late to watch a special programme, you can bet your life Charlie will insist on the same. But we became real friends when we discovered a mutual passion for fags and gin.

'You think *you've* got problems. At least you married Phil before you had kids. I have to explain how come I've got Charlie, but no divorce, and no hint of a long-standing partner anywhere. Am I a tragic victim of fate like a scullery maid out of a Catherine Cookson novel, or a lesbian who got lucky with the turkey baster?'

'Yes, I suppose so. It's so bloody unfair. You know, I reckon my two would be better off if it *had* been a DIY job. I mean, Charlie seems so settled, he's never seen his dad so he doesn't feel rejected, whereas my two feel like they've been dumped, just like me.'

And with this she starts to cry.

'Oh, Kate, don't. I know it's tough, but you love them and you put up with Phil's crap so they still get to see him. They'll be fine, I know they will.'

'Yes I know. But it's just not fair. It's not their fault but somehow they think it is. It's such hard work, and it never ends. And then you get some old bag telling you you're a monster.'

'I think they're jealous.'

'What?'

'Well, think about it. If you spent your life with some boring old bugger who treats you like a doormat, wouldn't you get a bit narky with women who just miss out on all that and get on with having lovely babies?'

'Well, yes, a bit, I suppose. But what about Roger and Sally? They seem really happy.'

'I know. One day our princes will come. But until then I'm fine, you're fine, the kids are fine, and that's what really matters.'

'God, Annie, you sound like one of those bloody therapy people.'

'OK, try this. Stop whining and make some coffee.'

'OK. Do you want Hobnobs?'

'What a stupid question.'

We drink coffee and eat a whole packet of Hobnobs. I tell Kate about the impact of James and his sausages on my morning, which cheers her up a bit, and soon we're laughing, chain-smoking and planning an evening out soon. We decide on the local pub because at least we can walk home. But we agree to limit our consumption of booze as last time we ended up singing along to the karaoke machine only to discover that the pub doesn't actually have a karaoke machine and it was meant to be background music. We suddenly spot that it's nearly half past one and we both have huge lists of things to do, so I race off to do the shopping, desperately hoping one gin does not count as drunk driving.

I ponder on the usual single-parenting dilemmas during the drive to the supermarket: Will Charlie grow up to be a crack-cocaine dealer due to his tragic lack of a male role model? And what is wrong with me that I don't have a husband lurking somewhere in the background, at least paying child support if not actually playing happy families? How come I managed to end up with Adam, who was so keen on not becoming a father that he chose to emigrate shortly after I discovered I was pregnant? Actually we'd only just got back together again after a five-year gap, during which time he'd married someone else. He turned up out of the blue one night, and said he was getting a divorce. Apparently she was boring, and I was the one he loved. He had huge shoulders and bright-blue eyes. He was also fond of telling long stories which didn't really have endings, but you can't have everything. A few weeks later it turned out that I was the one who was boring, and she was the one he loved. She'd lost two stone and got a new haircut, they had a grand reunion and I lay about weeping.

They were happily settling back into Mr and Mrs Land, when I rang with my thrilling news. He said they'd agreed they weren't having kids, and he didn't want one popping up now, thank you very much. And then he got a new job in Toronto. Facker, as Kate would say. But at least he didn't bugger about pretending to be interested and then never turning up. I truly think I'd stab anybody who did that to Charlie. And once I got over the initial shock of finding myself going solo, it worked out fine. My sister Lizzie was great, and her partner Matt offered to have a crack at the male-role-model thing because I went on about it so much: he even offered to buy an electric drill if I thought it would help. Mum and Dad were pretty thrown by it at first, but ended up being very reassuring, and Mum spent hours knitting. My friend Leila opened a platinum account at Baby Gap, and then the sheer magic and terror of being pregnant took over, and I spent so long worrying that the baby would have flippers, or hate me on sight, that I stopped obsessing about Adam and started obsessing about scans and due dates instead.

I even dragooned my poor sister into coming to NCT classes with me, and they all thought we were a lesbian couple for the first few weeks and nobody would sit next to us. Lizzie thought it was hysterical, and kept putting her arm round me. The newspapers seemed to be full of articles saying that children from single-parent families are doomed; but then I read a brilliant piece which said if you took out poverty as a factor and compared like with like then children from single-parent families actually do slightly better than their two-parent counterparts. That cheered me up for weeks. And at least I earn enough to support us both. Working as a freelance producer in advertising does guarantee me a healthy income, and I can do a lot of work from home, even if it gets a bit frantic at times. God knows how I'd cope trying to live on benefits.

I'm still sporadically haunted by the idea that somewhere out there is a perfect dad for my boy, who would teach him to play football and do things with wood. But so far he doesn't seem bothered. He hates football, and seems perfectly happy with Lego. I've shown him photographs of Adam, but he only glanced at them and then asked if we could watch a *Star Wars* video. I do get really jealous of women with perfect loving partners who cook and can entertain under-fives for hours with horse impressions. But I know that for every one of them there are at least six women whose partners rarely make it home before bedtime, and can be heard at weekends shouting, 'Christ. Can't you get him to stop doing that.' I must try to remember this next time I'm feeling overwhelmed and exhausted. In other words, tonight.

Safeway's is hateful – full of ghastly people going round and round saying, 'That's only forty-three pence in Asda.' Why don't they all bugger off to Asda then and get out of my way? As usual I've forgotten my list so I trot round trying to visualise what is in the fridge and remember what vital bit of bathroom kit we've just run out of. Get home to find we now have seven packs of Flora. But no coffee. I'll have to go to the village shop on the way to school, so I can avoid taking Charlie in on the way home. I can't face entering a heated debate, yet again, as to why holding your finger over the 8 does not mean an 18 video magically turns into a 1, and is therefore suitable for rental.

Arrive at school to find the other parents are ahead of me, yet again, and the line of parked cars stretches almost to the other side of the village. I park and jog back to the school, and I'm still clinging on to the fence trying to breathe normally when the doors open and all the kids rush out trailing their bags. There's no sign of Charlie's class, but then I remember they've gone swimming which means that the coach could arrive at any time during the next hour and a half depending on the mood of the driver. It's pointless to stagger back to the car as I know from bitter experience that just as I sit down the coach will whizz past, and I'll fail to catch up with it in time to stop Charlie getting off and looking bereft when he can't see me. So I stand freezing in the playground with all the other mothers, and a couple of dads.

One of the dads is an Older Father, a regular. He's very genial and on the parish council, so he's made a huge fuss of by all the mothers trying to stop their neighbours getting planning permission to build extensions. The other father is young and not a regular, and is also wearing a suit, so he's left to stand on his own in the furthest corner of the playground. One woman spent half a term stuck there in exquisite clothing, until she switched to jumpers and jeans like the rest of us and was asked to join the zigzag rota. She now stands at the gate longing for some-one to park on the yellow zigzags painted on the road, so she can rush over and stick a rude leaflet under their windscreen wipers.

Where you stand in the playground can be vital. Too close to Mrs Harrison-Black and her gang, and you'll be down on a list to bake a coffee sponge before you know it. And standing in a playground trying to flog slices of your rather flat cake to people who can make much nicer cake themselves, thank you very much, is no fun. I slide into my usual place, skulking by the bushes, with Kate and Sally. Sally, mother of William, who is Difficult, and Rosie, who is Not, points out that Mrs Harrison-Black is lurking by the gate with her clipboard and so we go on red alert.

Mrs Harrison-Black is a large woman, chairman of the PTA, and formidable. She usually wears blouses tucked into pleated skirts with elasticated waists, which make her look like she's sitting on top of a smallish marquee. Her sidekick, Mrs Jenkins, the treasurer, has taken to dressing in a similar manner. They have matching padded waistcoats, and both drive Volvo estates with 'I slow down for horses' stickers in the back window. I've always thought those stickers should actually say 'I slow down for horses but speed up for ramblers', since invariably this is what they do. A determined-looking mother who does cooking with Year 3 (Hell. Grey pizza, burnt fingers and it takes hours to scrape the dough off the floor) is making a beeline for us, and we are madly avoiding making eye contact and trying to think up watertight excuses when the coach miraculously appears.

Today's coach driver is a new one, looks to be about twelve, and is practising his Formula One driving technique. The coach races round the bend on two wheels, and screeches to a halt, catapulting all the children forwards in an extremely dangerous manner which they all naturally

14

adore. Miss Pike manages to stagger off but looks to be in deep shock. She doesn't normally do swimming, but Mrs Oliver, who usually goes with them, is off sick. I suspect the coach driver may have finally finished her off after what must have been a very trying afternoon. The parent helpers then get off the coach looking like they have just had roles as extras in *Titanic*: soaking wet, shivering, pale-faced and traumatised.

The children on the other hand are Lively, and I bet they've been eating sweets on the coach as they all leap off and begin running round and round the playground screaming, and whirling swimming bags above their heads. We parents split up into our usual groupings, identifiable by different parenting techniques. The Come Here Wayne or I'll Hit You division win hands down at getting their children into the car quickly. The Hello Darling Was Swimming Lovely I've Got Something Interesting to Tell You in the Car approach works fairly well, combined with determined eye contact and firm holding of hands, and Kate, Sally and I are off, madly inventing interesting things to talk about. But the dithering approach of Stop That George mixed with attempts to chat to other parents means that a fair number of people are in for a long night.

'So, was swimming lovely, darling?'

'Yes, but Miss Pike said I'm never to go in the deep end again, which is totally not fair as I'm a very good swimmer now and that man should not have got me out.'

'What man, darling?'

'The man who sits on the ladder thing. He put a long pole in the water next to me and told me I had to hold it, but I didn't want to. And then I think he said a swear word, and anyway I did hold it and he pulled me back to the side and said I had to stay in the shallow end until I was a bit bigger.'

'Oh, Charlie, you know you shouldn't go in the deep end. What was Miss Pike doing?'

'Oh, she was helping Laura who'd swallowed a lot of water and was coughing, and Jack Knight's dad took our group swimming and me and James swam off on our own and it was great and then the man stuck the pole in but I was fine. And then Jack's dad said, "Thank Christ," and got me and James and made us go right down the shallow bit and James said he was a sod, but he said it quiet so I don't think he heard.'

'Well, James was being very rude. Jack's dad was quite right to keep you safe.'

'Hmm.'

'Well, he was.'

Oh God, I've just remembered I'm on the swimming rota next week. A tactical error in the playground: I stood too close to Mrs Harrison-Black without back-up, as Kate was late. Probably emergency sausage shopping.

'Anyway, next week I'm coming swimming, so I'll be able to keep an eye on you.'

I can hear distinct sounds of muttering involving swearing, but decide to ignore it as we're nearly home. If we get caught up in an argument now we may have a replay of last week when he refused to get out of the car, and demanded to be driven to the local branch of the NSPCC, because 'Cruelty to children must stop, you know, Mummy'. All because I had suggested we might do homework before television. I was reduced to screaming through the window, 'Yes, but what about cruelty to parents?', and then a woman came round collecting for the Red Cross and gave me a very funny look.

'I'm very starving. What's for tea?'

'You can choose. Tuna, or pasta.'

'Sausages.'

I come up with an inspired plan and make tuna sausages by mixing tuna with mashed potato and squidging the resulting mess into sausage shapes. Covered in grated cheese and grilled for a couple of minutes, they're a huge success. Actually they taste rather revolting, but Charlie eats without complaint. Then we move on to a mad homework sheet on fractions, and I come up with a very clever idea of drawing a cake and then dividing it up into quarters etc. Which really helps until we get to sixteenths and then it all gets rather fraught and I snap my pencil in half. I manage to avoid a huge tantrum on my part when I'm told I should just sit quietly and let him get on with it, because 'To be honest, Mummy, I don't think you really know what you're doing'. I could have told him this for free, almost from the minute he was born. But instead I lie on the sofa sulking, and he finishes off his worksheet without my 'help'.

We embark on the required twenty minutes of reading with his school reading book. There's nothing quite so nice as having your small child read to you, even if it is from the most boring school reading book in the world.

Bathtime goes well, without the usual bathroom flooding. In retrospect, having a submarine and a battleship as bathroom toys was not a good idea: the battles always involve huge tidal waves that threaten to float the bath mat along the corridor. While we're putting on his pyjamas, doing his teeth and generally trying to waste as much time as possible before going to bed, he starts his Random Chatting Routine – always guaranteed to take up at least half an hour.

'I think it's a good idea that the Gherkins get pensions now, Mummy. It was on the news, don't you think it's good?'

'The Gherkins? Who are they, sweetheart?'

I'm frantically trying to imagine why pickles are now getting pensions, whereas I, according to my financial woman, will get nothing if I don't start chucking 150 per cent of my income into a pension starting yesterday, and will have to recycle string and live on cat food.

'You know, those soldiers.'

'I think you might mean Gurkhas.'

'Yes, them. It's good, isn't it?'

'Oh yes, marvellous, darling. You don't need that much toothpaste, you know, it will fall off. You see, just like that. Now that's wasted.'

'No it's not. Look, I've got it back on.' He shoves his toothbrush down the plughole so it bends alarmingly, retrieving a tiny bit of toothpaste. 'And anyway I hate this toothpaste, it's too tingling. James has nice toothpaste.'

'Don't tell me, sausage flavour.'

'Don't be silly, Mummy, his is strawberry.'

'Well, you said the strawberry tasted like sick.'

He ignores this, as he does all contradictory factual evidence.

'If I have a terrible dream tonight, can I come in your bed?'

'Yes, but start off in your own bed.'

'But sometimes I'm so scared I can't get up. Isn't that awful, Mummy, to be so scared you can't get up?'

He pauses for the full horror of this to register.

'It would be much better if I started off in your bed and then I would already be there.' He grins, very pleased with this logic.

'Yes, but then I'd only have four inches of mattress to sleep on, with a tiny bit of duvet. You should start off in your bed and you'll probably have lovely dreams.'

18

'I won't. I'll have horrible dreams and it will be all your fault. Actually I'm starving, Mummy. Can I have a satsuma in bed?'

'No, because last time you sat on it and made a terrible mess.'

I'm shoving him along the corridor now and succeed in getting him into bed, where he instantly transforms into an angelic vision in pyjamas and does his special pleading look, but I manage to stand firm and he eventually agrees to stay in bed if a) I stroke his back for five minutes in circles, not lines because they itch; b) he can have his little light on; c) he can have a satsuma for breakfast, with all the peel taken off and all the white bits; d) if I see a werewolf on the stairs I will smack it sharply on the head.

I check on him again after twenty minutes and he's fast asleep, doing that thing that only small children do where they look like they fell asleep unexpectedly, in the middle of doing something else. His arms and legs are stretched out and he's clutching bits of Lego in one hand and a small dagger in the other. I realise, not for the first time, that however much you love them you always love them that little bit more when they're asleep.

I wake up early the next morning, because Charlie has crept into my bed at some point during the night so I'm freezing cold with a small bottom pressed into my neck. He has taken up the entire duvet, my head is bent into a weird shape, and I'm marooned on the furthest edge of the mattress. It's extraordinary how one small boy can take up so much room, and he could do it even when he was a tiny baby. I know it's useless to try to get back to sleep, so I get up, make some tea, and refill the bird feeder which hangs outside the kitchen window. Then I spend ten minutes watching the birds get hysterical in a bid to eat as much food as possible and still be able to fly. A bit like children's parties, really, but with no jelly.

Breakfast goes very well, the satsuma is a big success, and we set off for school thankfully minus the milkman slowing down progress. Everything is fine until we spot a pheasant wandering in the woods at the side of the road. Pheasants are Charlie's favourite, and we have to stop the car and chat to it or he will descend into a sobbing fit and cling on to the car door when we arrive at school. We've discovered that pheasants run like hell if you try to get near them, but if you stay in the car they obviously feel safe and will peck about quite near. Presumably it's considered bad sport to actually shoot them whilst sitting in your car. I feel very foolish, but Charlie is thrilled, and I am so busy watching him I lose track of time.

Finally the bloody thing moves off into the distance and Charlie agrees we can now drive on – a good job because we are now late. The headmistress, Mrs Taylor, is standing by the gates looking pointedly at her watch as we walk in. Charlie, as usual, makes the whole thing much worse by saying, 'Oh, hello, Mrs Taylor, we've just seen a lovely pheasant so we stopped to have a chat,' which makes her look at me like I'm a complete moron. Which she already suspected, because she still hasn't got over Charlie insisting he will not go to Assembly any more because he is a Pagan. I don't know where he got the idea of pagans from: he insists they did it on *Blue Peter*, but somehow I can't quite imagine this.

I get home to discover the man who does the garden, Bill, has got his pruning shears out and is looking at the trees in the front garden with a smile on his face. This is very bad news. What he's supposed to do is mow the lawns and generally dig things, and stop the weeds reclaiming the garden entirely, for an hour a week for a fiver. Brilliant. What he must not be allowed to do, as various villagers have impressed upon me with great force, is prune anything or the garden will end up like theirs: a curious mixture of traditional English cottage garden meets bonsai. I have to make tea, and generally divert his attention, and then ask him to tidy up the herb garden to avoid him reducing the apple tree to a stump.

He potters off eventually and makes the herb garden look pristine, so we're all happy. The garden is not really that big and I could just about cope with doing it myself. But mowing the grass takes hours in the summer, even though both the lawns are tiny, and last time I tried it I managed to mow over one flip-flop and half the paddling pool so it seems safer to leave it to Bill. I feed the rabbits, and wonder if I should ring the vet and ask if it's OK for them to spend so much time humping each other. Let them out in their run, and the bastard things begin digging a burrow in the middle of the lawn. Bill is outraged by this and has them back in their hutch in thirty seconds flat. It usually takes me at least half an hour to catch them, and I think they rather enjoy diving about and watching me fall into flowerbeds. But they are furious at Bill's more assertive technique, and begin a mammoth sulk in their hutch. I'm longing for Charlie to get bored with them so I can put them in a cab and send them to Rolf Harris or the producers of *Pet Rescue*. It's all their fault anyway, because the endless barrage of pet programmes meant Charlie was desperate to adopt everything from a donkey with three legs to a foul-looking lizard.

He tried to hold out for a St Bernard, or possibly an Irish wolfhound, but I made it clear if he wanted to be dragged through the mud by a large stupid animal he could go horse-riding like everybody else. So rabbits were the easiest solution to the I-Must-Own-A-Pet-Or-I'll-Die crisis. They're very sweet, but make a terrific noise at night leaping about. I keep thinking they're being eaten by foxes and have to rush out into the back garden with a torch. Last week I staggered out into the pitch black clutching a fish slice to ward off predators, only to find them perfectly happy in their hutch, staring at me, and smirking. I feed the goldfish in the pond, who are my kind of pets. A bit of food every now and again, and they're happy. They managed to have babies last summer so there are lots of tiny little fish hurling themselves about. Very sweet. Realise with horror that time is getting on: I need to fix up meetings for next week when I'm in the office, sort out childcare, and there are sausages to buy. I can't really afford to spend half the morning pretending to be Dr Dolittle.

Chapter Two

This Sporting Life

WAKE UP EARLY, AND plan a relaxing day mucking about until I remember I'm on the bloody swimming rota. Charlie wakes up, and is not pleased. He makes me promise not to wear my swimming hat, and then moves on to his new campaign for me to buy more exciting breakfast cereal – preferably a brand which makes the milk go an unusual colour. I ring up Leila for sympathy, but she is having none of it, and says she'd love to go swimming, as it's bound to be much nicer than the day she's going to have: she's got a big pitch for a new account, and the client is famously neurotic and demanding.

Leila is Charlie's godmother, and she's been my best friend for years, ever since we worked together at a huge advertising agency which is thankfully now defunct as it was crap. She takes her godmotherly duties very seriously, and was most put out when I refused to have a proper christening. She wanted to publicly renounce the devil: apparently she'd seen it in a film, and had already bought the perfect hat. She turned up at the hospital when Charlie was born with a beautiful silver spoon from Tiffany's, engraved with the words 'For Charlie'. Apparently Tiffany's were rather anxious about this until she reassured

23

them that it was for a two-day-old baby, and not illegal substances. She's MD of a huge advertising agency, earns bucketloads of money, and is very good at spending it. But she does have to work incredibly hard and is always threatening to quit and go off and live a different life. Her latest fantasy is that she's going to be a crofter on a remote Scottish island. The plan is to buy a few sheep and a spinning wheel, and knit wonderful jumpers. She's started on a scarf, but it's gone a bit triangular.

I wish her luck with her meeting, and she says if the swimming gets too tough I should just go off and have a sauna or a massage or something. I'm not sure she's entirely grasped the range of facilities on offer at the local pool. Perhaps she is thinking of her gym, which has every bit of kit going, a restaurant, a juice bar, and comfy leather armchairs in reception. The reception area of our local pool consists of cracked lino and one metal bench.

Charlie refuses to put on his school uniform and wants to go to school in his pyjamas, but I have a flash of inspiration and divert his attention by suggesting that he might be able to have soup in a flask as part of his packed lunch. He is thrilled with this unexpected news, and spends ages choosing which soup he'd like, and then the trip to school is accomplished in record time, and I'm back home and out in the garden before I know it. Start digging the flowerbed which I plan to turn into a mini vegetable patch so Charlie can grow some carrots. After digging for about five minutes, it gradually dawns on me that the ground is frozen solid so I abandon the spade and poke about in the herb garden for a bit and chat to Buzz and Woody. I'm tempted to let them out for a run, as they are being so amusing, but know this would be a big mistake as it took nearly an hour to get them back in at the weekend, and I don't think missing swimming because I was chasing rabbits round the garden will be deemed an acceptable excuse.

I turn up at school just as lunchtime play is finishing, ready for the afternoon swimming session. The dinner lady is just clocking off, and when I explain I'm going swimming with the children she says, 'Never mind, dear, it will soon be over,' which I don't think is very nice. I've taken the precaution of putting on my swimsuit under my jeans to save time and potential embarrassment in the changing rooms: I had visions of fourteen little girls staring fixedly at my huge bottom. But wearing my swimming costume means that I can't stand up straight without the straps cutting off the circulation in my arms. I've developed a sort of hunchback walk, which Charlie thinks I'm doing on purpose to amuse his classmates. Mrs Oliver is off sick again, so Miss Pike is coming with us. She looks delighted. We get on the coach after a slight delay because this week's driver, who looks about ninety, cannot remember how to open the doors. I just hope he can remember the way to the swimming pool. Miss Pike sits next to me with a plastic bucket. It looks rather ominous, and all my worst fears are confirmed when she explains that someone's always sick on a coach journey, and it's best to be prepared. Lovely.

We eventually arrive at the swimming pool, after going round the same roundabout twice. The driver looks exhausted, and says he'll wait for us on the coach, and have a little nap. The children all swarm off the coach and charge into the changing rooms. A very severe-looking swimming instructor with a crew cut appears, and starts blowing his whistle and marching about like he's in the army. The children ignore all his requests for them to line up, until

Miss Pike claps her hands and asks them nicely, whereupon they line up instantly. The swimming instructor is not pleased. I get to the side of the pool and find two other swimming instructors lurking. The children are divided into Drowners, Slow Drowners and Almost Swimming. Charlie is in the Almosts group, and so Miss Pike puts me with the Drowners: she's obviously learnt from bitter experience that it's hopeless putting parents into the same group as their children. I like being with the Drowners because they go in the baby pool which is about six inches deep, with tepid water. The other parent helper, who's the father of one of Charlie's friends, Tom, is put with the Almosts which means he has to go in the freezing-cold main pool and try to stop them from reaching the diving board.

There are lots of whistles blowing, and a frantic holding of polystyrene floats, and they're all given tips on how to put their faces into the water, and not inhale. This goes quite well with Charlie's group, who all plunge their heads underwater quite cheerfully. But a small girl in my group is having none of it, and becomes hysterical. I'm debating whether I should try to intervene, or slap the swimming instructor who is glaring at her in a most unhelpful way, when Miss Pike marches over and says, 'Now come on, Cecily, if you don't want to do it just say no thank you nicely.'

Cecily stops shrieking, and cheers up. I wish I'd thought of this: the poor thing was obviously frightened out of her wits and I'd done nothing to help. She then astounds us all by saying she'd quite like to have a go, if Miss Pike will hold her hand. Miss Pike kneels down at the side of the pool and holds her hand, and looks like she'll fall in at any moment. Cecily puts her face very close to the water, and gets a spontaneous round of applause from all the other children. I'm almost moved to tears, and realise that, despite the general *Lord of the Flies* motif that surrounds group activities with children, they can actually be very sweet.

This impression soon disappears as the lesson draws to a close, and we have to try to get thirty shivering wet children dressed. An extraordinary amount of time is taken up trying to reunite them with their socks, and I'm sure some of them are not wearing the same clothes that they came in. The girls seem much better at coping than the boys, except for Cecily who cannot get her shoes on and bursts into tears again. I help her, and she gives me a look of undying devotion and whispers that she has sweets in her bag, and will give me one on the coach if I will sit next to her on the journey home. Not sure if I should encourage sweets, but I thank her anyway and promise to sit with her, as Charlie has made it perfectly clear he'd rather die than have me anywhere near him. Although he's ignored me for most of the afternoon, he now decides I may come in useful to do up his shoes.

'Did you see me doing my swimming, Mummy?'

'Yes, darling, you were brilliant.'

'Can we buy chocolate from the machine now, like we did when we came last time?'

'Last time we were on our own, Charlie; today we're with your class and we can't get chocolate for everybody.'

'Cecily has sweets in her bag, you know, Mummy. She always has sweets, and then she's sick.'

Oh marvellous. I hastily renegotiate the seating arrangements, and promise Cecily I will sit with her next time, but I need to sit with Charlie today as I think he might get a bit silly. Luckily this is all too believable and she accepts without a murmur.

The coach driver has fallen asleep, so we have to bang

on the coach doors to try to wake him up. Miss Pike asks me if I know how to resuscitate people. I don't, and neither does she. We knock a bit more quietly, and I get my mobile phone out ready to dial 999 if he starts going blue. But thankfully he wakes up, and once he's found his glasses and remembered how to open the doors we all pile back on. I do feel a bit mean when I notice Tom's dad sitting down next to Cecily, but it's the only spare seat left by the time he gets on the coach. I wonder if I should warn him, but decide that he probably usually relies on his wife to deal with children being sick, so the experience will be good for him.

The journey back to school takes ages, and the children get very silly. Miss Pike has to stand up twice and clap her hands. Tom's dad gets lots of practice with the bucket and a packet of Wet Ones. We finally reach school to find groups of parents waiting in the playground looking slightly anxious. Kate says, 'Christ, you look exhausted,' and then we concentrate on getting our kids into cars and home. Swimming has obviously totally knackered Charlie because we have a lovely relaxed evening sitting by the fire watching telly, and he even does his school reading without a murmur. Bedtime goes well, but at the last minute he bolts for freedom. It turns out it's vital that he checks whether a werewolf has hidden itself under the bed in the spare bedroom.

Unfortunately he finds a long-lost piece of Lego under the bed, a crucial bit which means he can now fix the portcullis back on his Lego castle. Very tricky negotiations follow, and I confiscate the offending piece because if I don't he will be up until midnight.

'I hate you, Mummy.'

'Well, I don't hate you. But it's late, and you've got school tomorrow. What about if we get up early and do Lego before school, and I might make crispy bacon for break-fast?'

There's a long silence while Charlie weighs up the merits of accepting this deal, or continuing to throw a fit in the hope that I will cave in and let him get cracking on the castle. I put on my special determined face, hoping it will sway him. It does.

I wake up late, and so does Charlie who has managed to stay in his own bed all night. I start grilling the bacon and the smoke alarm goes off, as it always does, and I have to bash it with a wooden spoon. The noise is so piercing I'm sure it's caused a crucial blood vessel in my brain to burst as I develop a sharp headache shortly afterwards. The bacon is pronounced crispy enough, and his Lego castle is coming along fairly well, although it's already caused him to exclaim 'bugger' twice, and 'bloody stupid thing' once. I pretend I didn't hear, because both phrases have been picked up from me in previous Lego-building sessions, and we set off for school in fairly good time, although there's a last-minute panic when we realise I've totally forgotten his packed lunch. I make a hasty cheese sandwich, and try not to think of other mothers sending in their children with fresh pasta and small green salads. Charlie discovers a packet of chewing gum in the glove compartment and is in bliss.

'Why is it called a glove box?'

'I don't know, that's just what they're called.'

'That's stupid; they should call it the chewing-gum box.'

'Yes, well, anyway, you've got to finish your chewing gum before we get there, Charlie. You know it's not allowed in school.'

'Why not?'

'Charlie, stop asking silly questions.'

'It's not a silly question. Honestly, Mummy, you are *rude. Oh look, there's James. Stop the car.*'

'I can't park in the middle of the road, Charlie.'

'Why not?'

I manage to park and remind him that he has to finish his chewing gum, and miraculously find a tissue in my coat pocket for him to put it in. But he has a much better idea: he will try to spit it on to the roof of the mobile classroom. He gets so excited arguing about the merits of his plan that he swallows the chewing gum, nearly chokes, and is furious.

'You did that on purpose, Mummy.'

'I didn't do anything at all, Charlie, you did it yourself. Now calm down; look, James is waiting for you.' With this he stamps off across the playground and begins briefing James on my appalling behaviour.

Drive back home and ring up Edna, to arrange for her to come in tomorrow and look after Charlie while I'm at work. Edna lives in the village, on her own since her husband died, although her grown-up son does come to visit her occasionally, usually to ask for a loan. She doesn't like her daughter-in-law, who she refers to as That Woman. With good reason, though, as the woman does sound like a complete cow. Edna is very kind and gentle, and adores Charlie. She also needs the money, since she keeps having to bale out her son. She loves cleaning, and has a passion for bleach and polish and can get a shine on any surface. I have to rush about making sure nothing is too hideously filthy before she arrives.

I agree with her that she'll turn up at seven am tomorrow like she usually does. She says that she wakes up early anyway and likes an early start. Can only hope that one day I'll feel the same. She offers to do the ironing, which is brilliant. I wash the kitchen floor, which is revolting, and then forget and go into the garden and walk back across the wet floor leaving muddy footprints. Great. I'm in the midst of wiping the floor again when Edna rings to ask if I want anything at the shops, as she's just about to go out. I tell her, not for the first time, that I think she should be officially recognised by the Church of England as Saint Edna, Patron Saint of Working Mothers. She is very pleased.

Charlie has games practice today after school, which means I have to lurk about on the freezing playing field trying to be encouraging. Harry Chapman's dad has been 'volunteered' to run these sessions by his wife, who has her sights set on a seat on the PTA committee. They're doing hockey today, and nobody has a clue. Charlie is especially hopeless, but likes the running-about bits and is very keen on using his stick as a submachine gun. Just as I've lost all feeling in my feet, and am thinking about heading back to the car for a five-minute warm-up, there's a hideous scream and Charlie runs towards me wailing, with blood pouring from his nose. Apparently Harry has whacked the ball hard, and much to his surprise it's flown up into the air and managed to clout Charlie sharply on the nose during its descent. It's the only ball Charlie's managed to stop for the entire session.

I gather Charlie in my arms and make soothing noises, and then realise that my newly dry-cleaned mac now looks like it's been involved in some sort of accident at an abattoir. Charlie is distraught and claims Harry did it on purpose, which clearly isn't true as Harry is lurking about at the edge of the field looking close to tears. Finally I manage to get Charlie to accept an apology from Harry, and Harry compliments Charlie on all the blood. Charlie is suddenly transformed into a bloody-but-not-defeated hero, and rushes back to finish the session. All the other boys clap, and Charlie is absolutely thrilled. Eventually it is over and we can go home. I must remember to never let him attempt hockey again, or the dry-cleaning bills will be astronomical.

Charlie is very stroppy all evening, and keeps saying his nose might be broke. He rings up Nana and Grandad to tell them about his hideous sporting injury, and they commiserate. Mum suggests we get an X-ray and I have to spend ages reassuring her that he is exaggerating somewhat, and his nose now looks perfectly normal. My mac, on the other hand, does not. Mum is hugely relieved and says I once did exactly the same thing with a cut on my chin. I'd been playing on the swing in the back garden, and decided to try to get off head first. Apparently I managed to completely ruin her favourite pink angora jumper.

Edna turns up at seven in the morning, but unfortunately I'm still fast asleep. She creeps into my room with a cup of tea, and I nearly have a heart attack. Admittedly she's a bit tiny for a burglar, and they don't usually bring you a cup of tea, but I have an anxious moment before I wake up properly. Edna goes off to make toast, as she insists that I don't leave the house without eating something. I get dressed in about five minutes flat, bash the smoke alarm with the wooden spoon, give Charlie a quick kiss goodbye, and escape to the car before he can think of any vital questions to detain me. Halfway up the motorway I realise that I've forgotten to put on any earrings, and I have one black sock on, and one navy. Bugger. Barney is bound to notice and make sarcastic comments.

The traffic is inexplicably light, and I reach the outskirts of London in record time. I decide to treat myself to a bacon sandwich at my favourite café, run by a nice woman called Maggie in the backstreets of Deptford. I met her when we did a shoot nearby and the catering van didn't turn up. As I walk into the café I notice that the floor is wet, but realise too late to avoid skidding right up to the counter. I manage to avoid falling flat on my face by grabbing hold of the till to steady myself, and we all agree that £1,379.98 is a bit steep for a bacon roll. The café is full of workmen, who all compliment me on my graceful slide. Maggie explains that they've been having a marvellous time watching customers skating up to the counter, and have persuaded her not to dry the floor because it's so entertaining.

I sit down, and two BT workmen come in. One manages a very impressive glide, and the men sitting at a nearby table hold up paper napkins on which they have written 5.9, 5.8 and 6. They start doing a pretend commentary, saying Ivan has managed a triple toe loop with double dismount. The BT men join in the fun and anticipation builds for the next victim to enter the café. It turns out to be the man from the paper shop next door, who scores 5.9,6 and 6. Maggie then says she has got to dry the floor because someone will hurt themselves soon, and we all reluctantly agree that this is probably a good idea. I get back in the car to discover that the traffic has become completely solid while I was in the café, and I get stuck in a terrible traffic jam on the Old Kent Road, which turns out to be caused by two lorry drivers having a fight. Finally make it into Soho and the office, only twenty minutes late.

Jenny, who does reception, seems very happy to see me, and I arrange to have lunch with her and Stef, Barney's PA. This will keep me up to date with the office gossip, and give me the inside track on what Lawrence might be up to. Lawrence is the Executive Producer, and I am the general Dogsbody Producer, who Barney calls in on shoots because he hates having Lawrence. Lawrence is great at all the meetings with agencies, pitching for new jobs and generally crawling to anyone important, but he's crap on shoots because he gets very anxious and fusses around Barney, which usually results in Barney throwing a fit and sending him home. I go into the office once every couple of weeks for meetings, and to generally pay court to Barney. I've worked for him for years, and he's a brilliant director, if rather prone to tempestuous outbursts. But then they all are, and at least Barney gets loads of work and vaguely knows what he's doing, which means I get to work regularly too.

Jenny warns me that Lawrence has been fiddling with my chair again. He keeps adjusting it, ostensibly to fix it. What actually happens is that just when I am least expecting it my chair suddenly descends about three foot, and I end up with my knees up around my chin. Usually I'm holding a cup of coffee at the time. I swap my chair with the one at Lawrence's desk: all the chairs look the same so he won't know until he sits on it for a while. Jenny thinks this is excellent, and Stef moves her computer so she will have a clearer view of Lawrence's desk and can report back as to exactly what happens.

Lawrence arrives, and as usual greets me with an expression of horror and demands to know why I am in, again. He doesn't like anyone getting too close to Barney, and he's on a constant mission to undermine me and get me banished. We're standing in reception waiting for Jenny to sort out the post when Barney sails in. He says, 'Thank God you're in,' which makes Lawrence wince, and then says, 'Great suit, by

the way, but did you know you've got odd socks on?'
Lawrence smirks.

'Yes, Barney, thanks so much for sharing. I got dressed in
the dark so I wouldn't wake Charlie up. Anything else you'd
like to criticise about my appearance, or shall we get on?'

Barney laughs and wanders upstairs to his palatial office
which takes up the entire first floor of the building. I can see
that Lawrence is furious, and can't understand how I can
talk to Barney like this, as every time he tries it Barney ends
up shouting at him. Stef rushes off after Barney, because
he's got a new coffee machine up there and doesn't know
how to work it. If she's not quick coffee is likely to cascade
down the stairs.

Lawrence glares at me, and sits down at his desk. Jenny
brings him a cup of tea, and just as I'm about to go upstairs
the chair does its thing and he ends up with his knees higher
than his head, desperately trying to avoid tipping boiling-
hot tea all over himself. Marvellous. I extend my sympathy
to him, and say that my chair does that too, and maybe they
have a design fault. Marvellous, marvellous. His face is a
wonderful mixture of fury and suspicion.

I go upstairs for my meeting with Barney, and run
through the arrangements for the porridge shoot. The
script is pretty bland, a bit like the product really. A bloke
gets off his fishing boat early in the morning. He walks up
the cobbled streets in a tiny fishing village, opens the door
of his cottage, and then we see him sitting at a table in a
tiny kitchen eating a bowl of porridge with a beatific smile
on his face. Barney says it's the most pathetic idea he's
come across in ages, but he may be able to turn it into
something worth watching. I have a horrible feeling this
will involve something tricky with boats, but am trying not
to think about it.

Lawrence keeps coming upstairs and loitering, hoping Barney will ask him to join the meeting. In the end he irritates Barney so much he asks him to fetch us both a cup of tea, which goes down really well. I don't risk actually drinking the tea when he brings it, because he's probably put bleach in it. I spend the rest of the morning wrestling with the computer and budget sheets, and praying that Lawrence's chair will collapse again because Stef missed it and is furious. Then we have lunch, and I catch up on the latest gossip, and all the annoying things Lawrence has done in the last couple of weeks. Apparently he told Barney Jenny had forgotten to give him a vital message, when she had told him twice, and he tried to get Stef into trouble over a missing script which it turned out he'd taken home. And he bought himself a new pair of black velvet trousers last week, and Barney asked him to roll about on the Persian rug in his office because the cleaner never vacuums it properly, and the velvet would be an excellent way of picking up all the fluff. We all agree that we adore Barney. Stef then points out that Barney threw a complete fit last week because his astronomically expensive new Italian desklight did not look quite how he thought it would when he put it on his desk. We all agree he can be a tad annoying sometimes, but at least he has charm, some of the time, and is a bloody good director. Unlike Lawrence who has no charm whatsoever, and is crap in a real crisis, which is what being a proper producer is all about.

The rest of the day is taken up with making hundreds of phone calls to check on the availability of crew, and sending tons of emails. I also spend ages wandering around the West End buying a variety of white china porridge bowls and milk jugs, because Barney wants a choice – and when he says get a selection he means at least twenty. When I get back to the office I start haggling over the budget sheets with Lawrence. Barney wanders over and says, 'What the hell are you two arguing about now?' and Lawrence says I'm demanding a totally unreasonable amount of equipment, and the budget won't cover it. As he finishes he realises he's made a huge tactical error. Barney launches into a passionate speech, the gist of which is that He decides what kit he needs on his jobs, and if I've said we need something it's because we bloody well do. If Lawrence thinks he knows better he can fucking do the fucking film himself. Or better still he can get a job at a production company which does crap jobs for no money, and see how many awards he ends up with on the office walls.

The crack about the awards is a bit of a sore point, because Barney wins quite a few and Lawrence decided they would look impressive hung up in reception. Barney said this looked pathetic and made him take them all down again and put them on a back wall. He told Lawrence he wouldn't know subtle if it punched him on the nose. Barney storms off upstairs, and we all creep about until he's calmed down. Lawrence is furious with me, and keeps glaring. I glare back. I go upstairs to say goodnight to Barney, and find him perfectly happy, lying on the sofa watching telly. He waves goodbye, but doesn't take his eyes off the screen.

Get home to discover that Charlie is asleep, and Edna says he dropped off like a little lamb. I point out that he never does lamb impressions when he's with me. Collapse into bed exhausted, and wake up what seems like minutes later at seven am, freezing cold, to find Charlie curled up inside the duvet, snoring loudly. He surfaces and announces that he forgot to mention it before, but he has to make a model of a Viking ship, with oars, to take into school this morning. I tell him he must be joking, but he says he's not, and gets very agitated. We do the best we can with a Shreddies box, felt pens and long wooden barbecue sticks, and make a sail out of a piece of old tea towel. It ends up looking quite good, but I could have done without this kind of challenge first thing in the morning.

Miss Pike is thrilled, and says the homework was actually supposed to be *thinking* about how to make a model of a Viking ship. But this one is lovely and can go on the art table. Charlie is very pleased with himself. Must remember to check with Kate next time, before any last-minute model making. I get home and decide to continue the arts and crafts theme for today and paint the old bathroom chair bright yellow with the leftover paint from my bedroom. It looks very nice, and I'm inspired to have a go at the tiles in the bathroom, which are a hideous green colour. Sponge away madly all over the tiles, and have to restrain myself from starting on the walls.

I go upstairs to work in my office for a bit, and confirm with Edna that she will turn up early again tomorrow, so I can drive up to the studio for the porridge shoot. Then I rush off for my aromatherapy massage, with a woman in the next village who Kate recommended. The massage is wonderful, although I'm not keen on the music she plays – lots of flutes, and the sounds of whales apparently having some sort of emotional crisis. I'm not sure that whales are a useful image to conjure up in people's minds when they are lying draped in towels, wearing only their pants.

The aromatherapist says I have very tense shoulders, and must relax more. I think this is very good advice, and if she'd like to collect Charlie from school and cook his supper I feel sure I'd get much closer to total calm. She gives me a little bottle of the massage oil and recommends I put it in my bath tonight, and she also gives me a small bottle of mineral water, stressing that it's vital to rehydrate. I promise to do as she says and nearly drive into a hedge on the way home: I'm dutifully rehydrating by taking giant swigs from the bottle of water, with one hand on the steering wheel, when a car suddenly appears out of nowhere in the middle of the road. A Volvo, naturally. The driver is an ancient old man who can barely see over the steering wheel, and appears to be balanced on a pile of cushions. He waves cheerfully as he drives past, and I wave back. Unfortunately the hand I wave with is also holding the bottle of water, so the entire car is soaked and my trousers now look like I've had a very unpleasant accident.

I do feel more serene than usual, though, once I've changed my trousers, and decide to see if it'll work on Charlie, who says he is not tired, refuses to have a bath, and wants to stay up and play Snap. I hate Snap. Think it would be a much better game if it was called Slap. I massage his legs, which he thinks is lovely, and he begs to have his back done. Put a towel on my bed and he lies on it. I start doing his back, he falls asleep, and so do I. Wake up at ten to find the last bit of oil has dripped out of the bottle and seems to have soaked the entire duvet. I check the answerphone and there are six messages, all of which are about work tomorrow. Decide to have a bath.

The water is boiling, and the room fills with steam. Gingerly sit down and lie back ready for a nice long soak. I'm admiring the newly painted tiles when I realise that the new paint is slowly sliding down and collecting in yellow puddles on the edge of the bath. It then starts dribbling down into the bathwater. Leap out, and start frantically wiping up paint. Two flannels later I realise I need a proper cloth, go into the kitchen to get one and leave footprints all over the carpet. A hideous half-hour follows, involving paint stripper, rubber gloves, carpet cleaner, and lots of swearing. The bath is finally restored to its usual colour, but I need nail-varnish remover to get the paint stains off my feet, and the bottle is almost empty. The soles of my feet remain pale yellow. I will never paint tiles again. Ever.

Collapse into bed in a wildly agitated state, and wake up what seems like moments later to hear Edna arriving. I creep about getting dressed and manage to leave before Charlie stirs. I arrive at the studio early, to supervise the final touches to the kitchen set which was built yesterday. The builders are bound to have hit some unexpected snag which will need sorting out before we can start setting up the lights. Barney is due to tip up mid-morning and will be furious if things are not ready. The set looks fine, apart from one cupboard which they've put in totally the wrong place. I have a frank exchange of views with the builders and refuse to pay any extra for them to put the cupboard where they were supposed to put it originally. They finally wander off muttering, but fix the cupboard into the correct position, and then the lighting man starts faffing about. The actor turns up and confesses that he actually hates porridge – it makes him want to vomit, and he hopes he won't have to eat any. Think he might have mentioned this at the casting, as the whole of today's shoot centres around him sitting down at the table eating a delicious bowl of hot porridge. Of course he doesn't actually have to eat bowls of the stuff, but it's not going to be easy if he heaves at the sight of it.

The crew turn up, and start larking about until Barney arrives. Barney, as usual, spends ages fussing around the set and then gets obsessed with the milk jug, rejecting his earlier choice. I knew he'd do this, and feel very smug about bringing all the other alternatives even though he said this was a waste of time. My smugness quickly vanishes when he declares they're all crap, and a fisherman would not have a white china milk jug anyway, any idiot can see that. I'm just about to stick someone in a cab and send them to Heal's to get a whole new selection, and am trying to get Barney to share his vision of a fisherman-type milk jug with me, when he spots an old chipped blue stripy jug on a tray with mugs of coffee which the studio has provided. Barney says it's perfect, thank Christ, and peace is restored.

During the jug crisis the crew have got increasingly bored, and by the time we're ready to start it's nearly lunchtime, and they're all whining that they're starving. When I point this out to Barney, he tells me to shut up. The crew increase their moaning. This is tricky because if I don't act quickly they'll really start acting up, just like toddlers do when they're over-tired and end up biting you at unexpected moments. I ask Barney if he's sure he's not hungry, after all the hard work he's done this morning, and luckily he misses the sarcasm and agrees to stop for lunch. The crew cheer up enormously except for the electrician, Dave, who can't find his cigarettes because Kevin has hidden them. I sort this out by threatening to slap Kevin if he doesn't behave. This is a mistake, because half the crew then launch off into favourite S&M fantasies and beg to be slapped.

Barney is oblivious to all this, and suddenly announces he would quite like to get some work done, if everybody could stop buggering about. The crew swiftly finish eating and snap into action, and content themselves with occasionally sniggering and calling me Miss Whiplash. The client doesn't turn up, which is a blessing, and the actor manages not to vomit, but only just. We end up putting brandy into the porridge, to stop him heaving. This works rather well, but thankfully we're finished before he gets totally plastered and his eyes go glassy. We have a tea break, and then move on to doing hundreds of pack-shots, and shots of bowls of porridge, which bore Barney completely so he keeps wandering off.

We break again for supper, and then we aim to finish the pack-shots before hitting the magic hour, midnight, when we have to pay the crew double time. The crew try to slow things down as much as possible, as they are very keen on 'double bubble'. But I'm wise to their tricks, and so is Barney. Finally we get enough pack-shots to satisfy even the most picky client, and the crew start disappearing pretty sharpish. Barney says he'll ring me tomorrow and will see me next week in the office so we can plan the shoot in Cornwall, where we are doing the tricky bits. I can't wait – the combination of boats, British weather and an actor who doesn't like porridge is bound to be great fun.

I get home to find Edna half asleep by the fire. She says Charlie was a little lamb again tonight, and she has signed his sponsorship form for his sponsored walk, bless him, but don't I think five miles is a long way? I think it's a bloody long way. I know nothing about a sponsored walk, and ring Kate in the morning, who says the walk is scheduled for this weekend, and is being organised by the PTA so attendance is pretty much compulsory. Apparently Miss Pike forgot to give out the forms earlier. We are to meet at eleven am outside the pub, and bring wellies and waterproofs. Brilliant.

Saturday morning, and we are gathered outside the pub in wellies and anoraks, carrying rucksacks full of food for our epic journey. Mrs Harrison-Black comes over and says she's so pleased everyone has made such an effort, and we aren't to worry if we can't finish the whole course, just do as much as we can. Roger whispers that he thinks this is a bloody cheek, and with a bottom like hers she's in no position to give other people lectures about fitness. Sally says she has brought brandy in a flask in case Roger collapses. Roger says if all he's going to get is sarcasm then he might as well have stayed at home and read the papers.

They always bicker like this, but it's affectionate bickering rather than that hideous I-really-wish-you-were-dead stuff that other couples seem to go in for. They met at university, and have been together ever since. They never have serious arguments, have never 'gone through a bad patch', and never had second thoughts. Enough to make you hate them really. Roger is a solicitor with a local firm, but he doesn't make much money because he's always helping people out and not charging them properly. Sally teaches part-time at the local secondary school, and is constantly exhausted. The combination of looking after William and Rosie and teaching A-level history to stroppy teenagers is not an easy one. Kate and I have told her that if she tells us one more story about dysfunctional teenagers we won't stand next to her in the playground any more. As Kate says, we would rather not know. Then when James and Charlie dye their hair blue and insist on speaking in a new dialect based on how drug dealers talk in Detroit, it'll be a nice surprise.

People start moving off, clutching their route maps. Some of them are Very Keen. Whole families have appeared in matching tracksuits, and appear to have enough kit to climb Everest.

'Good God, look at that man, the one who just ran past. He's got one of those watch things on; you know, those things that count your pulse and beep when you're going to have a heart attack.'

43

'Roger, dear, I think you'll find that's to measure his pace.'

'Oh, so that's what a pacemaker looks like. I thought you had to have them sewn into your chest, not wear them like a watch. Oh, I might get one now I know how jazzy they look.'

'Do shut up, Roger.'

'But really, look at him, jogging all over the place. What an utter prat, on a school sponsored walk. Honestly.'

We all agree, especially as Pacemaker Man keeps yelling at his two little boys to keep up. They look very miserable.

'When are we going to stop for lunch?'

As we have barely got out of the pub car park, I have to explain to Charlie that we'll have to go a bit further. This is greeted with howls of outrage. Kate opens a packet of wine gums as a diversion, and peace is restored. James, Charlie and William announce that the wine gums have made them drunk, and start doing silly walks. The gap between us and the rest of the group is growing steadily, and the really keen types who set off at a brisk trot are now tiny dots on the horizon. The route veers off into the woods. Things get increasingly muddy. This is going to be a very long day.

The boys now have so much mud on their wellies they can barely lift their feet up, and we have to keep stopping to help them wipe it off. The children start to whine, and then move into advanced whining mode. Roger starts a game of I Spy, and cheats shamelessly, claiming to have seen a tiger, and a Red Indian. The children almost believe him, and keep peering into the trees. We decide to stop for a rest, but the ground is far too wet to sit on so we balance on fallen tree trunks, and drink coffee while the children eat. We all have swigs from Sally's flask, and agree that really the countryside is very beautiful. Roger slips off his tree trunk

44

and sits in a muddy puddle, and the children think this is the most hysterically funny thing they have ever seen. Ever. Luckily Roger is not the sort to go off in a huff when being laughed at by five children and three women. A very rare man indeed.

He informs us that even his pants are wet, which sets us all off again. Sally finally stops laughing, and gives him a kiss. The children think this is revolting, and make noises as if they're being sick. Kate and I exchange envious glances. We set off again, much happier, and emerge into open countryside. We pass one of the matching-tracksuit families, in the midst of a blazing row. The parents are arguing very loudly about whose fault it is that they forgot to bring their flask of coffee, and the children are arguing about whose turn it is to carry the map. One of the children has clearly fallen head first into a puddle, and is covered in mud from head to foot. We are now almost in sight of the main group, and pass another family where all is not well.

William says maybe it will turn out like the tortoise and the hare and we will actually be the winners. We all say how clever of him to have thought of this, but the chances of us actually winning are slight as some of the jogging tracksuit brigade have probably already finished, and are back home having cold showers. I give William a mini Mars bar as a reward for such positive thinking, and Charlie sulks.

Then it begins to rain. Hideous nightmare half-hour follows where nearly everyone is on the brink of tears and tantrums, and we run out of sweets. I find a packet of Polos in the bottom of my bag, but sadly no four-by-four off-road vehicle which is what we really need. Still, the Polos work wonders for a while. William says that the dentist told him Polos are the worst sweets in the world, and he's not allowed to have them now. James and Charlie look at him like he is an orphan from a war zone, rather than a child with parents who have a firm policy on sugar. Roger says he once bit his dentist when he was a small boy, and the children all look at him with admiration. Roger hastily launches into a long explanation about how it was years ago, and dentists are lovely now and give you stickers. The children look unconvinced. Sally says Roger can take William to the dentist next time. I wonder if they have stickers that say 'I bit the dentist today' as well as the usual ones about Tommy Toothbrush.

The rain continues and we trudge on. The route is now taking us back along the road at the other side of the village, and the end is in sight. We finally reach the finishing point, and Mrs Harrison-Black says, 'Oh, thank God, we were just about to send out a search party for you. Ha-ha.' Kate fixes her with one of her special withering looks. Apparently she learnt how to do it at Finishing School. I can't believe she actually went to a finishing school, but she says it was her mother's idea and as it meant she got six months in Switzerland to flirt with ski instructors she agreed to go. It obviously paid off because she's very good at withering, and even Mrs Harrison-Black takes a step backwards. The children suddenly discover reserves of untapped energy, and run around saying hello to all their friends. I invite Kate and Sally and Roger to supper, and say I'll make pizzas. Kate says she'll rent a couple of videos and Sally and Roger offer to bring the wine. The children all get madly excited and Charlie wants balloons so it will be a proper party.

The pizzas are a huge success, and the boys disappear upstairs to Charlie's room to play with Lego. We keep hearing sounds of muffled crashing, and the mess in Charlie's room is phenomenal, but I try not to think about it. Phoebe and Rosie watch *Little Women* on video, and adore it. As do we all, except for Roger who keeps snorting at the more saccharine moments, and says the film should really be called *Boring Women* and when will there be a gunfight?

The film finishes and everyone starts to leave. William throws a fit and clings on to the sofa sobbing that he doesn't want to go home. I finally bribe him to go by lending him a cowboy hat, and a bow and arrow, which Charlie reluctantly agrees to part with, but only if he looks after them. William solemnly promises he will, and they all pile into the car and William waves his hat out of the window as they drive off down the lane. James then bursts into tears and says he doesn't want to go home either, and he wanted to borrow the cowboy hat. Phoebe says he's being a stupid baby, and James kicks her. Kate frogmarches them to the car, and Charlie hops up and down saying Phoebe is the most horrible girl in the world and deserved to be kicked. I tell him to shut up, and he tells me I am very rude. Could get a great deal ruder, but decide instead to ignore all his protests and get him into pyjamas and into bed before he has time to think of any diversionary tactics.

'Mummy.'

'Yes.'

'Can we go on another walk tomorrow?'

'No.'

'Can we have pizza then?'

'No.'

'I hate you, Mummy.'

'Goodnight, Charlie.'

He's asleep almost as soon as his head hits the pillow. I creep out of the room because the floor is covered with a layer of small pieces of Lego. There is even Lego in the bathroom sink. Perhaps I'll be able to throw some of it away tomorrow when he's not looking. On that happy thought I collapse into bed, and have complicated dreams about sponsored walks through porridge, with Barney shouting at us all to hurry up, because the light is going. I hope this is not an omen for the shoot next week.

Chapter Three

Sex and Drugs and Sausage Rolls

A PPARENTLY A LOCAL POLICEMAN visited school today and gave a drugs talk in assembly. Charlie has clearly been most impressed by this, and is sitting in the bath giving me a lecture.

'Mummy, I'm going to say no to drugs, and you must too.'

'Of course I will, Charlie.'

Though right now I'd say a very definite yes to a large gin and tonic.

'Good, and if anyone offers you extra tea you must say no.'

'What do you mean, extra tea, darling? Tea is alright, isn't it?'

Christ, I'm not even going to be allowed to drink tea now, without lectures from Charlie on the evils of drugs.

'You know, Mummy, extra tea, it's a drug and the policeman said it looks like a sweet sometimes. Isn't that awful – you might think it was a nice sweet and it would be a drug. So you must never take sweets from strangers either, Mummy, because it could be extra tea.'

'I think you mean Ecstasy, darling, not extra tea.'

'How do you know, has someone tried to give you some?'

Charlie narrows his eyes and looks at me very hard, scanning my face for signs of drug abuse.

'No, of course not, but I saw it on the news and it's definitely called Ecstasy.'

'Well, if anyone tries to give you some you must say no and tell a ponsible adult, like Miss Pike. Who will you tell, Mummy, because Miss Pike is not at your work, is she?'

No, thank God. I have visions of her trying to get everyone to sit nicely, and Barney telling her to fuck off.

'The word is responsible, Charlie, not ponsible. And I *am* a responsible adult, so I won't need to tell anyone.'

Charlie does not look convinced that I qualify as a responsible adult, so to avoid an ugly scene I change the subject.

'Anyway, darling, it's great that you listened so well and know all about drugs. Did the policeman say anything else?'

'Oh yes, loads. He told us all about stranger danger, and if you see a stranger you're allowed to do anything to them and then run away. Even biting.'

He pauses for the full marvellousness of this to sink in. I can tell he's thrilled at the prospect of biting the first stranger he meets. I must act now to avoid the possibility of legal action in the not-too-distant future.

'Biting is not allowed, Charlie, not unless you're really sure you're in danger, not just because you don't know someone. You can shout and kick and run away far better than hanging about trying to bite somebody. And anyway it's very rare that anything ever happens with strangers, so don't worry too much about it.'

I hope this is the right line to take; I hate these kind of conversations and know sooner or later I will have a vivid nightmare where Charlie is being dragged off by nutters and it's all my fault because I told him not to bite them.

Charlie meanwhile sits calmly in the bath singing rude songs of his own devising. We wash his hair, and he claims I am trying to drown him. I must book a hairdresser's appointment soon: his hair is getting so long he can barely see out from under his fringe. I did try to cut it myself once, but lots of little tufts sprang up out of nowhere and he ended up looking like he'd had a rather major electrical shock.

I finally get him into bed and am tucking him in, when he sits up and I can tell from the look on his face that he has important news to share.

'Mummy, you know sausage rolls?'

'Yes.'

'Well, James had them for his packed lunch, and he let me have a little bit and it was brilliant, though I didn't get much sausage because James was saving it. Can I have sausage rolls tomorrow?'

'Not tomorrow, darling, I won't have time to go to the shops.'

'We could go to the shops before school.'

I have a strong suspicion that this is a ploy to try out his new police-approved biting technique.

'No we can't, I've got to go to work tomorrow and Edna's coming. But I'll get some tomorrow while you're at school.'

'Alright, but get proper big ones not the little tiny ones, because they're no good. I'm really hungry now, Mummy. Can I have a snack?'

'No, it's bedtime. Now stop chatting and settle down, it's sleep time. Sweet dreams, darling.' I back out of the doorway swiftly before he can think of anything else to say.

I go up to check on him half an hour later, expecting to find a sleeping child. Instead I'm greeted as I open the door with a red-faced Charlie saying furiously, 'Go away, Mummy, I'm having a waggle.'

I'm not quite sure how to react to this. I've been adamant that playing with your willy is fine in private, but not in Marks and Spencer's, however long the queue. But somehow it feels deeply dodgy to have interrupted him. I have visions of family therapy at some point in the future, where I'm accused of hampering his psycho-sexual development. I decide it might be best to simply ignore it.

'I just wanted to say goodnight. You should be asleep really, you know.'

'That's OK, Mummy. I love my willy. I bet you wish you had one.'

Apart from late on Saturday night when the gin and chocolate supplies have run out, I can honestly say I never have, but naturally do not share this information with Charlie.

'No, darling, I like what I've got.'

I know this is a pathetic euphemistic defence of female sexuality, but I'm too tired for anything more robust.

'Well, I think willies are much better. You know, if you have a hole in the front of your pyjamas you can poke your willy right out. You can't do that with your bottom, can you, Mummy?'

Not unless I am very drunk, no. But I can't let this slur go unanswered.

'No, I can't. But you wouldn't have been born if everyone had willies, so both sorts are good. I love my bottom and you love yours, so that's great. Now go to sleep, you've got school tomorrow.'

Please God he does not share this conversation with Miss Pike.

I go back downstairs feeling shattered, and make a cup of

tea. I'm halfway through it when Leila rings. She thinks it's all terribly funny, and vows to adopt waggling as her new word for the week. The conversation moves on to other favourite euphemisms and we end up nearly hysterical. Our favourites are tinkle and hampton. We both think they'd make very jolly names for characters in a children's series. We finally get round to what she rang for, which is to fix up a visit at the weekend as she thinks it's too long since she last saw Charlie. The lovely prospect of a day with Leila is only slightly marred by the fact that she tends to ask what time Charlie goes to bed about half an hour after she arrives. She adores him, but her boredom threshold for child-centred activity is very low, in common with most of my friends who don't have kids. Last time she came down she got involved in a Lego-building session which nearly sent her into a coma. Also she usually wears some item of exquisite clothing that Charlie manages to stain permanently. I make her promise to wear something washable and arrange for her to come down on Sunday. I also confirm we're meeting for supper tomorrow night, for some Charlie-free gossip time. If the weather is nice on Sunday we can go to the beach and Charlie can run about getting soaked. I can't wait.

Edna is due at the crack of dawn tomorrow, so I set the alarm clock extra early so I can get up and clean the kitchen before she arrives. I wake full of good intentions, but end up standing in the kitchen watching the birds building a nest in the hedge opposite the window. I'm tempted to put some kitchen paper out for them to make duvets with, but suspect they prefer the twigs and straw from the field next door. I do manage to remember to spray Jif cleaner all over the kitchen surfaces, which suggests a recent cleaning spree. And even through I know this won't fool Edna for long, it makes me feel better. I'm dressed and ready to go by seven thirty, when Charlie belts downstairs and starts telling me all about his dream about Egyptians. Smiling vaguely, I try to steer the conversation away from pyramids and then Edna diverts his attention by offering to cut up fruit and take all the peel off for breakfast. Charlie is thrilled because I usually refuse this kind of fiddly task. We all troop into the kitchen and Charlie does a dance while listing all the different kinds of fruit he's going to eat. He finally decides on pineapples and strawberries, and I beat a hasty retreat to the car before he discovers that we only have apples and a mouldy old orange.

The motorway is a nightmare: a lethal mixture of lorries, heavy rain and lots of people clearly desperate to get into hospital as quickly as possible by crashing their cars into the central reservation. I find myself stuck behind an old git in a Mini Metro doing fifty miles an hour in the middle lane trying to overtake lorries but failing dismally. Each time I try to get into the outside lane some bastard in a BMW speeds up and refuses to allow me to move out. It feels like I will be stuck like this for ever. Eventually I lose my temper and accelerate so I'm almost inside the exhaust pipe of the old git and then I move sharply into the outside lane without giving the BMW driver time to speed up and block my way. He is furious and starts flashing his lights at me. I retaliate with my new favourite trick, which Barney taught me. I switch on the rear fog lights which light up the back of the car in a major way, suggesting I'm about to make some sort of emergency stop.

It's very stupid of me to get drawn into such ridiculous behaviour, but most gratifying to see that it works, and the BMW driver brakes and pulls back. He's obviously decided I'm mad, and I proceed to confirm his conclusion by moving back into the middle lane once I'm safely past the old git in the Metro. The BMW instantly speeds up to pass me but he can't resist slowing down when he's level with my car to give me a threatening look, whereupon I give him a one-finger salute while keeping my eyes firmly on the road. I've got purple nail varnish on, which I think adds a touch of style to hand gestures. I know, without looking, that he is distraught. Brilliant.

I finally make it to Soho and the car park, only to discover that the few remaining spaces are on the roof, up a hideous wobbly metal ramp which shakes as you drive on it. An idiot in a Range Rover gets halfway up and then loses his nerve and reverses back down, causing havoc as two cars are behind him. What is the point of designing cars with four-wheel drive and the ability to climb cliffs if they sell them to idiots who can't park them? All the car parks in Soho are awful, but the train costs a fortune, takes hours, and there are only two choices home at night: five pm or five fifteen pm. After that you have to go via Aberdeen. So I'm stuck with the car. I manage to drive up the wobbly ramp and park, and make it into the office with just enough time to realise I have left a crucial folder in the car, but no time to go back and get it. Perfect.

Barney is already sitting in the meeting room looking thunderous. It turns out he came in early and tried to make a cup of coffee with his new machine, and managed to scald his thumb with boiling-hot water by pressing the wrong button at the wrong moment. Stef warns me that he's behaving as if amputation might be the only way forward, and has told her to bugger off, twice, and take that bloody machine with her. I make a huge fuss of his thumb, which has a tiny red mark on it, and produce one of Charlie's dinosaur sticking plasters from my handbag and offer to stick it on, to 'keep the wound clean'. He is almost tempted, but finally recovers himself and tells me to sod off. I find some Savlon in the office first-aid kit, and insist on smearing his thumb with about half the tube. Barney is delighted, and cheers up hugely now he has had ointment and a proper fuss made of him. Just like Charlie, really, but with less screaming and slightly more swearing.

We're talking about plans for the shoot in Cornwall next week, when Lawrence bustles in. He hates not being in meetings, and says do we need him? The honest answer would be no, but Barney can't resist the temptation of telling him all about his dreadful injury. Lawrence says oh he knows all about scalds, he burnt his whole hand once on a kettle and it was agony. Barney looks at him with utter contempt, and asks him where on earth did he get those trousers. Lawrence is wearing brown leather trousers today – a serious mistake not least because the sofas in the meeting room are also leather, so comic sound effects are produced every couple of minutes, much to his embarrassment and Barney's delight.

The accountant, Ron, turns up and he and Barney go upstairs. Barney has clearly forgotten telling Stef to bugger off, and asks her if she would make them some tea. Peace is restored, and we all get on with some work. I then have a tedious meeting with Ron trying to explain Barney's expenses from the last couple of shoots. As Barney's filing system consists of stuffing receipts in his pocket and occasionally chucking them all in a drawer, this takes some time. We discover receipts for all sorts of things I have no memory of, and have to be very creative. Finally Ron agrees to let me go, but says he may have to call me on a couple of things in the next day or two. Lovely.

The list of messages on my desk makes me feel faint, so I

go out and eat cake and drink so much black coffee that I have a major caffeine rush and wonder if I'm having a heart attack. I suddenly remember sausage rolls for Charlie's lunch tomorrow and try all the smart patisseries on Old Compton Street, but they look at me like I'm mad and can only offer spinach quiche. Finally I have to trudge to M&S in Oxford Street, and buy two packets of large sausage rolls as instructed. I do not allow myself to even consider buying anything else or I'll be there for hours trying to visualise what's in the fridge. The woman on the till looks at me with pity, obviously assuming I'm having some sort of food crisis and am about to eat eight jumbo sausage rolls for lunch. I get back to the office to find the list of messages has grown even longer, but I rally and manage to make a huge number of calls and confirm most of the crew before I realise it's nearly six and I haven't called home.

Edna is fine, but Charlie is not. He hated the pizza Edna made for supper, and wants to know if he can stay up late to watch *Buffy the Vampire Slayer*, which will give him nightmares. Complicated negotiations follow, which eventually result in him agreeing to go to bed at the usual time if he can watch a video of *Buffy* tomorrow night with me, which means I can distract him by tickling him during especially scary moments. This annoys him intensely, but it does mean he won't wake up screaming in the middle of the night. Edna doesn't know how to use the video – in fact I've only just persuaded her that using the microwave won't affect her perm. So I have to go through a long instruction process which I know will result in her taping the world bowls final.

I'm meeting Leila in a trendy new club for an early supper. I arrive late, as usual, and she's sitting by the bar looking wonderful in a new suit, which must have cost a fortune. It did, but it makes her look fabulous, so, as she quite rightly says, it's really a bargain. The place is full of skeletally thin young women who appear to have come out in their underwear and very little else. Lots of lacy slips, very high shoes and tiny little cardigans. Floral is back in, apparently, but only in acid colours. And only if you are a size eight. Otherwise long black jackets are still popular. I feel about eighty, and don't think my long black jacket is long enough. But will this stop me having pudding? Not a chance.

I'm not drinking as I'll be driving later, but Leila is making serious inroads into a bottle of champagne and is on top form. There are loads of advertising types milling about, so we do lots of useful but exhausting networking. I'm reminded yet again that my ability to remember people's names is less developed than it should be. Leila remembers everyone, including the names of their children and pets. I can barely recall the name of a really nice woman I worked with last year – and we spent all night bonding in the hotel bar listing all the things we hated about directors, men in general, our thighs, and hairdressers who cut your hair too short.

Finally we move to our table, and a very complicated ordering process begins. Leila is on some new diet, and can only eat very odd combinations of foods, but also has to make sure that the things I order are the things she really wants, so she can eat mine and it won't count because she didn't order it. It's all going well until we get to the chips, when I suggest it might be best if we order two portions, and she gets cross and says I'm not playing the game properly at all. In the end we settle for a large bowl, and thankfully when the food arrives the bowl turns out to be enormous and barely fits on the table, so all is well. I tell Leila that Mum has booked a villa in Spain for a week, for the half-term holidays after Easter, and has invited me and Charlie. It'll be a brilliant way to escape the usual spring weather of gales and torrential rain. Mum says she fancies a little holiday and Dad has invented a golf tournament so he doesn't have to come. He's not keen on holidays with the under-tens. Leila thinks a holiday is an excellent idea, and is planning something similar. Her idea of something similar turns out to be a week in Venice, and I offer to swap but she is having none of it and says Charlie would be bored in the Cipriani, and would be honour-bound to fall into the Grand Canal. Sadly I have to agree, and promise to bring her back a straw donkey.

We move on to general gossip, and Leila makes me laugh so much I nearly choke at one point, and have to be banged on the back by the waiter. To be honest, I don't think he needed to slap quite that hard, but composure is regained and Leila points out it could be worse: he could have tried the Heimlich manoeuvre. I almost wish he had, as trying to lift me up would have wiped the smile off his face. The puddings are glorious – Leila's new diet positively encourages crème brûlée, apparently – and the coffee and the bill arrive without the usual half-hour wait. Perhaps the waiter thinks I may start choking again. Leila insists on paying and makes me promise to put my share towards a present for Charlie, but only if it's something noisy and plastic. She is now off to meet a new man and go dancing. I cannot imagine where she gets her energy from, as I can barely stagger back to the car.

The lift is not working and by the time I make it up to the top floor I'm in need of oxygen and a lie-down. It's pouring with rain and the ramp has gone all slippery. Nearly fall over twice. I finally make it back to the car, and collapse exhausted. I could do with a nice little sleep, but make do with taking my bra off to get more comfortable, without taking my jumper off, which involves various contortionist-type movements. Just as I'm pulling my bra out of my sleeve, I realise the car opposite is no longer unoccupied. The man in the driving seat stares blankly at me, and I don't think he's actually seen anything as he's trying to work out how to drive back down the ramp without aquaplaning into the wall at the bottom. But the woman in the passenger seat is most amused.

The drive home is much more relaxed than the journey in. A Merc flashes past at well over a hundred, and about five minutes later I spot it on the hard shoulder, accompanied by a police car. Hurrah. Finally the motorway police have done something useful. The police car is lit up like a Christmas tree so I can't imagine how the Merc driver didn't spot it, but presume driving at over a hundred in the outside lane used up his entire brain. When I get home, Edna is dozing by the fire. She's remembered to put the outside lights on, so I don't fall into the flowerbed when I get out of the car, like I usually do. It's the perfect end to a long day, and she says Charlie was an angel, which I know is a downright lie but nevertheless very nice to hear. The video has worked and she's thrilled. I decide not to tell her that she's taped the wrong channel.

The sausage rolls are a huge hit next morning, and inevitably Charlie is desperate to eat one for breakfast.

'Mummy, don't you think sausage rolls are brilliant?'

'Marvellous.'

'Yes, and whoever thought of them deserves a medal, don't you think?'

'Yes. Now hurry up and put your socks on or we'll be late.'

'Can you get a medal for things like sausage rolls?'

'Charlie, I don't know, put your socks on.'

'Alright, alright, there's no need to shout. I was just asking. Honestly, you need to relax more, you know, Mummy.'

He gives me an angelic smile, and I'm strongly tempted to put a sausage roll up his nose.

'I love you, Mummy. Can there be sausage rolls for tea as well?'

'Yes, Charlie, I expect there can.'

I've booked a hair appointment for Charlie in honour of Leila's visit, and have promised him lunch at Pizza Express in an attempt to convince him it is actually possible to leave the house on Saturday morning without watching the entire range of children's cartoon programmes. He's unconvinced, but relents when I say he can also have ice-cream for pudding. The hairdresser, Tracy, is very sweet and asks Charlie what kind of haircut he would like.

'I want deadlocks – they're very trendy, you know.'

Tracy is not quite sure what deadlocks are, but if he means dreadlocks his hair is not quite long enough.

'OK, but not too short because my ears get very cold, you know.'

She busies herself snipping away, and I begin reading a chapter from *The Lion, the Witch and the Wardrobe*. Last time we came I forgot to bring a book, and we ended up playing I Spy for what seemed like hours. Charlie won with a word beginning with F, which worried me a lot so I insisted we went into whispering mode, and the answer turned out to be Fat Lady. So a book is a much safer option. I've nearly finished the chapter when Tracy announces his haircut is done, but would I mind reading to the end of the chapter because it's such a lovely story, and isn't the Snow

Queen a cow. I finish off the chapter while Tracy very slowly brushes imaginary hair off his neck.

Leila arrives early the next morning, and says Charlie's haircut is the most stylish thing she's ever seen, and we drive into Whitstable. As soon as we get out of the car, Charlie hurtles off towards the sea, and manages to get thoroughly soaked within five minutes. I've got a spare set of clothes for him in the car but timing is crucial: if I change him too early he'll soak the new clothes before we get into the restaurant for lunch, and if we hang about too long he'll get hypothermia. His legs are already pale mauve. Leila and I sit gossiping on the pebbles, which are incredibly uncomfortable after about two minutes, though undeniably picturesque. Leila is wearing various shades of cream, with marvellous pink sandals that look very delicate. She can't actually walk in the sandals, but she doesn't care because they're so pretty. I quite agree, and want a pair myself.

Leila's new man is shaping up very nicely. He's single, with no obvious psychological disorders, not married, no extra-curricular children, and he earns a fortune. He is also fantastic in bed, and does a very clever trick with his tongue. He works in the City but is not boring, according to Leila. I can well believe it if the trick with his tongue is not something he saves for special occasions only. He's called James, which Charlie says is a very good name, just like his best friend. Leila thinks this is an omen, and is clearly very smitten. She admits to thinking about how good he would look at the altar, which is a very bad sign since she usually doesn't get to wedding fantasies quite so soon. She asks Charlie if he would agree to wear a kilt and be a pageboy, and he says yes, and then we explain what a kilt is and he looks at us like we are both mad.

'Mummy, you should get married, and then I could have a dad. I'd get extra toys then, wouldn't I?'

'Not really, Charlie, you'd get the same but they'd be from both of us.'

'Oh. Well, anyway I think it'd be nice.'

Oh God. Does this mean the poor little thing is traumatised and longing for a father figure, and I haven't noticed? Feeling crushed at my selfishness I give him a cuddle. Leila gives me an anxious glance.

'Do you really want a dad then, darling?'

'Well, a bit. A nice man might come along, you know, not too fat and not with red hair.'

Damn, that's my ideal man out of the picture.

'Not like Homer Simpson, and with lots of money and a dog. A big dog. And then you could take it in turns to go to work, and we could have a swimming pool. If I get married I'm not doing it in a church, I'm going to do it in a box office.'

'I think you might mean registry office, Charlie.'

'Yes, and if you were too tired to go swimming he could take me.'

'Yes, darling, but you'd have to share more, you know, and if we all went out in the car then you'd have to sit in the back.'

Charlie pauses to consider this giant flaw in his picture.

'OK, what about just getting a dog then?'

Leila chokes with laughter, and I'm hugely relieved that he doesn't appear to be harbouring a terrible yearning for a patriarch in his life. Charlie charges off to play an imaginary pirate game which involves running into the sea up to his knees and then running out again, screaming very loudly.

It suddenly starts to rain, and we take refuge in the Whitstable Oyster Bar. I practically have to carry Leila off the pebbles in her new sandals, and Charlie thinks this is brilliant. I've booked a table so we manage to get in, but the place is heaving and the waitress looks on the point of hysteria. Charlie announces he is starving, and starts looking longingly at the food on other people's tables. If I don't act quickly he'll start sidling up to people and asking them if they need their chips. I manage to get the waitress to take our order, and at the last minute Charlie pipes up that he thinks he'll have a lobster. I tell him to shut up and have fish and chips, but Leila overrules me and says she will pay, because children must be encouraged to have adventurous palates. The lobster arrives with a small dagger to crack the shell: Charlie is thrilled and sets about smashing away, and even uses the dagger to eat his chips.

Leila and I are soon covered in bits of flying lobster, and the people on the next table stop smiling indulgently at the small boy being so grown up, and start ducking. I wrestle the dagger off him and he returns to his knife and fork, but he's sulking with all his might until Leila asks him if he would like to try an oyster. He would, so she orders half a dozen. He slurps away, and says it's just like drinking sea water but more chewy, and can he have another one, please? I'm half thrilled he's being so adventurous, and half terrified he will be sick at any moment. Leila says he must always remember he had his first oysters with her. Then we all have fantastic ice-cream for pudding, and Charlie rushes back outside to the sea and his pirate game. We sit drinking coffee and watch him. I try to work out if he'll have time to drown himself before we can belt out of the restaurant and retrieve him from the sea. I decide that we will, but only if Leila takes her new sandals off.

The restaurant is full of families with children and babies. Some sit very happily: content to chew on a piece of bread and occasionally wave it about a bit. But others are passed around like parcels, wriggle, try to get down, throw bread, and generally act up. I tell Leila that I think it's terribly unfair that some people get happy little plodders who will sit for hours, and the rest of us get stroppy little buggers who will not sit still for a minute. I used to think it was simply faulty parenting, but shortly after Charlie's birth I realised it wasn't. If you've got a stroppy one, you just have to get on with it. They should write baby books with this in mind. A Plodder at twelve months will be walking a little, his first word will be yes, and his favourite toy will be a teddy. A Stropper will be running, his first word will be no, and his favourite toys will include your hair, the contents of your handbag and the telephone – but only when you're talking on it. As we pay the bill I give a smile of solidarity to a woman with a toddler who will only eat other people's chips.

We finally get Charlie back into the car, with a combination of bribery and threats. Leila makes up a fabulous story on the way home about a magical pair of pink sandals that can fly you anywhere in the world, and we end up with Charlie wearing her sandals and wishing to go to Never Never Land. Leila is very pleased with her storytelling skills, so I don't tell her that she'll be asked for another chapter of this story every time she sees Charlie for the next five years. I got stuck with a similar situation last year when I bribed him to throw a crab back into the sea. After about six weeks of nightly requests for another chapter of The Adventures of Charlie the Crab I was desperate, and invented a disaster on an oil rig. All the crabs had to migrate to avoid all the pollution, and left no forwarding address, and I had to buy a huge number of new story tapes to make up for the sad loss.

Leila stays for tea, and is just about to head back to London when Charlie insists he needs another chapter of Pink Sandals before he will be able to cope with her departure. Leila looks desperate and suggests Mummy might tell him the next adventure, but Mummy says she knows nothing about pink sandals and is going to do the washing-up. Leila makes a very rude hand gesture, but settles down on the sofa for Chapter Two. She's eventually allowed to leave, and practically sprints to her car.

After sorting out his school uniform for tomorrow, making his packed lunch, doing school reading, having a dispute about watching a *Star Trek* video, and countless other diversionary tactics including a mammoth Random-Chatting Routine, Charlie is finally settled into bed, hair washed, teeth brushed, and pyjamas on. And I am totally knackered.

'Mummy, we had a lovely day, didn't we?'

'Yes, darling, but now it's sleep time, it's a school day tomorrow.'

'Yes. I love oysters, Mummy, and lobsters. And Leila. Don't you, Mummy?'

'Yes, darling,' I say, backing out of the doorway.

'When I grow up I'll marry Leila in a box office, and she can bring her pink sandals and we'll have oysters for tea. And you can come and do the cooking.'

'Oh, thanks very much, Charlie. Now go to sleep.'

'Yes. But we won't have crab, because that's cruel. Mummy, can I have one of my special Charlie the Crab stories, where he goes on an adventure with a whale and meets a mermaid with pink sandals?'

'No.'

'Tomorrow night, maybe?'

'No.'

A heated argument develops, involving lots of hurling the duvet about. Finally I get him to agree that the crab stories will not be resurrected, and Pink Sandals will remain Leila's special territory, but an extra-special video from Block-buster's might be possible tomorrow night if the silly behaviour stops and his duvet returns to his bed. I wish I could find a way of winning arguments without using bribery, but without resorting to the use of an electric cattle prod my chances seem slim. I can foresee a bitter dispute tomorrow, while I hold out for Disney family entertainment and he insists that *The Spy Who Shagged Me* is perfectly all right. Go back downstairs, wondering just how 'bad' *The Spy Who Shagged Me* really is, and who can I ring to find out without appearing a total fool.

Chapter Four

Sex, Lies and Videotape

I LEAVE HOME VERY early to drive down to Cornwall for the porridge shoot. Edna's looking after Charlie until this evening, when Mum and Dad will arrive. The journey is pretty but exhausting. The signposts are all particularly unhelpful, and I manage to get on to a succession of small roads going in entirely the wrong direction. Sunlight streams through the trees lining the road, so shafts of light almost blind me every few seconds, like a sort of ecological strobe-lighting effect. Wonder if there'll be time for me to pull over before I find myself in the midst of a tricky neurological episode due to the unaccustomed effects of flashing lights on my brain.

I finally find my sunglasses at the bottom of my handbag, but they have only one arm, as the other one has mysteriously disappeared. I balance them on my nose very carefully, and achieve a kind of Rayban meets Retard look. I'm singing along to Aretha Franklin, and every time Aretha and I reach a really belting bit my glasses fall off.

Eventually I manage to locate Cornwall and the hotel, which turns out to be one of those hideous modern types with lots of grey concrete and an enormous car park, which is full. I finally find a space but have to walk miles back to the hotel entrance carrying my bags, because I just know that this is the kind of place which takes six hours to get your bag from your car. And then delivers it to your room just as you step into the bath.

The hotel is packed with financial services people on a conference. They are all quite excited about this. I'm sure Lawrence booked me in here on purpose, knowing it would be full of delegates. Barney and the crew are staying in a much posher hotel at the top of the hill overlooking the bay, but Lawrence claims there were no single rooms left, and either I had to share with the crew or stay here. Reception is awash with men, and a few women in navy suits, shouting greetings to each other and swapping business cards. I plan to have a peaceful night of uninterrupted sleep, and then do a last-minute run-around before Barney turns up tomorrow afternoon with the crew. Then we'll have just enough time to start setting up, but not long enough to get into any serious trouble. I hope. The combination of a film crew and water is not a good one. I wonder if I should have put the local coastguard on standby.

My room is very bland and plastic, but child-free so I promptly fall asleep. Wake up starving, and feel sure room service will take hours and be horrible, so I rush downstairs in old jeans and a jumper to find that the restaurant is full of financial services people in cocktail outfits. I beg a waiter to find me a table, and he finally relents and says he will ask 'the gentleman' if he minds sharing. Before I can stop him he has shot across the room and asked a man sitting on his own by a window. Brilliant.

I walk over to the table feeling sure I'm doomed to spend the entire meal being given a lecture about pensions by a conference delegate who's so unpopular nobody will sit with him, but instead an incredibly gorgeous man stands up. I thank him profusely for allowing me to share his table, and wish with all my heart I was not wearing such tragic clothes. He says that perhaps I should wait until I've tasted the soup before thanking him too much. He says this in a marvellous Scottish accent, a sort of cross between Sean Connery and Mel Gibson in *Braveheart*. I smile and study the menu, and decide to avoid the soup. The financial services people are getting very loud, and begin telling each other that there's going to be a film shot in the harbour over the next couple of days. There's rumour that Tom Cruise will be turning up. I'm not sure he actually does commercials for porridge, but I bet he'd be marvellous if he did. Might blow the budget a bit, though.

Everyone gets very excited about the prospect of rubbing shoulders with stars, and they all vow to rush down to the harbour the minute filming starts to see if they can make friends with Tom. This is going to be great. Barney is so patient with people trying to get their five minutes of fame. My dining companion introduces himself as Mack – I'm not sure if this is his first name or his surname and don't like to ask. He asks me what I'm doing in Cornwall, and I decide not to mention anything about my work mainly because I feel sure the men on the next table will overhear me and launch into their audition pieces. I say I'm having a little holiday and he tells me he's an art dealer, down looking at a few local artists.

The food arrives, and is fine, though Mack has clearly tasted better and is deeply amused by his carrots, which have been cut into flower shapes. I have given up on a first course and gone straight for steak and chips and salad. The conversation dribbles on; the other diners are getting very rowdy and have started doing impressions. Mack is not happy, and suggests we have coffee in the bar. His accent is divine, and I go off into a fantasy where he's wearing a kilt, and then I'm wearing a kilt and he's wearing nothing at all. I must get a grip or I'll make a total fool of myself. We get our bills and the waiter gives me a sickening smile and a sort of wink as we leave the restaurant. The bar turns out to be full of more conference people, and one of them is trying to liven things up a bit by standing on one of the tables dancing.

Mack asks if I'd like to have coffee in his room, no strings attached, as it would be nice to talk some more. I agree very happily, and then think I should have been more reluctant. I'm secretly hoping there'll be lots of strings attached, but not before I somehow manage to get back to my room and change out of my disastrous old underwear. Mack is even more gorgeous standing up, very tall, and he smells divine, which reminds me I have no perfume on. He also has the most amazing grey eyes and dark curly hair which is the perfect length. Not even a hint of a ponytail, or earrings, or any other art-dealer-type accoutrements – though, to be fair, I don't actually know any art dealers, so the lack of a ponytail may be totally understandable. We get to his room after a rather embarrassing silence in the lift, and I discover it is in fact a suite, with three sofas, and acres of pale-blue carpet. There's no bed in sight, but there are two sets of doors off the main room, as well as a balcony overlooking the sea. Mack explains that as the business is paying he thought he might as well get a decent room. Quite agree, and only wish I could make Barney follow this kind of logic.

Mack orders coffee and launches into a long debate with room service as to whether they can provide petits fours to go with it – no not chocolates, no not biscuits, good God doesn't anyone know what petits fours are, yes marzipan bits and little biscuits. Thank you. Then he says he thought I might like some sort of pudding as we had to flee the restaurant early. I think this is an excellent idea, and also find his explanation rather reassuring as I was beginning to wonder if he had some sort of fetish about marzipan.

We sit about chatting for ages, the coffee arrives, with little biscuits which almost count as petits fours, and brandy is discovered in the mini bar and turns out to be rather nice freezing cold. Mack tells me he got divorced last year, and has two children, Daisy and Alfie. He shows me photographs and they look very sweet. Alfie looks just like him, only smaller and with more amusing hair, and wearing a Batman outfit.

In the midst of general chatting he suddenly blurts: 'Look, I'm terribly sorry. But I'm crap at this sort of thing, and I really want to kiss you, quite badly actually. So would that be OK, because I don't want to make assumptions, or get a black eye or anything. So would that be OK?' He finishes with a special pleading look which I know he knows is irresistible. This makes me laugh so much he is almost offended, until I manage to say that I can't think of anything nicer. Then he says he'll wait until I have stopped laughing, if I don't mind. Which makes me stop instantly.

It's marvellous how quickly you get back into the swing of kissing, and I'd be quite happy to stay on the sofa all night but Mack seems keen to move to the bedroom and then the pace really hots up. My appalling third-division underwear proves no major impediment to the proceedings, although Mack does give my tired old grey bra rather a quizzical look. I explain that I do have girly satin ones, but was not expecting a high-performance-bra sort of an evening, and anyway I prefer comfy ones. Having your chest forced up under your chin is no laughing matter, and plunging cleavages are all very well but tend to trap biscuit crumbs if you are not a very careful eater. Mack is highly diverted by the concept of plunging cleavages and requires a demonstration. He then goes on to say all sorts of very rude things in his marvellous accent. I fall asleep exhausted at some point and wake up at five am completely disorientated. I'm about to creep out when Mack wakes up and demands to know where I'm going. I say I really need to get back to my room so that I can sleep without distractions, which he reluctantly accepts, but then we spend ages saying goodbye and I don't leave the room until six thirty.

Feeling very smug and gorgeous, I collapse into bed in my room after deciding to try to sleep for an hour before attempting to work out how I'm going to summon up the energy to get through today. But I discover that I can't get to sleep, as I keep having an action replay of last night whenever I close my eyes, which is most unsettling. I order breakfast and have a shower. Nearly drown in the shower as weird partial paralysis seems to have set in, my legs have gone like jelly and my back is killing me. I feel about ninety-five, and my hair has gone into a massive tangle at the back of my neck which will require scissors to sort it out. I've got the start of a huge bruise on my shoulder, where I fell off the bed at some point last night and landed on my shoes.

Huge quantities of coffee and toast arrive and I start to feel slightly more human, and less like someone who has just survived an earthquake. I'm about to call Leila for a therapy session when my mobile rings. It's Barney, in a foul mood, asking me to run down to the harbour and make sure the bloody boat is still there. I end up with a huge list of little jobs to do. I can't work out what to do about Mack, but the hotel phone rings and it's him, to say thank you for a lovely night. And he's found one of my earrings in his shoe, and would I like it back because it doesn't really suit him.

Wonder how he got my room number, but I'm glad he did, although it's not very inspiring on the hotel security front. I say it was my pleasure, and we flirt for ages and agree to meet up again tonight in the hotel bar. Mack says he's going to look at some pictures in St Ives, and should be back around nine. I'll just have to hope I'm actually back at the hotel by then, and not stuck down at the harbour fending off audition pieces from over-excited conference delegates.

I'm not quite sure what to do about the fact that the crew will be floating about tonight and I will be meant to be keeping an eye on them, but decide to worry about that one later. Maybe I'll just explain to Mack and blame last night's subterfuge on understandable caution. I make a quick call to Charlie, who announces Nana is being very stupid and has made him eat Shreddies, so he might have to be sick at any moment. Nana grabs the phone and points out that he asked for them specially; in fact he refused point blank to even consider eating anything else. I say he often does this, and we both agree it's very annoying. She suggests I follow her example and buy only one type of cereal, so there's no choice. This reminds me that I still hate Weetabix, and we agree that really there is no answer. I rush off to the harbour to try to persuade the man with the boat to hang around all day, and surreptitiously check how many life-jackets he has.

Barney and the crew arrive just after lunch and generate the usual mêlée of equipment and shouting, but gradually we work out what we're going to do tomorrow. Barney wants to start at dawn so we get the early-morning light, which he says will be Magic. The crew aren't keen. The man who owns the boat is definitely not keen, and keeps asking me if Barney really means he has to be there at four am. Sadly, yes he does. Just as we are about to call it a day, a huge black Mercedes drives down the harbour road and heads towards us. I'm about to send a runner to tell them to fuck off, when we realise it must be the Agency, turning up early. Typical. The car stops and Lucy, the agency producer, gets out. She's followed by an odd-looking man who is bound to be the client. Barney looks on the point of apoplexy, and the client looks nervous, but determined.

We knew Lucy was coming, but no one said anything about the client. Barney hates it when clients turn up, because they always ask lots of stupid questions and need to be made a huge fuss of. They also often come up with 'ideas', which are always crap, and want their product to be in sight constantly, preferably slap in the middle of every shot. In fact Barney is notorious for telling clients to fuck off. And agency producers too, come to think of it, if they start coming up with ideas. On one famous occasion, luckily before my time, during a shoot on a beach, he actually drew a line with a stick in the sand and said if anyone, agency or client, stepped over it he was going home. They thought it was a joke, and stepped over the line. He went home.

With a sinking feeling, I realise that this is bound to be another Lawrence moment. Lucy rushes over and says, 'Look, I'm sorry about this but he insisted on coming down early, and Lawrence said he'd told you all about it and it was fine,' and Barney glares at me and says, 'Did you forget to mention it, or what?' Great. I'm about to explain that Lawrence didn't tell me anything, as usual, when I see that the other passenger door of the car has opened, and a man is getting out who seems oddly familiar.

It's Mack. He goes pale, and hesitates by the car, but then walks over and starts wittering on to Barney, who seems to know him, and then they wander off to look at the boat. I chat to Lucy and the client, who has had a major personality-bypass operation somewhere along the line, and generally try to work out how to handle this unexpected turn of events. Lucy says that that Mack is the new creative head of the agency who gave us this job, and he decided to come down unexpectedly because he wanted to see Barney in action. Perfect. I'm tempted to share with Lucy quite how unexpected things are turning out to be for me in particular, but resist because the client is telling us how he wanted to come down early so he could really get to grips with things, and see how on earth we're going to spend all that money. Lucy and I spend an anxious ten minutes persuading him that getting to grips with Barney would not be wise, and then Lucy risks taking him over for a quick chat while I make frantic signals behind her back telling Barney to be nice.

Mack sidles over. 'Who are you waving at?'

'Fuck off.'

'Christ, Annie, I'm sorry about this. Look, let's just get on with it and we can talk about it tonight.'

'Fuck off, and buy some paintings, why don't you?'

'I hope you won't mind me saying this, but I find your vocabulary rather limited, sweetheart.'

'Fuck off.'

'Charming. So tell me, how are you enjoying your little holiday by the sea?'

'Fuck. Off. I had a better reason to lie than you did. You could have been a nutter. Well, actually you are a nutter, so I was right. Do you have any idea what Barney will do to me if he finds out? This is so unprofessional. And as for the crew, if they get wind of this I'm doomed.'

'Yes, I know. Which is why I suggest we just keep cool and then we can talk about it tonight. Nine pm, hotel bar, don't be late.'

And with this the bastard walks off and starts steering the client back into the car saying that they'll explain everything to him back at the hotel, and they will see us all tomorrow morning, bright and early, ha ha ha.

Barney knows something is up, but frankly he doesn't care because a vital bit of kit has gone missing and he's in the midst of throwing a major tantrum. I rush about sorting out the crisis, and try to stop the crew pretending to push one another into the sea because sooner or later someone will fall in. They ignore me. Someone falls in – Dave the electrician – and has to be fished out by our boatman who does not think it is funny at all. Dave stands wringing out his pockets and emptying water out of his hood. The crew, and Barney, think this is fabulously funny. Everyone cheers up hugely, and we finally finish dithering about and Barney is happy that we can start tomorrow with the camera pointing vaguely in the direction where the sun rises, so we all troop off back to the posh hotel and start running up a major bar bill.

Barney wanders off to his room saying he has calls to make, and I say I'm knackered and am going back to my hotel to sleep, but he can call me on my mobile if he needs me. It looks like the entire crew are ordering bar snacks and watching sport on satellite television, so I can slope off back to my hotel without half of them trailing after me demanding food.

As soon as I'm back in my room I ring Leila for an emergency therapy session. She thinks it is very funny.

'Look, Leila, it's not bloody funny. If Barney finds out he'll go berserk.'

'Oh stop it, he's always going berserk about something, you can handle him. You know the deal: screw the agency if you must, but never screw the crew. Now tell me more about this man.'

'Well, he's called Mack.'

'Christ. Not Mack MacDonald?'

'Yes, apparently.'

'Oh honestly, how could you not have recognised Mack MacDonald? They call him Mack the Knife, you know, everyone's terrified of him. He's from Glasgow and once threatened to stab a client at a big pitch which wasn't going very well. He did that brilliant campaign last year for Persil.'

'What? That awful one with the baby?'

'No, you idiot, the one with the dog. He's the new man at BLG, which is now BMLG. As in Bates MacDonald Lightfoot and Grace. That MacDonald. Ring a bell now? He's fantastic, a brilliant creative type but good with money too. They're paying him a fortune and they had to give him a chunk of the agency to woo him away from DDT. For God's sake, you must know who he is now?'

'Yes of course I know the name now, but he didn't give me his surname last night, and anyway Lawrence does all the agency crawling, you know that. And we don't work for DDT, not since Barney stormed off that Jif shoot and refused to go back. So how would I know what he looks like?'

'Oh yes, I'd forgotten about that. Well, anyway, now you know what he looks like better than most of us. Actually, now I come to think of it, I met him a few months ago at a party and tried flirting with him, but it was like trying to flirt with a tree – all rugged and gorgeous but totally blank when it came to chitchat. He's gorgeous, darling. Hurrah, hurrah, you finally got laid by someone who doesn't look like a refugee.'

Leila has always disapproved of my choice of men, preferring matinée-idol-type looks rather than my pale and wistful working-class-hero types. Mack is actually a bit of both.

'Yes but, Leila, what do I do with him now? I'm supposed to meet him in the bar, but I just know someone will see us. I can't handle this at all, and I haven't brought any decent clothes, and anyway I'm totally knackered.'

'Oh stop it, and have some fun. What clothes have you got? Oh God, not those awful jeans.'

A rather painful conversation follows where Leila declares she does not know why I insist on going round dressed like a runner, and she told me to throw out that hideous old bra years ago. Then she redeems herself, as she always does.

'Well, it's a good job you're so gorgeous, because you really are hopeless. Just wear a white T-shirt, tight, use safety pins at the sides if you have to, and that horrible old leather jacket but don't do it up, and the cleanest jeans you can find. And don't wear your woolly hat. And not those awful old deck shoes, have bare feet if you have to. Have you got lots of condoms?'

'Leila, shut up. We are going to have a professional chat and sort this out so it's not a problem tomorrow.'

'Yes, and then you are going to shag him senseless. Have you got condoms?'

'Yes. I've got my emergency packet in my washbag, the ones you made me buy last year.'

'Good. Have they gone past their sell-by date?'

'Leila, I'm warning you.'

'OK. Well, be careful, darling, and have fun. And you can tell me all about it when you get home. Love you, bye.'

And with that she is gone. I ring Mum and chat to Charlie, who is staying up late as a special treat.

'Nana made sausages for tea and they were great. Much better than you do them. You should do them in the frying pan like Nana, you know, Mummy. And Grandad is taking me fishing tomorrow, and we may catch a shark.'

I tell him I'm not sure there are sharks in the local lake, and he tells me I know nothing about fishing and should leave it to him and Grandad.

I still can't work out what to say to Mack, but put on the outfit suggested by Leila just in case. At five to nine I go downstairs, find a quiet corner in the bar and order a triple vodka. All the financial lot from last night are still in the restaurant, so the bar is blissfully quiet. Mack saunters in and orders a beer, then comes over and sits down.

'Look, I really am sorry. I just didn't want to talk about bloody advertising all night, but I never thought you would turn out to be the bloody producer.'

'What do you mean by that – don't I look like a producer?'

'Well, to be honest, no. You don't look demented enough.'

I'm secretly rather charmed by this, but try not to let it show.

'So, what do you suggest we do now? I think we should pretend it never happened, and get on with the job.'

Actually seeing him again has made me realise I think the direct opposite of this, but I don't want to appear to be a total pushover.

'Yes, well, I've been thinking about that. And you see the thing is I really don't want to do that. So I don't really think that's an option.'

I'm half thrilled by this, and half furious. Christ, it's like being fifteen again. As if it's just up to him to decide. I'm about to tell him exactly how annoying he is when he leans over and kisses me. Hard. We are in the midst of a passionate clinch when two of the crew, George and Kevin, walk in.

They stand completely still in the doorway and watch, with their mouths slightly open.

'You total fucker, two of the crew have just walked in.'

'Shit.'

George and Kevin sit down at the bar, and pretend not to see us. But I know they have, and they know I know.

'I know. I'll go up to my room, and you can chat with the boys and then follow me up.'

'And that's your plan, is it?'

'Yesh, Moneypenny, and it's a damned good one.'

I can't help laughing. But also do a bit more swearing, and add that I will not follow him up to his room like a well-trained puppy because this will be totally obvious.

'In that case I shall be forced to sit here and kiss you at unexpected moments throughout the evening.'

'You wouldn't!'

'I bloody well would, you know.'

'OK, OK. You go up to your room like you said and I'll try and think of something to stop the boys grabbing their mobiles the minute I leave.'

'OK. I'll wait for you by the lift. You have ten minutes. Or I'm coming back in.'

With this he gets up and walks out.

George and Kevin look over and try to appear surprised to see me.

'Wasn't that Mack, the bloke from the agency?' says George. 'What have you been doing to him? He looked well pissed off.' Then he snorts into his drink in a most annoying manner.

I get up and walk over slowly. Staring hard at George, I tell him that if he breathes a word of this to anybody, even his mother, I'll ring his wife and tell her about that waitress in the Little Chef last summer. George goes white, and

Kevin sniggers. I tell Kevin that I will also ring George's wife if Kevin says anything, and George is a lot bigger than Kevin. I think this will do the trick.

I walk out of the bar to find Mack loitering beside the lift, getting some very odd looks from the woman on reception. The lift arrives and we get in, and Mack begins kissing me. I'm enjoying myself immensely when the lift stops and an elderly couple join us. Since I don't want to get arrested for performing an indecent act in a hotel lift, as apart from anything else it would be bound to get back to the PTA, I glare at Mack until we reach his floor. We get out, the doors close and then we hear the elderly couple laughing. Mack doesn't seem to care at all, and as soon as we reach the safety of the other side of his door, neither do I.

Eventually we realise we're both starving so we order sandwiches and coffee and then try to work out how we're going to handle the shoot, which is due to start in a few hours. We agree that we'll just have to play it by ear and hope George and Kevin will keep silent. I finally stagger back to my room at two thirty. I have no idea how I'm going to stay awake for the next twelve hours and manage to speak, let alone work. I'm dithering about trying to decide what to wear, as it will be freezing, when the phone rings.

'I just wanted to say that I think you're lovely, and I want to see you back in London if that would be OK. Just in case I don't get a chance to say so later.'

He seems rather embarrassed by this outburst, and promptly puts the phone down. I'm thrilled, and suddenly feel much more energetic.

The location manager, Johnny, turns up to collect me and we get to Barney's hotel at three fifty-five. He's hopping about in reception. He takes one look at me and says, 'God, darling, you look totally fucked.'

Nearly choke on my coffee in the polystyrene beaker which Johnny has magically provided, but Barney begins chattering on about plans for the morning and was just being his usual charming self. The boatman looks freezing, but the catering van has turned up, so all the essentials are in place, and the weather is fine although the sea is pretty rough.

Amazingly, things go without a hitch, and we get all the shots we need of the actor stepping off the boat in the early-morning light, although as usual it turns out that the sun actually rises in a totally unexpected point no one had anticipated, which requires frantic repositioning at the last minute. No one falls in and things are looking good, when Barney decides it would be nice to get a shot of the boat coming back into harbour. It will look great, the light is wonderful, and he's the director so that's what we'll do. The actor is not keen on heading out to sea, and neither is the boatman, but Barney insists and we finally persuade them all that it won't take long. We put Chris, the first assistant, on the boat with a radio so Barney can tell him what he wants. He's not keen either, and says boats make him puke.

Just as they head off to sea Mack turns up with Lucy and the client, and we explain what's going on. The client is a bit dubious and wants to know if it will cost extra. Mack says, 'Oh, for God's sake,' and Barney looks at him with a glimmer of admiration. Lucy rushes the client off to have breakfast and soothe his ruffled feathers. We're all huddled on the dock watching the boat head out beyond the harbour walls, where it begins to pitch about alarmingly, and the strangled cries from Chris on the radio suggest all is not plain sailing.

'It's fucking heaving out here, guv, can we come back now?' There are muffled sounds of swearing in the background.

The waves are getting quite big now; in fact it looks almost like a mini storm is brewing. The sky is fantastic, with the sun breaking through the clouds and sending shafts of light on to the sea. The tiny little boat comes bobbing back through the entrance to the harbour, and Barney, as usual, is right: it does look brilliant. The boat gets close in, but Barney says they have to go out again because the sun went in just at the crucial moment. Terrible language can be heard on the radio when Chris breaks the news to the boatman.

I notice with horror that the client has brought his own video camera and is standing right behind Barney trying to record over his shoulder. He then plays back the tape and peers at it. I can tell, and so can Lucy and Mack, that he's about to start asking questions. Barney turns round and fixes him with a terrifying glare. Lucy and I surround the client and Mack grabs his arm and we manage to walk him over to the car where he starts blathering on about the light not being very bright. We go into all sorts of technical detail, some of which is totally made up, and eventually manage to persuade him to stop worrying. Lucy assures him that if he doesn't like it we can always cut this bit from the final film. She whispers this because if Barney hears he'll have a fit. Mack then suggests coffee, and begins asking the client all sorts of questions about his lovely camera, and they wander off quite happily. Brilliant, and you'd never know they were faking it if you couldn't see them making rude gestures behind his back.

The boat goes back out, and comes back in, three more times before we get the right combination of light, clouds and the boat bobbing up and down looking like it won't make it back into harbour. Then Barney makes them go round and round inside the harbour, almost docking and then going off again, so we can get that bit just right. The actor has been sick, and the boatman is furious. Finally we get what we need, but now Barney wants the boat to come right up close to the harbour wall so we can get a shot of the actor throwing rope off it.

The actor isn't keen, and says nobody told him he would have to throw ropes about, but we tell him to pull himself together or Barney will make them head out to sea again. This does the trick, and he hurls ropes about countless times. It's really getting rough now and on about the tenth run a huge wave hits the boat, bashing it into the harbour wall with a sickening cracking sound. The boatman slams on the engines and moves the boat away from the wall, but the damage has been done and the railing at the front is cracked and hangs off looking pathetic. Everyone says, 'Oh fuck,' and then frantically looks away pretending to be doing something else.

After a short silence Chris comes on the radio. 'Um, guv, this guy is seriously pissed off now. Can't stress that enough, really. Have we got enough to call it a day, because I really don't want to be the one to tell him you want to go again.'

Barney agrees they can come back in for real now. We all huddle around the camera, and try not to look at the boat. It starts to pour and the waves are getting gigantic. The boat finally ties up, and the boatman gets off and storms towards us looking murderous. He is huge – I hadn't quite realised this before – and we all cower behind Barney. Just as he is about to reach us, an enormous wave breaks over the side of the harbour wall and drenches us all. Barney is soaked from head to foot, and stands dripping water, holding out his hand saying, 'Look, I'm terribly sorry.' Luckily this sight cheers the boatman up no end, and he begins to laugh.

We promise to pay for the damage to the boat, and invite him to join us at the hotel for a drink. He accepts, but makes us promise to tell everybody that Chris was steering, because this is his home port and if word gets out that he drove his own boat into the harbour wall he'll never live it down. I brief the crew and make sure that everyone knows this is the line to take, and after their initial disappointment that Barney is not going to get punched they all start teasing Chris about what a crap job he did steering straight into a wall. We start to pack up, and plan to rush back to the hotel in convoy, with the aim of getting dry, and then drunk, as quickly as possible.

The client has been sitting in the car during most of this, and Lucy says he is now bored and wants to go back to London. Mack asks if he can have a lift with us back to the hotel, as he doesn't want to go back in that car with that idiot client under any circumstances. Barney thoroughly approves of this and takes Mack off with him in his car, which I imagine is not quite what Mack had in mind but he makes the best of it. He begins telling Barney how he has always wanted to work with him, and just had to come down and watch a genius at work. This goes down very well indeed and Barney is beaming as the car drives off.

The crew pack up in record time as it's now really freezing and tipping it down. We get back to the hotel and I feel sure I'm in the first stages of hypothermia, but hot coffee and brandy help. Mack says George and Kevin have been giving him very funny looks and sniggering a lot. I don't get a chance to answer this because Barney starts talking about what to do this afternoon. We need the actor to walk up from the harbour, up the cobbled streets to the front door of a cottage, but preferably not in torrential rain. It looks like this afternoon will be a washout, so we plan to start bright and early tomorrow morning, and if it's still raining we will just have to make do.

Barney says he's off to have a sleep and the crew are all in the restaurant having lunch, so Mack and I have a quick cup of coffee in the bar. He's due to leave in a couple of hours, but suggests he might invent a reason to stay another night. I regretfully decline, because if I don't get some sleep soon I'll collapse. In the end we agree that we'll speak once we are both back home, and then George and Kevin wander into the bar and sit watching us. I begin writing things down in my notebook to make it look like we're having a meeting. Mack tears out a sheet of paper, writes something and folds it up. Then he gets up to leave, and winks out of sight of the boys. As he walks out I read the note which turns out to be his home number, mobile, pager, email and direct line in the office. I want to rush off and call Leila to check the significance of this gesture. Instead I have to sit and chat to the actor, who comes in and wants a lot of fuss made of him because he got wet. Also he doesn't like boats, has been sick twice, no one told him anything about throwing ropes at the casting, and now he's got a blister on his hand. George and Kevin sit sniggering behind his back, and generally make it very difficult for me to keep a straight face.

When I'm safely ensconced in my hotel room, I call home. Charlie has just got back from his fishing trip, very pleased with himself because he caught a trout.

'That's fantastic.'

'Yes. Actually Grandad got it on his rod, but he said he needed my special strong arms to help him. He's getting old, you know. And Nana is going to cook it for us, and we've got ice-cream. Shall we save you some?'

'No thank you, darling, you eat it all up, I can have some next time.'

'Yes. When are you coming home?'

'Tomorrow night, darling.'

'And will there be a surprise when you come home?'

I'm tempted to say yes, your mother will be in a light coma with strange marks on her back. But I know he actually means a toy, so long negotiations follow over what this might be. I've already bought some Lego, to save the trauma of trying to find something in a motorway service station. But of course he doesn't know that so he runs through all possible options with prices ranging from about £10 to well over £1,000.

I manage to get some sleep, and then check in with Barney who says I am to meet him at eight tomorrow morning as it's still pouring. He's going to watch telly and sleep, and the crew are all in the bar doing the hokey cokey and drinking like fish. I'm allowed to go to sleep as well, but only after I have made it clear to Chris that the crew are to use their own money for booze from now on. I sort this out and collapse into bed, but manage to remember to book a wake-up call for seven am. The morning goes very well, although a few of the delegates from the hotel spot us and try to loiter in the exact part of the cobbled street where the actor is due to walk. But they soon get bored when Tom Cruise doesn't show up. We also eventually manage to persuade the owners of the cottages adjacent to the one we're using to stop looking out of their windows and waving.

I don't get home until midnight, and after a brief chat with Mum and Dad fall straight into bed. Mum says a nice-sounding man phoned, and said he'll call back tomorrow. I hope it was Mack and not the plumber, who was supposed to have fixed the outside tap but failed to turn up. The phone rings. It's Mack.

'Hi.'

'Hi. Hang on, how did you get my home number?'

'Well, I called Lawrence. God, he's really wet, isn't he? I told him I'd left a vital folder down at the hotel and wanted to know if you'd found it.'

'Oh, very clever.'

'Yesh, Moneypenny, and I thought of it all by myself. Is the kid asleep?'

'Yes.'

'Oh good. Then we can have a nice long chat.'

'No we cannot. I need to go to sleep.'

'Oh. I do very good phone calls, you know.'

'Yes, I'm sure you do. But I'll be asleep any second now, so it'd be a bit of a waste.'

'Oh alright. Look, if I offered to take you out to dinner would you start all that dreadful swearing again?'

'I might.'

'What, come out to dinner, or start swearing?'

'Fuck off.'

'Charming. Just what I was afraid of. A simple yes or no would do, actually.'

'OK. Yes to both.'

'Great. Friday night. I've got the kids for Easter, so it'll have to be the week after next. Meet me at work at eight and I'll take you to dinner at the Ivy. Have you got a little black dress? It's pretty posh, you know.'

'OK, OK, I get the message, Friday at eight. You want to take my little black dress out to dinner. I'll bike it over to you. Do you want to borrow high heels as well?'

'Oh yes, definitely high heels.'

'OK. I'm writing this down. Black dress, high heels, bike them to you at the office for eight. Now go away and let me sleep.'

'Sweet dreams.'

If this relationship is going to work I'll have to teach him to end telephone conversations by saying goodbye rather than simply putting the phone down. Fall asleep feeling very chirpy, although I'm already debating exactly what to wear. The only little black dress I own is very old and is now two sizes too small, due to the combination of having Charlie and eating countless packets of chocolate Hobnobs. I can only wear it if I don't sit down, so it might not be ideal for dinner unless I can arrange for us to go to a buffet somewhere. I'll ring Leila and arrange an emergency shopping session.

Spend the next few days catching up with chores and having endless conversations with Barney, who is editing the Cornish film, which he says will be an award-winner if he can persuade the fucking client not to insert twenty fucking seconds of fucking pack-shot into a thirty-second film. I find myself standing in Safeway's trying to calm Barney down, with call waiting bleeping on my mobile. I hadn't actually realised I had a call-waiting facility, and don't know how to use it. I manage somehow to press a secret button which means Mrs Jenkins from the PTA suddenly launches into a conversation with Barney. I end up having to offer to bake Easter fairy cakes for the cake stall on the last day of term, just to get her off the line. Barney is furious. 'Who was that mad fucking woman going on about cakes? For fuck's sake get a new phone.'

I have lots of talks with Leila and Kate about the

potential pitfalls of embarking upon a passionate affair with Mack, should this turn out to be on offer. They both heartily recommend getting as much action as possible while it's available, because you never know when you'll get another chance. But I keep dwelling on the potential pitfalls if a brief affair turns into something more long-term. Apart from worrying about Charlie's reaction, I know Mum will launch into mother-of-the-bride fantasy land at the merest whisper of a man. I find myself day-dreaming about Mack in a variety of unlikely locations, and having panic attacks at the thought of seeing him again. I'd forgotten quite how tricky it all gets. Try very, very hard not to think about it, and fail.

Everyone comes to me for Easter lunch. Mum and Dad have bought Charlie the biggest Easter egg I've ever seen. In fact it's the size Mum always refused to let us have when we were children. My helpful little sister Lizzie has done the same. She offered to do lunch this year but she and Matt, both being architects, live in minimalist heaven in a huge converted warehouse in Whitechapel. The entire place is done in shades of white, and I simply can't stand the strain of taking Charlie there. I wish I'd agreed now, because getting chocolate stains off white sofas would serve her right for buying such a big egg. I tell Lizzie about Mack and she says it's about time I had some fun, and when can she meet him? I'm not even sure if I'm going to meet him again if my current level of panic continues, so I beg her to change the subject before I start having palpitations, and we talk about her work. Her latest clients are very rich but totally mad, and keep changing their minds.

'Honestly, they're driving us nuts. If they alter the plans

for the kitchen one more time, I'm going to get the builders to brick them up in the utility room.'

'Good plan. That's bound to have new clients flocking to your door.'

'Yes, but it'd be worth it.'

Charlie eats so much chocolate he practically needs to be sedated after lunch. We go for a walk in the woods, and there are bluebells everywhere. The scent is marvellous, and Charlie insists on stopping to chat with the sheep in a nearby field, who all have lambs busy bouncing round like Zebedee from *The Magic Roundabout*. Mum starts telling us what she plans to pack for our holiday in Spain, which is only a few weeks away now.

'Do you think it would be handy if I brought my toasted sandwich maker? It's very light.'

Lizzie and I exchange glances, as we both know she's not joking, and try to convince her not to bring any major items of kitchen equipment or the plane will never get off the ground. We get home and eat the special cakes Charlie has made for tea. They're sort of chocolate nests, some more nest-like than others, but they taste delicious and we all have far too many and then feel sick. Everyone then beats a hasty retreat before the second sugar high of the day can kick in. I spend a hideous couple of hours trying to stop him from causing major structural damage. Finally he's so exhausted he only registers a faint protest as I bundle him into bed.

'Mummy, we had a lovely day, didn't we?'

'Yes, darling. Now go to sleep.'

'Yes and the cakes I made were brilliant, weren't they?'

'Yes.'

'I could make cakes and sell them like you did at school,

but I could keep all the money and buy a dog, couldn't I, Mummy?'

'No you couldn't. Goodnight, Charlie.'

'I hate you, Mummy. I really do. Goodnight.'

Chapter Five

Home Thoughts from Abroad

T HE DAY OF MY dinner date with Mack finally dawns, and I feel very nervous. Kate has offered to have Charlie to stay the night.

'I've put pyjamas and everything in his bag, and also his special blanket. He's almost given it up but he might want it tonight.'

'OK. Although I doubt they'll sleep at all.'

'True. Thanks, Kate, he's really excited. I'll do the same for you, anytime.'

'Chance would be a fine thing. Anyway James is thrilled. He was so excited this morning he even tidied up his room. Now look, off you go and have a fabulous time. Charlie will be fine. I promise I'll ring you if he starts throwing up or anything.'

'OK. Although it's me that's likely to be sick. I feel so nervous it's ridiculous, but it's so long since I've been on a date date, if you know what I mean.'

'You'll be fine. Oh, that reminds me, I thought you might like to wear these. They always brought me good luck – well, apart from Phil of course.' With this she pushes a small black leather box towards me, looking very embarrassed. Inside is a pair of beautiful earrings, with green stones which I have a horrible feeling might be real emeralds.

'God, they're beautiful. But I'd be bound to lose one or something.'

'Don't be silly. I want you to wear them. At least my earrings will be having a hot date even if I'm not.'

I give her a hug, and promise to ring later, and race up to town to meet Leila. She drags me into countless shops and we finally find a little black dress which doesn't make me look like I am six months pregnant with triplets. It's black velvet, and costs a fortune. I also buy some fantastic black suede shoes, so high I can't actually walk in them. But they are beautiful. Then Leila insists we get our nails done and starts lecturing me about underwear while the manicurists smirk. Eventually I agree to buy a new bra to shut her up. I feel like a trussed-up chicken. I also feel a burst of defiance coming on and ask Leila why I can't just wear something ordinary and if he doesn't like it he can bugger off.

'Don't be ridiculous: you're going to the Ivy, not Burger King. Anyway, it's about time you bought some nice clothes. Everyone needs a perfect black dress. If he doesn't turn out to be Mr Right, you can still wear the dress.'

'I suppose so, but the thing is I don't really want a Mr Right, I want a Mr Friday Night.'

'If a man said that you'd say he was a creep.'

'If a man said that he'd be gay, so shut up. You know what I mean. I like my life the way it is, thank you very much. I can't be bothered with all this sitting up straight and wearing uncomfortable bras. If it works out it will be complicated and tricky, and if it doesn't it will be mortifying and tragic. I can't win. I should have stayed at home.'

'OK, Little Miss Optimistic, ring him up and say you're

cancelling because you don't want to have to sit up straight. I'll take you to dinner at the Ivy, and you can slouch and I'll wear your vest. Now stop whining or I shall scream.'

We have lunch at Leila's office because she needs to get back to her desk. She orders sushi, and almost as soon as she puts the phone down her secretary arrives bearing little trays and chopsticks. I can't work out if she has trays of sushi ready at all times hidden in her desk, and if so is it safe to eat, or whether the delivery service is just very speedy round here. I demand a fork as I hate eating with chopsticks, which seem designed to make you look like a total berk or a smug bastard who has spend hours practising. Then I lounge about reading magazines while Leila runs about shouting at people and having countless phone calls where she's charming and seems to be having a chat with an old friend, and then puts down the phone and says, 'What a total prick.'

For some reason this reminds me of Lawrence, and I'm tempted to wander off to the office just to annoy him. But Barney's away, so there really isn't any point. I ring Charlie and discover he loves being at James's house, and they are having sausages for tea, and Coke, so he's in bliss, but can't stop to chat because he is playing a marvellous game with James which seems to involve running round the house screaming. Lucky Kate. I get changed in Leila's office and then totter round to the car park in my new shoes to stash the bags in the car. Walking turns out to be a bit of a challenge. I wish my new shoes had stabiliser wheels like Charlie's bike. I manage to get back to Leila in one piece, but have had to hold on to one lamppost and two sets of railings.

Kate's earrings look brilliant with my new frock, and Leila insists we go out for a quick drink to celebrate my transformation. I confess I can't actually walk in my new shoes, and she marches me up and down the office giving me handy hints. Apparently you need to tip your head back, chest out, and hips forward, which I can just about do, but you also need to clench your bottom and pull your stomach in, which I cannot. We walk to a local bar, and I nearly fall over twice and have to have a vodka to try and calm down. Leila starts telling me all about James, and how brilliantly things are going.

'He makes me laugh, and the sex is great. What more could a girl want?'

'Can't think of anything off-hand. So have you told him about the wedding yet?'

'Not yet, and anyway I've gone off all that church stuff, it's so obvious. But I think a blessing somewhere magical would be nice, somewhere remote like the Sahara.'

'Leila, I am not trekking through the Sahara just to hold your flowers.'

'Well, perhaps not the Sahara. But somewhere exotic, with great light so the photos look fantastic. Maybe Barney could do the snaps.'

'Good idea. If you really want to do twenty-six takes of your wedding, I'm sure I could persuade him.'

As always, Leila meets people she knows, one of whom she slept with last year. I'm sure she could parachute into the middle of the Amazon rainforest and within five minutes she would bump into two old friends and a former lover. We get involved in a long riotous conversation. Suddenly I realise with horror that it's five to eight and I'm going to be late. Leila helps me stand up and sends a waiter off to find a taxi. She gives me a huge hug, which nearly makes me fall over again, and wishes me luck, and then tells everyone that I am off on my first hot date for decades. The entire bar wishes me good luck. Could slap Leila sometimes but the taxi arrives before I have time to thank her for sharing my pathetic private life with a roomful of total strangers.

I arrive at Mack's agency at eight twenty, which I suppose is slightly cool – not like me at all so I'm rather pleased. Mack is pacing up and down in reception, which is not cool at all, so I feel I have a slight advantage. Good thing too, because I practically fall out of the taxi on to the pavement, just as Mack looks round. I pretend I meant to get out this way, and pay the driver. The agency has revolving doors. Mack walks towards them smiling and begins to push the door from his side. I manage to push the door in totally the opposite direction so the whole thing judders to a halt. Mack then takes a step back, the doors revolve very quickly indeed and I am catapulted into reception at great speed. I'm able to slow down before I hit the reception desk, and mercifully do not fall over, but it's not entirely how I'd planned to make my entrance.

Mack looks at me for what seems like hours, and says with a smirk, 'Do you always launch yourself into buildings like that? Great dress, by the way.'

'Thank you. I'm breaking in the shoes for a friend and they're still a bit lively. I seem to remember you insisted on a black dress last time we spoke. I've got my jeans in the car, so I can always change.'

'No, no, keep it on. Well, at least while we eat.' He grins, and the security man sitting behind the reception desk coughs and drops his newspaper. Mack glares at him. 'Look, my car's downstairs so let's go off to dinner unless you want a tour of the office.'

'No, that's fine. I'm not sure these shoes are up to touring. Food sounds good to me.'

The lift arrives, and Mack explains that he was lurking in reception because Bill, the security man, has the IQ of an ironing board and doesn't like using the telephone. So he just tells everyone who turns up after six pm that the person they've come to meet has gone home. We descend to the basement car park. The atmosphere is electric, and I'm having difficulty breathing in anything approaching a normal fashion. Mack keeps looking at me, and then looking at his feet. The lift doors open and we walk to his car, which is a grey BMW, one of those special huge ones that looks like it's been designed to carry the entire Bundesbank to lunch. Mack fumbles in his pockets for the keys and presses a button whereupon the car goes into a little disco routine complete with flashing lights before the door locks click open and the lights come on.

'Oh I say, how very 007.'

'Yes, but don't touch any buttons or you'll blow us all to kingdom come.'

'OK. Can I drive?'

Mack hesitates for a second, goes a bit pale, and then says, 'Sure, why, are you into cars or something?'

'No, I just wanted to see your face.'

'Oh very funny. Well, be my guest, but if you drive it into a wall I'll refuse to speak to you for the entire evening.'

'I thought these kind of cars usually come with little men in peaked caps to drive them.'

Mack looks embarrassed.

'Don't tell me you actually have a chauffeur. Where is he, in the boot?'

'He's not a chauffeur, he's the company driver. I've told him I don't need him tonight, since you'll be driving. Actually it saves us a fortune on cabs.'

'I bet it does. Economy drive, really.'

'No, really it does. Anyway it was part of the set-up when I arrived. Give me some credit: I wouldn't actually choose this car, or a driver, come to that. But our chairman is rather keen on all that kind of bollocks. And if he has one we all have to have one.'

'What, the whole company? Or just the top boys? Because if everyone gets a BMW and a driver I'm applying for a job here tomorrow. I suppose secretly you're yearning for a Reliant Robin.'

'Are you going to be sarcastic all night?'

'Probably. I'm nervous.'

'So am I.'

'Shall we start again?'

'What?'

'Come here and I'll show you.'

Mack grins, and visibly relaxes.

'If you're going to do what I think you're going to do, I'd rather wait until we're out of the car park, if you don't mind, and off the security monitors. Otherwise poor old Bill will have a heart attack.'

'Fair enough. Do you actually know how to drive this thing?'

'Shut up and get in.'

We race out of the car park at astonishing speed, and I sit back and enjoy being driven by someone else for a change. A hideous noise suddenly belts out of the CD player, very loud 'Smack Your Bitch Up'-type music. Mack brakes and grabs the disc.

'Sorry about that, I was listening to it this morning for a pitch we're doing next week. It's awful, isn't it?'

'Not the kind of thing you can really sing along to, unless you hate women and have a serious drug habit.'

'Quite. Describes our client perfectly. So, do you really want to go to dinner?'

'Yes.'

'Bugger.'

'This dress cost a fortune. It might as well go somewhere posh for dinner.'

'Couldn't we just drop the dress off at the Ivy, and go home?'

'No. Leila made me promise to write down all the famous people I see.'

'Leila?'

'Leila Langton; she's my best friend. Do you know her?'

'Christ, I know her. She's terrifying. Do you have lots of frightening friends?'

'Loads. And she's not frightening, she's lovely.'

'Not if she thinks you're trying to nick one of her clients, she isn't.'

'Oh, that explains it. She said I wasn't to worry if she turned up at some point during the evening and took you outside for a quick word.'

He laughs, and then suddenly pulls over and stops the car. 'Now what was it you were going to show me in the car park?'

Never made it to dinner. Barely made it back to Mack's house. End up ordering pizza at two in the morning. It's bliss to be in London where you can order things at two in the morning. It's bliss to be in Mack's bed. Bliss, bliss. Dress is a resounding success, I lose track of my shoes entirely, and my new bra is awarded a certificate of merit for effort, but is soon discarded as surplus to requirements. I'd forgotten how nice it is to spend hours in bed with a desirable man – it makes a change from chocolate Hobnobs and the remote control although it's infinitely more exhausting. In between passionate interludes which seem to go on for hours, we talk and talk.

We finally surface at lunchtime on Saturday. I realise I'll

have to leave soon if I'm going to get home and change before picking up Charlie. Mack startles me by suggesting he drives me home and meets Charlie, and then we drug him so he goes to sleep early. I point out that I don't think Charlie will appreciate me turning up with a stranger, and will probably refuse to get into the car, let alone take drugs, so we end up deciding that I'll go home and Mack will drive down later tonight.

Drive home in a daze. Kate takes one look at me and says, 'Wow. He must be quite something.'

'Yes, and he's driving down tonight for an action replay. Do you think I should try to be a bit more cool?'

She looks at me and we both start laughing.

'Oh Christ, I forgot. Your earrings. Oh God, I've no idea where they are.'

I ring Mack on my mobile and ask him to try to find them. He calls back five minutes later and says he's found one under the bed and another on the stairs, and are they real emeralds, because if so he's keeping them. I explain to Kate that her jewels are safe, and then Charlie bounds down the stairs and nearly knocks me over, and we have a long cuddle while he tells me all the marvellous things he's been doing. I feel sure they aren't as marvellous as what I've been up to, but naturally do not say this. His list includes drinking Coke in bed, and throwing wet flannels at Phoebe while she was asleep, and then running away and hiding in the garden. I'm about to remonstrate when Kate explains that Phoebe got her own back with the garden hose, which is why Charlie's bag is full of wet clothes. I thank her and promise to meet her for coffee at the earliest child-free opportunity.

Charlie is exhausted, and sits happily watching a video and occasionally telling me fabulous snippets from his overnight stay with James. He's even willing to have an early bath and supper. I tell him I have a friend coming down later, but he will probably be asleep before he arrives.

'Is it Leila?'

'No, a new friend. He's called Mack.'

'Like Old Macdonald?'

'Not really. Anyway, you'll probably be asleep. But if you're still awake I'll bring him in to say hello.'

'OK, Mummy. Mummy, you know Coke?'

I assume he means the fizzy drink – I hope he does – and say, 'Yes.'

'Well, I want it for my packed lunch. It's brilliant.'

'Charlie, you know the school rules. Water or juice.'

'That's just stupid. Can we have Coke tomorrow for lunch? It's the weekend, you know.'

'Yes, probably. We'll see. Now let's get you into bed.' I hope he goes straight to sleep. Sometimes when he's very tired he falls asleep really early, but sometimes perversely it means he stays up extra late jumping on his bed. He's chatting to his collection of soft toys as I creep out of the room, telling them how fantastic Coke is.

Mack turns up at nine. He's brought supper, which is lucky because I have no food in the house and would have had to resort to cheese and crackers, and not much else. We sit by the fire eating, and Mack complains that the village is not on his map, and he had to take compass readings and consult a madman at the local garage to find his way here. I point out that the London A–Z does not cover the villages of Kent, and he throws salami at me. We indulge in a minor food fight, and then begin kissing. The door bursts open and Charlie marches in. He takes one look at Mack and says, 'Oh, you've got cake.' Indeed there is a cake, a posh chocolate one with lots of swirls of chocolate on it, still in its white box from a smart Soho patisserie. Mack introduces himself, and I refuse point blank to sanction cake-eating in the middle of the night, but agree to put it in the fridge for the morning.

I march Charlie back up to bed, and he seems totally uninterested in who the strange man was on the living-room floor. But somehow I feel like I've been caught out in unsuitable behaviour. I've never brought anyone home before. Not that there have been a huge number of opportunities to bring anyone anywhere, but on the few occasions where it has been an option I've always gone for their place, or hotels. Somehow Mack is different, but I don't know why, or whether this will turn out to be a weekend fling, in which case I don't want Charlie involved. Have a mini meltdown on the stairs, and explain to Mack that I'm feeling rather overwhelmed. He says he quite understands, and he'll go if I want him to. Which I don't. I make coffee and decide the best plan is to stay right where we are, with the door barricaded shut, so if Charlie does come wandering in again at least we'll get some warning. At about three in the morning the living-room floor finally proves too uncomfortable, and the sofa too narrow, so we stumble up to my room to find Charlie asleep in the middle of the bed, doing his starfish impression. Mack smiles, and says he'll sleep on the sofa, and I should get in with Charlie and let him wake up with just me. Which I think is very sweet. I tell him so, and we end up back in the living room, clinging on to the sofa until we both fall off. Stagger off to bed at dawn, feeling totally shattered, but happy.

I wake up with Charlie, who is frighteningly lively and bounds off into the living room and switches on the television before I can stop him, so poor Mack is woken by cartoons at full blast. Thank God he has kids of his own and can cope with early-morning TV. Charlie seems totally unfazed by Mack, and merely asks him if he agrees that Shreddies are disgusting and no one should be forced to eat them. Mack says it depends, which I think is an excellent answer. Charlie wants to know what it depends on, and Mack says, 'Whether your mother is about to give you a bowl of Shreddies, and I'll get thrown out of the house for saying they taste like cardboard.' Charlie is delighted, and so am I.

'Don't worry. If she makes you go out in the garden you can stay in my house; it's got a door and everything.'

'That's good to know, Charlie, thanks.'

I haven't the heart to tell him the 'house' is actually a filthy old shed, full of mud and sticks. Charlie disappears into cartoon land, and I offer Mack the chance to catch up on some sleep in my bed while I have a bath and make breakfast.

We decide to go to a pub for lunch before Mack heads back to London. Charlie plays happily in the garden, which has a swing and a stray dog which has appeared out of nowhere but seems very friendly. Mack and I talk, and it turns out he's feeling a bit shellshocked too but does not want to go home, and is thinking of ordering a new extra-large sofa to be delivered in time for next weekend. The logistics of this are going to be tricky: we want to fix up something for next weekend, or sooner if possible, but Mack has his kids for the weekend, and I don't want to dump Charlie again. A motorway service station doesn't seem a very auspicious place for a liaison. We end up deciding to talk later as there must be a solution, and then we go home and finish reading the papers, and Charlie does jigsaws. Mack finally leaves at teatime. Charlie is engrossed in his wildlife programme and merely waves, and Mack and

I spend twenty minutes saying goodbye in the kitchen, both agreeing that it's been an extraordinary weekend. He says he'll call in a couple of days when he knows what his plans are.

I feel a terrible pang as his car disappears down the lane, but also a huge sense of relief as the combination of both Mack and Charlie is somehow totally draining. Gentle questioning of Charlie during bathtime reveals that he thinks Mack is all right, but he prefers Leila because she brings toys and not just cake. Then we move on to why I am incapable of buying toothpaste which does not taste like sick. He finally goes off to sleep after two escape attempts, clutching a sword and wearing a plastic helmet.

I ring Leila for a debriefing session. She says it all sounds great, and is expert at decoding phrases like 'I'll call you in a couple of days'. I'd forgotten just how complicated this all is. It's a bit like cracking the Enigma code really. If he hasn't called by Friday afternoon I think it means he's a bastard, but Leila says not necessarily: he may have outstanding commitment issues. We move on to how I should react if he does call. Screaming 'Thank God, I've been sitting by the phone for the last three days' is hopeless, apparently, and will guarantee disaster. And you are not allowed to ring them, because this signals that you are a desperate bunny-boiler. I just have to be calm, and if possible leave the answerphone on, so I can play back any messages to Leila and work out an appropriate response.

I feel catapulted back in time, and seem to have turned back into my teenage self waiting for Gary Johnson to ring and ask me to the school disco. Which he didn't, so I wish I hadn't thought about it, really. I decide that, despite brilliant advice from Leila, I will simply answer the phone when it rings, and if he hasn't rung by Wednesday I'll call him and ask him what the fuck his problem is. Leila says this is hopeless, but may turn out to be right because she is halfway through a new book which says that playing games is wrong, and you should just go with your instincts. As my instinct is to hide under the duvet for the next six months, this may not be entirely helpful either. I tell Leila that really I'm not even sure I want him to call, because life is complicated enough already. She doesn't fall for this, and says very sweetly that if I don't stop being so pathetic she will drive down right now especially to slap me.

Charlie wakes up in the middle of the night and launches himself into my bed saying he has had a horrible dream about a fox eating Buzz and Woody. We end up having to troop outside with a torch to reassure him they are still alive. They are very pleased to see us in the middle of the night, and put on a little cabaret performance, running up and down the hutch and hurling straw about. I put Charlie back into bed, but have to stroke his back for twenty minutes to get him calm enough to fall asleep. I wake up a few hours later feeling like I have had no sleep at all. Charlie is very grumpy, and is on the point of tears and tantrums when I come up with an inspired plan, suggesting we get dressed and then put Buzz and Woody in their run and eat our breakfast watching them. Charlie is desperate to let them out so they can run round the garden and flatten all the plants. But I persuade him that the ground is too wet from the overnight rain, and they'll get sore feet from all the mud because they don't have wellies. Charlie offers to lend them his.

Mack rings on Monday, and Tuesday, and Wednesday. Leila says he has obviously not been reading the right books, because he is showing classic signs of being a stalker. It looks like next weekend is going to be too tricky, but we arrange to meet up the weekend after that. Lizzie agrees to come to stay – Matt is away at a conference – and she gets very excited and starts planning a thrilling itinerary of things to do with Charlie. Her list includes swimming, making a cake and going for long walks. Charlie's list includes toy shopping and renting unsuitable videos from Blockbuster's. I have a day in town in the office, but manage to resist the temptation to call Mack to see if he wants to meet for lunch. Apart from anything else, there's too much work to do on various new jobs. Barney is very cheerful because his cut of the Cornish film is being hailed as a minor classic by everyone who sees it.

Lizzie arrives at teatime on Saturday and is greeted by a small mountain of jigsaws which Charlie has got out specially. A heated debate follows as to when exactly they can drive to Blockbuster's. I leave before pieces of jigsaw start flying about, and arrive early at Mack's. He opens the door dripping wet and draped in a towel. He greets me with a kiss and invites me to join him in the shower. I can't face stripping off in broad daylight so make him turn the bathroom lights off, and then fall over. Eventually manage to get into the shower, which is enormous, all marble and frosted glass with water jets everywhere, and a whole panel of buttons. I press one inadvertently during a passionate clinch, and the water jets instantly turn into powerful torrents which nearly knock us both over. It's a bit like being in *The Poseidon Adventure*. Mack resets the controls with one hand and manoeuvres me into the corner furthest away from the buttons with the other. Emerge half an hour later feeling very happy, and also very, very clean.

'Christ. That was fantastic. I knew spending a fortune on

that bloody shower would come in handy one day. I'm starving. What do you fancy? Chinese or Italian?'

'Chinese, I think.'

'Great. I'll just make a call and we can eat here.'

The takeaway turns out to be rather different from the usual five tinfoil containers delivered by moped. A waiter turns up with countless little padded bags, and there's no special fried rice in sight. He decants the food into bowls, and produces chopsticks, napkins and a small vase of orchids. The table looks beautiful, and he's even found some candles and lit them. Finally he asks if we want him to serve the food. Mack says he thinks we can manage, and he departs clutching what looks like a £20 note.

'Don't tell me this lot only cost £20?'

'Darling, that was his tip. I've got an account. Trust me, you don't want to know what this cost. *I* don't even want to know.'

Mack rejects chopsticks in favour of a fork, saying he thinks chopsticks are a cunning ploy to serve smaller portions and humiliate customers simultaneously. I could get to seriously like this man. We talk about music, and discover a mutual love of Motown, Mahler, Sinatra, Elvis Costello and Italian opera, but only if the sopranos don't get too shouty. We end up dancing to Frank Sinatra, which quickly descends into a passionate clinch on the sofa when it turns out that neither of us can actually dance to 'New York, New York'.

Hours later we collapse into bed and I sleep for a few hours, and then lie watching Mack sleep. I could get very fond of him indeed, and hope to God this doesn't all end in tears and sick.

I'm admiring the curve of his shoulder when he opens one eye and says, 'For God's sake, stop staring at me like that and do something useful, Moneypenny. If you make me a cup of coffee, I'll be yours for ever.'

'Shaken but not stirred, right?'

Mack laughs and I go downstairs to make coffee wearing his dressing gown, which is much nicer than mine. I wonder if I can smuggle it out with me when I leave. I ring Lizzie who sounds exhausted. Apparently Charlie persuaded her to rent *Jaws* and then got terrified, and she had to spend half the night assuring him that great white sharks cannot swim up stairs.

We have breakfast in bed, and resurface at lunchtime. I grab a quick shower, after insisting Mack goes downstairs to make coffee and does not join me in the shower or I'll be there for hours. As I'm leaving he says, 'I'll ring you tonight, shall I, and you can tell me how much you're enjoying wearing my dressing gown.'

'Blast. I thought you wouldn't notice.'

We end up spending so long kissing goodbye a small crowd gathers on the pavement.

I get home at teatime, and Lizzie and I have a quick debrief in the kitchen.

'He sounds lovely.'

'He is.'

'Lucky you then, right?'

'Yes, I suppose so. I mean yes, definitely. It's all a bit overwhelming, really. And I'm totally knackered.'

'Yes, but it's nice knackered. It's not like doing-the-ironing knackered.'

'No, Lizzie, it definitely beats doing the ironing.'

Charlie is delighted to see me. He and Lizzie have spent the entire morning making a cake, and he's eaten most of the icing. I make a cup of tea and Lizzie leaves, and I get Charlie into the bath. After a bit of scrubbing I manage to get the icing sugar off his arms and legs. We have supper watching telly, and I agree he can sleep in my bed. He finally falls asleep at nine thirty after a long random-chatting routine. I call Mack who says he's been listening to 'New York, New York' again, and thinks he has come up with a dance routine which will score well if we ever find ourselves on *Come Dancing*.

I talk to Leila and Kate who both agree that Mack sounds wonderful. I'm not sure I can cope with the full implications of this, so decide to try not to think about it and just see how it goes. I then spend hours thinking about it, and end up feeling sick. I'm due to go off to Spain with Mum soon, for the half-term holiday. Mack has to work this weekend, and has his kids next weekend. He asks if I want to bring Charlie up to stay but I think it might be a bit early to start introducing children into the picture, and anyway I have a million things to do before we leave, so we agree to meet up once I'm back from Spain. I half wish I wasn't going away at all, but know it's never a good idea to drop everything as soon as there's a man on the scene, however tempting this might be. And anyway, Mum would kill me.

'At least I'll have brown legs by then.'

'I'd rather you had white legs and didn't go at all. Where are you going anyway?'

'Lanzarote. And don't make any snobby jokes. I couldn't face another half-term holiday in the rain.'

'Sounds good to me. Will my dressing gown be going?'

'Yes, probably.'

'Good. I shall program it by remote to keep an eye on you.'

'Don't be daft: with Charlie in my room and Mum next door the only thing that will need keeping an eye on is my blood pressure.'

'Will your mobile still work in Spain?'

'No. Mainly because I'm not taking it. Otherwise Barney will ring every day.'

'Fair enough. I tried that once, but the agency sent a messenger to the hotel with a new phone.'

'Christ. Don't tell Barney.'

Gatwick. Six thirty am. This is going to be a very long day. Mum has an enormous suitcase and has brought her entire collection of Tupperware which she says is bound to come in handy. She also has an enormous first-aid kit which she is carrying in her hand luggage, although I'm not sure how useful four miles of crêpe bandage will be if the plane ditches in the sea. Charlie has packed so much into his rucksack he can't stand up straight, and has insisted on wearing his favourite hat, which unfortunately turned out to be a bright-yellow woolly bobble hat Mum knitted him. Sporting this combined with his new holiday shorts, he thinks he looks cool. At least we won't lose sight of him in a crowd.

Have a mini crisis in duty free because I can't work out if Lanzarote is part of the EC, and therefore duty free is defunct. I have visions of buying duty-free cigarettes, being strip-searched at customs and spending the entire holiday in a *Midnight Express*-type nightmare with the local police. Finally a saleswoman with a bright-orange face, purple eyeshadow and blue hair comes over, squirts me with disgusting perfume and asks me if I need assistance. She confirms I can purchase duty free, so I buy cigarettes and a bottle of Chanel, to cover up the horrible smell which is actually beginning to make my eyes water.

The flight is awful. The combination of couples having blistering rows and slapping toddlers is not conducive to relaxation, and we discover the airline has invented a new game to amuse the cabin crew: shrinking the seats so that only under-tens can actually sit down in them without dislocating their hips. I have lost all feeling in my feet before the plane even takes off. The food is indescribable, but Charlie likes all the little packets, opens them all, and then refuses to eat anything. Mum says her chicken is Nasty so she will just drink tea, if they ever bring it round. Apparently, however, hot drinks are only served five minutes before landing. Mum has packed snacks in her capacious bag, but it takes us ten minutes to get it out from under the seat, and then Charlie's tray goes flying up into the air and deposits plastic cutlery and packets of butter all over the people sitting in front of us. They are very pleased.

I spend ages loitering by the loos so I won't need reconstructive surgery for my knees upon arrival. The plane starts to descend. It actually looks like we'll land in the sea, and Charlie gets worried. I tell him it'll be fine: the plane has special inflatable aprons like a hovercraft so if the pilot misses the runway, we will simply float back into the airport. The woman in the seat behind us tells her husband, 'Isn't it marvellous, Trevor, they think of everything, don't they?' We land without use of inflatables, and the captain tells us to stay sitting down with our seatbelts on, and not open lockers and give fellow passengers concussion until the plane has come to a complete stop and the crew can make a quick getaway if things turn nasty.

The luggage takes hours to appear, and we get through customs without being arrested, and locate a gaggle of reps, all in dazzlingly bright polyester outfits. The glare given off by the combination of orange and cerise is almost blinding, and I get a slight electric shock from the Welcome Pack. I find the queue for pre-booked car hire and discover everyone is making a huge fuss about being asked for 5,000 pesetas as a deposit for petrol. When it's my turn I offer to pay 15,000 pesetas, but only if they can upgrade our car. The other passengers stare at me with undisguised contempt. One man even tries to explain to me that it's only 5,000. I learnt this trick from Barney, who says it always works, but it is vital not to try it in Germany or they think you're taking the piss and give you an old Volkswagen camper van.

The car-hire man gives me a smile and the keys to a brand-new Renault Laguna estate. Everyone else gets keys for Renault Clios. They all glare at me as we make our way up the ramps to the car park. The car is very swish, with hundreds of buttons with totally inexplicable symbols on them. God knows what $\pm$ is supposed to stand for, but I decide not to press it just in case it turns out to be some sort of Gallic joke and inflates the airbags. I keep forgetting where the gearstick is and try to change gear with my left hand which hits the electric window switch, producing a small hurricane effect inside the car. Charlie thinks this is delightful.

I manage to find the villa by sheer good luck, but pretend I had a cunning plan all along. Mum is very impressed but cannot undo her seatbelt, which seems to have locked. I spend ages trying to get it undone, and then realise Charlie has got out of the car, put his rucksack back on and disappeared through the front gates into the villa. Mum and I exchange a horrified glance, and then we hear him yell, 'There's a pool,' followed by an ominous splash. Sprint to the pool. Charlie has jumped in still wearing his rucksack, and has sunk to the bottom like a small boulder. I'm just about to leap in when he bobs up, minus his rucksack, and says the water is lovely. Grabbing him, I begin a long safety lecture about never jumping into pools, especially

114

wearing rucksacks. I hope to God this really is our villa, or the owners may appear at any moment and call the pool police. We retrieve the suitcases from the car and unpack, and then we wander down to the main road which runs the entire length of the resort and find a pizza restaurant. The ice-creams come with sparklers, which Charlie adores.

We gradually settle into a holiday routine of swimming in the mornings, and trying to have a siesta, but Charlie thinks this is a ridiculous idea.

'Only babies go to sleep in the day.'

'Not in Spain. Everyone has a sleep when it gets hot, and then they stay up much later.'

'How late?'

'Oh, about nine or ten.'

Charlie considers this for a moment, and attempts to lie down and sleep, but gets up again after five minutes, just as I am starting to doze off, and says, 'It's no good. I can't sleep and that's final.' So we end up playing the Alphabet Animal game, where you pick a letter and name all the animals you can think of. Charlie insists that Amster is acceptable for A, and Big Squirrel is fine for B. We move on to drawing.

We attempt a bit of culture and visit the house of Cesar Manrique, a local artist and sculptor. It's all very beautiful, with wonderful volcanic pools and gardens, and an art exhibition. Charlie is not impressed with the art, but discovers a kitten in the café and feeds it ice-cream. Charlie, and the entire café, sit rapt with delight at the kitten's antics, and I know he'll remember this far more than he'll remember the art, and, I suspect, so will everybody else. We find the loos to wash his hands and discover that the doors have metal sculptures on them. The female figure has huge bosoms, and the male figure is painted bright green and has a coat hook in the form of a willy sticking straight out.

In fact I could have had my eye out, and walking into a toilet door and poking your eye out on the willy of a symbolic metal figure would probably not go down too well with the holiday-insurance people. Charlie thinks the toilet sculptures are the best thing he has ever seen, and insists we take photographs to show Miss Pike.

I'm slowly getting the hang of the hire car, but still have nightmare moments when for a split second I think I'm in the passenger seat and Charlie is driving. We visit the local hypermarket which turns out to be something of a challenge because Charlie insists on buying anything unusual-looking, as it might be lovely. And Mum insists on buying anything British. Supper consists of Spam, instant mashed potato and digestive biscuits, with Coke for Charlie to drink. He eats far too much, and then runs about screaming.

Mum suggests a slap might be in order. 'Be my guest, but I don't think it'll calm him down, do you?'

'Don't take that tone of voice with me, I'm only trying to help.'

'Oh right, and slapping him is going to do that, is it? He's not used to having Coke with meals, or so many biscuits.'

'Oh of course, I might have known it would be my fault. Children are never naughty any more, are they? They just have sugar highs or food allergies.'

'Mum –'

'Well, honestly.'

At this point Charlie pauses in his manic run-about and says, 'Mummy. Stop being horrible to my lovely nana.'

I'm sorely tempted to explain that lovely Nana is advocating slapping, but manage to restrain myself.

'Shut up, Charlie, you're being very silly. Stop running around and come and have a bath.'

'I hate you, Mummy, and so does Nana.'

116

Nana smirks, but says, 'Don't be rude, Charlie. Come on, you and me will go and get you a lovely bath.'

I'm left fuming in disgrace.

Mum reappears and says Charlie is now in the bath and will not stop splashing, so perhaps I might like to use non-violent tactics to get him to stop. I march into the bathroom and pull the plug out of the bath, and order Charlie to get out instantly as I've had enough.

'Enough of what, Mummy?'

'Charlie, don't push your luck. Stop splashing and get out now. Or there will be no ice-cream tomorrow. At all.'

I'm not sure bribery is an official good-parenting technique, but at least the NSPCC is not currently running a campaign against it, so I guess it'll have to do.

Later on, when Charlie is asleep, we sit on the balcony drinking tea, and Mum says, 'I'm sorry about earlier, I was just a bit tired.'

'Oh don't be daft, Mum, it's fine. I know he can be annoying – well, more than annoying really. Sometimes I wish there was a remote control for children and you could put them on pause for a while.'

Mum smiles. 'You were much worse.'

'Thanks, Mum.'

It's vital I head her off now before she can start on her When You Were Young stories. If I have to hear one more time about the day the vicar came to tea and I ate a whole box of Maltesers under the spare bed, and then came downstairs and was sick all over the living-room carpet, I shall definitely scream.

'I'll cook tomorrow, if you like. I could do pasta.'

'No, I want you to have a proper rest.'

'It's OK, Mum, I like cooking.'

This is a downright lie, but I don't want her to spend the

117

entire holiday cooking. She's actually a really good cook, but likes to rely on tins when she's abroad because 'you know where you are with a tin of corned beef'. Quite.

'All right then, that would be lovely. We're very proud of you, you know, your father and me. And you're doing a grand job with Charlie.'

'Thanks, Mum.'

We visit the volcano park on the island, and Charlie gets very excited and wonders if the tyres will burst driving over molten lava. Mum goes very quiet. We drive for ages over what was once lava, and the landscape is quite extraordinary. At the top of the mountain, there's a huge car park. Mum refuses to get out of the car, saying she has brought a flask of tea and would rather stay and drink it and read her book. I eventually persuade her to come with us by telling her that the car will not lock if there is still a passenger sitting inside it, and the alarm will go off. We walk up the path from the car park and join a cluster of people gathered round a series of small holes in the ground. A park ranger is standing by a hole with a bucket of water. I have a sinking feeling this will turn out to be one of those demonstrations where a tiny puff of steam is produced, and children get very bored. But instead he pours the entire bucket of water down the hole, and without warning a huge jet of steam shoots about fifty feet into the air and everybody screams. Mum drops her camera, and Charlie sticks his head up my sweatshirt.

Everyone then recovers and begins laughing, and Charlie re-emerges and says, 'Make him do it again.' It turns out he stands there chucking buckets of water down holes at five-minute intervals, and we see steam shoot out four more times before Charlie will agree to have a drink in the very stylish café built right on top of the volcano. I presume they have some sort of early-warning system to avoid the café being shot down the hill on a lava flow, but all the same Mum is not keen to linger over coffee just in case. We find a little stone hut built over what appears to be a large barbecue. Then we realise it's actually a huge iron grille over a hole which goes right down into the volcano. The heat is sufficient to cook whole chickens, and we peer down and see a distinct red glow. I manage to restrain Charlie by his hood, and explain that climbing on to the grille to get a closer look would not be a good idea, as apart from anything else his sandals would melt.

We gradually adjust to the slower pace of life, and I rediscover the joys of lying in the sun drinking gin. Bliss. I buy a huge inflatable whale for Charlie to play with in the pool. It takes hours to blow up and I nearly pass out twice. Mum keeps him plastered with factor 200 suncream, which makes him look like one of those nutters who swim the English Channel covered in a thick layer of goose fat. I ring Mack midweek – I've been thinking about him a lot. Being away from home has given me a whole new perspective. I miss him, but I've also managed to get myself totally panicky and wish we could go back to the *Brief Encounter* stage. I end up deciding that the whole thing is doomed, and can't work out what on earth he sees in me. Maybe I've just had too many gin and tonics.

I spend the first ten minutes of the phone call having a lovely flirty chat but suddenly find myself going all pathetic and saying, 'Um, Mack, I've been thinking.'

'Oh, God. You shouldn't do that, you know.'

'No, I was just thinking, you know, trying to work out what on earth you see in me.'

Christ, I can't believe I really said that.

'Well, you've got my dressing gown, for a start. Will that do?'

'No.'

'Bugger. Um, well, you make me laugh. That's important.'

'Yes, but I've been thinking and I'm not an obvious choice for a man like you.'

'What do you mean, a man like me?'

'Well, one surrounded by gorgeous young women all day long, with no kids and flat stomachs. And legs like giraffes. I mean, I don't know if anyone has ever told you this, but you *are* rather gorgeous, you know.'

'Thank you, Quasimodo.'

'Fuck off.'

'Oh great, back to the swearing now. Have you been talking to that Leila friend of yours?'

'No, and that may be part of the problem. I know if I rang her she would tell me to get a grip.'

'I like that woman more and more. Look, I don't know who these women are that are supposed to be surrounding me, but the only ones I meet can drink me under the table, and frankly they frighten me a little bit. Well, quite a lot actually. I don't have time for all that serial-dating stuff and anyway I'm crap at it. I'm sorry if things have gone a bit fast, but I don't like hanging about. I like you. You're strong, and you make me laugh.'

'Do you mean strong like carrying bags of potatoes on my head? Because I can't do that either.'

'No, and stop interrupting. I mean strong as in not clingy. And you know, it's funny, but I've never met a majorly beautiful woman who wasn't just a tiny bit vacuous and smug. And none of them are sexy. At all. Believe me.'

'You should go into advertising, you know; you're quite good at the old persuasive pitching. I feel much better now.'

'Good. So have I got the job, then?'

'Let's just say it's looking good, James, it's looking good.'

'Thank Christ for that. You had me worried for a minute. Sweet dreams, darling.'

And he puts the phone down. I wish he wouldn't do that. Arrive back at the villa with a very stupid grin on my face. It looks like I may have got myself a new dressing gown for a little while longer.

Chapter Six

Of Lice and Men, and 101 Dalmatians

THE JOURNEY HOME FROM Spain is horrendous. A family with a small baby sits behind us on the flight, and one with a lively toddler sits in front. Both scream for the entire journey. The toddler does let up for a bit, but only to try to steal his mother's food. She slaps him, and he starts up all over again. Think the NSPCC should do emergency training sessions on all charter flights.

Charlie is very pleased to get home, and rushes around touching all his toys and hurling duvets about, like a small animal marking out its territory. Kate rings and says the weather has been appalling, and she doesn't want to see me until my tan fades. Mack calls and wants to see me straight away, but settles for next weekend. Then Lizzie calls.

'So. Did she make you eat Spam?'

'Yes.'

'I knew it. Honestly, when is she going to get over this obsession with tinned meat?'

'I don't know, but it can't come soon enough for me.'

'Did she drive you crazy?'

'No, she was lovely actually. We had a bit of a scene one night, when Charlie played up and she wanted to slap him. Or rather she wanted me to.'

'Oh dear, I bet that went down well.'

'Yes, we had a frank exchange of views, but then we had a nice cup of tea and it was fine.'

'Oh good. Did you go anywhere interesting?'

'Not really. We went to the volcano and it took me twenty minutes to get Mum out of the car, but really it was just a lovely lazy week. Charlie had a brilliant time, and I think Mum did too.'

'Good. Lucky you, I've been driven nearly demented by those bloody people and their sodding kitchen.'

'Oh dear. Charlie's brought you back a really tasteful present – will that help?'

'If it's as tasteful as that hideous donkey you brought back from Turkey, then to be frank, no.'

It rains constantly, so my tan is fading fast. Charlie goes back to school, but the endless rain means they get no proper playtimes. All the children get very grumpy and are almost hysterical by the end of the day after being cooped up in a small classroom with the wet play box, which consists of old tattered board games and a couple of bean bags.

Mack has come up with a new plan for us to meet this weekend. He's arranged to pick up Daisy and Alfie on Friday, and will take them home at teatime on Saturday, and then belt down the motorway and spend the rest of the weekend here. I can't help asking how his ex-wife, Laura, feels about this. But Mack says they had a very amicable separation, which began at her instigation. She's now doing a course in homoeopathy, which is something she always wanted to do but Mack made fun of it. She's also found a wonderful new man, Troy, who's a herbalist and wears sandals, even in winter. Mack thinks he's a complete prat, but the kids like him.

123

Apparently Laura and Troy are rather keen to go to a lecture on Friday night, on the uses of common hedgerow plants, although I think Mack might have made this up, but it means it's all worked out rather neatly. And if I ever need miniature doses of belladonna Mack knows just where to get them. I'm secretly hugely relieved that there's no bitter ex-wife lurking about in the background, especially not one studying the uses of common hedgerow plants.

Charlie's school has a church service this morning, something they do once a term. Charlie is sulking, because he says he's a pagan. I tell him he can always stay at school and do maths worksheets with the school secretary, and he decides he might go after all. We get to the church, which is tiny and ancient and down a narrow lane surrounded by fields, which the recent rain has turned into a quagmire. Charlie steps into a huge puddle as soon as he gets out of the car. I do the best I can with a tissue, but he looks like he's been in a mud-wrestling tournament on the way to school, and lost every round. The sun comes out, and the scene is transformed into something from a Thomas Hardy novel. I love living in the country at moments like this: it's very beautiful and timeless and deeply relaxing. Apart from the mud.

Mrs Harrison-Black seems to have appointed herself church warden for the day, and is annoying everybody by standing at the door reminding people to wipe their feet. The children all file into the pews at the front and begin to wriggle. The parents are all at the back, and I manage to sit with Kate and Roger, who says Sally has told him to keep a close eye on William because he managed to get at the biscuit tin this morning and ate a whole packet of chocolate digestives while nobody was looking. Sure enough, he can be seen batting a small boy on the head with his hymn book. Miss Pike is oblivious, and seems to have fallen asleep, or maybe she is praying. Roger does his best with piercing glares, but to no avail. Finally he has to tiptoe to the front, lift William up out of his seat and whisk him outside before he can cause permanent brain damage.

We wait for the telltale sounds of slapping outside the church door, but thankfully Roger has gone for the Reasonable But Firm approach, and comes back in a few moments with William holding his hand, looking much calmer. He sits with us, and concentrates on swinging his legs backwards and forwards, just missing the pew in front each time. The vicar arrives, and begins a rather brave attempt at a modern child-friendly service. He asks the children what happens if we put a seed in the ground, and they all look perfectly blank, until one little boy puts his hand up and says, 'Does it grow into a beanstalk?' I assume he's hoping that the text for today might turn out to be *Jack and the Beanstalk*. The vicar says very sweetly, 'Well, sort of. But what I really meant was that from little acorns mighty oaks do grow,' and the children all go, 'Oh.'

The vicar then waffles on for what seems like hours about the importance of being kind, and nice, and how we should all sow the seeds today of the people we want to be tomorrow. I'm in the middle of a daydream where I find a packet of seeds which turn me into Cindy Crawford, when the children all stand up and begin 'singing' 'All Things Bright and Beautiful'. A very old lady has come to play the organ, and she's not exactly zippy in her delivery, so the children finish the song about three minutes before she does.

The vicar then launches into prayers, and thanks the children for behaving so nicely in God's house. They all look around them as if God will appear from behind the font at any moment. Then they all surge back up the aisle and cause a massive scrum by the doors in an effort to get back out into the sunshine and run around before their parents can grab them and get them into cars for the drive back to school. One dad is shouting, 'For Christ's sake, get into the car now,' just as the vicar comes out of the church. Roger and I start to laugh, and Kate says she once did something similar right behind Our Vicar at the harvest festival, and was so embarrassed she went bright red from head to foot and Mrs Taylor asked her if she was feeling ill. I offer to take William and Rosie back to school so Roger can get off to work, and he gives me a look of utter devotion and practically sprints to his car. William and Charlie sit in the back saying rude things about Our Vicar, and Rosie sits in the front telling me that when she's grown up she's not going to have any babies at all. And if she does they will not be boys. Definitely. Because everybody knows boys are stupid. Luckily the boys are too busy libelling the vicar to hear.

I spend the rest of the morning trying to sort out a pile of bills, bank statements and various other irritating bits of paper which seem to have arrived in the last few days. Barney rings and tells me about two new scripts: both dog-food commercials, studio jobs, and from Mack's agency.

'Great, Barney, I could do with the work. I've just been looking at my bank statement.'

'Oh, that's a huge mistake. You should just throw them in the bin like I do.'

'Well, if these jobs happen I won't have to worry.'

'Of course it probably didn't hurt us that you're shagging the creative director.'

'I beg your pardon?'

'Oh, don't play the innocent with me. I'm talking about you and Mack MacDonald. You know, the one that turned up on the shoot and you nearly fainted when he got out of the car. Honestly, I'm not totally blind, you know.'

'Yes you are, Barney. Don't you remember that job in Wales when the crew all changed clothes, and then put their coats on back to front? You were oblivious until they all put their hoods up and started falling over.'

'That was different. Anyway, Lawrence told me.'

'Told you what? Honestly, what is the matter with that man? Come on, tell the truth, you didn't notice a thing.'

'Look, don't get stroppy with me. I'm not complaining, you know – it's about time you found yourself someone to play with when Charlie goes to sleep.'

'Bugger off, Barney.'

'I was just joking, I think it's great. Just remember to tell Mr MacDonald that calling Lawrence about a folder he'd left at the hotel was a bit obvious, even for Lawrence. You know what he's like, he probably rang the hotel and sent forensics down.'

'Look, it's very early days yet; I was going to tell you when there was really something to tell. I know how much you adore agency people.'

'Well, he's all right, actually. We had a word in the car and he seemed to have a fairly good grip on things.'

'You mean he said you were a genius.'

'Well, yes, there is that, but that's a sign of good taste, nothing wrong with that.'

'So you're not going to go on and on about it then?'

'On the contrary, my dear, I shall whine and moan like I

always do, and if he turns up on one of my shoots and starts throwing his weight about you're fired. But apart from that, good luck to you. Oh, and by the way, I told Lawrence I knew all about it and was delighted. He's furious.'

'You are brilliant, Barney. Thanks.'

'My pleasure. When are you in next?'

'Friday, if that's OK?'

'Fine. We've got another crap script in, for fizzy orange or something – crap idea but I might be able to do something with it. Should be a nice job, it's got a piano going down a staircase. It'll be a huge budget.'

'Barney. I've told you, I am not doing any more jobs with you that involve stunts, and that's final. I still have night-mares about that helicopter.'

'Oh no, this one's not like that. I just need to work out how to stop the piano once it's come down the stairs, and it'll be a piece of cake.'

I tell Mack all about my chat with Barney when he phones, and he offers to track down Lawrence and punch him on the nose. I'm sorely tempted but decline. Actually it's a bit of a relief that Barney knows, which means the entire office knows. I won't need to make secret phone calls, and can call on the girls for support if I need it. I'm also pleased that Mack seems totally unconcerned that Lawr-ence is gossiping his way round London. I ring Leila to share the news with her, and she is jubilant and says we are now officially a couple and should have a dinner party at the first opportunity. I tell her I would rather stick pins in my eyes. She says she knew I would say that.

Work on Friday turns out to be frantic, because the timing on the dog-food films has suddenly changed and they want

128

them as soon as possible. I spend the entire day doing budgets, and arguing with Lawrence. Get home exhausted at ten, and Edna says Charlie was such an angel tonight she promised him she would ask Mummy to take him swimming tomorrow morning, and she hopes I don't mind but it was the only way she could get him out of the bath. We have a cup of tea and she tells me all about her son's latest request for a loan. Apparently he wants a new car this time. Bastard.

Charlie creeps into my bed at some point during the night, and wriggles so much I get hardly any sleep. I wake up very grumpy and tell him there's no way I am going swimming. He sulks, and I lose my temper and tell him not to be such a brat, and he bursts into tears. I spend the next half-hour reading him a boring book about badgers to make up, and then he launches into a mammoth Lego-building session which is still going on when Mack arrives. Mack is forced to build a Lego castle while I make supper, but he copes very well. He even manages to persuade Charlie to stop firing the Lego 'cannon balls' into the fire, which I have failed to do for most of the afternoon, by suggesting that they go into a special cage in the castle and are saved up until the invaders arrive.

I begin a long debate with Charlie as to what is the appropriate time for going to bed. I let him stay up late as a special treat – actually only an extra half an hour but he thinks it's midnight – and then he barely makes it up the stairs before falling asleep. I come back downstairs to find Mack is also asleep, so I leave him to doze and I'm doing the washing-up when he wanders into the kitchen.

'Sorry about that, the kids were exhausting last night.'

'No problem, do you want some more coffee?'

'Actually what I really want is some sleep. I don't suppose

there's any chance I could actually sleep in a bed, is there? I mean, with you, in a bed, waking up with you. You know the sort of thing.'

'Alright. But don't be surprised if Charlie bounds in at the crack of dawn.'

'Fair enough. I'll try to bear that in mind.'

It's lovely settling down to sleep with him like proper grown-ups, and my newly acquired tan is a great success. Mack turns out to be not tired at all, and I fall asleep in his arms hours later, feeling very content but a little bit worried in case Charlie charges in and is shocked at the sight of Mack in my bed. As it turns out he simply pushes Mack to one side and jumps into the middle of the bed at some point just after dawn. Mack merely groans, and has obviously had previous experience of being booted in the stomach by small boys because he doesn't even wake up. We all doze for a bit, and then Charlie suddenly sits bolt upright, shouts, 'Cartoons,' and rushes off downstairs, desperate not to miss a second more. I get up to make coffee, and return to find Mack is in the bath singing.

Everything seems very peaceful, and I'm in the kitchen when Charlie comes running in.

'Mummy, did you know Mack is in our bath, and he's got no clothes on?'

Oh God: I feel sure my response to this will be vital to Charlie's whole psychological future.

'Well that's alright, isn't it, Charlie? I mean, Mack can have a bath, can't he?'

'Yes, of course he can. But when I went into the bathroom he covered up his willy.'

I bet he did.

'Yes, well, that's OK too, isn't it? I mean, some people are shy about that sort of thing, you know, Charlie.'

'Yes, I know. But he used my flannel, Mummy. Tell him not to use my flannel.'

I think this might be some sort of defining moment: must stand firm, yet be reassuring.

'Charlie, don't be silly. You can have a clean flannel out of the airing cupboard at bathtime. There's no need to fuss. Now, do you want crispy bacon and scrambled eggs, or just crispy bacon?'

He yells, 'Bacon,' and rushes off back upstairs and then I hear him shouting, 'It's OK, Mack. You can use my flannel to wash your willy, Mummy says she'll get me a clean one for later.'

Mack eventually wanders into the kitchen, with a huge grin on his face.

'I promise to bring my own flannel next time. Honestly, I nearly had a heart attack. What happened to the lock on the door? Did you take it off specially to traumatise house guests, or what?'

'Charlie kept locking himself in. I nearly had to call the fire brigade the last time, so I took it off. I'm sorry he barged in on you like that.'

'Oh, don't worry. Alfie went through a phase of sitting watching me in the bath, and I got quite used to it. He didn't like me using his flannel either, but there's only so much silent staring a man can take.'

We spend the morning dodging Lego, but feel very calm and relaxed. Mack reads the papers and I cook lunch. I could get used to this. Manage not to burn anything, and Mack says it's the best lunch he's had in ages, which is a patent lie unless smart London restaurants have gone into terminal decline, but nice of him to say it anyway. We go for a walk in the woods, and Charlie tries to track down pheasants by leaping into bushes clapping his hands. He's astonished that this does not reveal a single one. Mack asks if we would like to come up to town next weekend and stay with him in his house, because Alfie and Daisy will be there and it might be fun. I'm rather staggered by this, but agree and say I'm sure it will be lovely. Can't help feeling that meeting his kids is another crucial landmark stage, and I'm not sure I'm ready for it. But at the same time I'm glad he's asked. Charlie says he would like to meet Alfie, but is not keen on girls because they are silly and whisper. Mack says he knows just what Charlie means, and I pretend to get annoyed which delights Charlie.

Mack leaves after tea, and drives off up the lane tooting his horn a lot which Charlie thinks is brilliant although I suspect the neighbours might not agree. Charlie and I spend ages wrestling with homework. He insists on drawing Viking warriors with machine guns, despite my assertion that this is both historically inaccurate and not what Miss Pike had in mind when she said they should write about what they did at the weekend. I ring Leila and Kate in the evening, and the general consensus is that meeting the kids is a vital next step, fraught with potential pitfalls, and bound to be a bit tense. But it also means he is serious. I go to sleep feeling dazed and confused, but very happy.

The next few days are frantic with work, because the dog-food jobs have got the go-ahead and the shoot is set for next week. Luckily the scripts are nothing to do with Mack, so I won't have to face working with him again just yet. One of his junior creative types, Paul, has written them, so he's the face of the agency for this job. I go into the office and have endless meetings with Barney, which Lawrence tries to infiltrate with a variety of pathetic excuses which finally provoke Barney into telling him to piss off. Paul turns up at the casting, and turns out to be rather sweet. I tell this to Mack and he gets all huffy and says he hopes I don't make a habit of having passionate encounters with agency personnel on shoots, because if I do he will just have to turn up unexpectedly to check how things are going.

A letter comes home from school to say lots of children in Charlie's class have got nits. I get busy with the comb and shampoo, and sure enough Charlie has got them too. Actually I only find three, but according to the leaflet they breed at an astonishing rate, so there could be seven million by morning. I feel sick, and wash my own hair, twice. Try very hard not to share my revulsion with Charlie, but I needn't have worried. He's delighted – he calls them his nitters and wants to keep them in a bottle, so he can try to teach them tricks. I veto this firmly, and have a hideous time in Boots buying multiple bottles of nit shampoo. I decide to buy all the embarrassing goods at one time, so I take the opportunity to stock up on condoms. The woman behind the till gives me a very funny look.

I ring Mack on his direct line at work, and he answers the phone with a very curt, 'What?'

'What a lovely way to start a conversation. You must tell me where you learned your phone technique.'

'Oh hello, sweetheart.'

He sounds very pleased to hear from me, which is always nice. I wonder if he'll be quite so pleased when I tell him he may have nits.

'Look, I'm just ringing to let you know that Charlie has managed to get nits, so you might be well advised to have a session with a comb fairly sharpish.'

There's a long silence.

'Oh dear, you aren't terribly pleased about this, are you, I can tell. Come on, say something.'

'Yes, yes, sorry. I was just thinking how delightful life with small children can be.'

'Tell me about it. I'm sure I can arrange for Charlie to draw you some pictures if you'd like. He's absolutely thrilled.'

'Please don't go to any trouble on my account. You know, come to think of it, I think the kids got them last year. Laura tried nettle oil or something, but then she gave up and we had to import some special Agent Orange stuff from the States because they got urban-guerrilla ones that nothing else would shift. Still, I'm sure Charlie's got a much better class of rural types – bit of sheep dip and you'll be fine.'

'Oh stop it, it's horrible. Oh, that reminds me, there's something else I should tell you.'

'Don't tell me, let me guess. Ringworm?'

'No, but I think I may have to have a new haircut, a bit like Demi Moore in that GI film. Would you mind terribly if I was bald next time you saw me?'

'I think I might slightly, yes. Unless you were planning on doing lots of press-ups wearing one of those tiny little vests. That might be OK.'

'Oh very funny. At least you've got short hair. I had a dreadful time in Boots buying nit cream, and loads of condoms.'

'Got plans for the weekend, have you?'

'Well, I hope so. But he might change his mind once he knows about the nits.'

'Oh I doubt it. I shouldn't think a few little headlice will put him off.'

'You couldn't be more specific, could you? I need cheering up.'

'Well, I would love to, darling, but actually I'm in a kind

134

of board meeting at the moment so if you don't mind I'll call you back on that one.'

'Oh fucking hell, Mack, why didn't you say?'

'I really must go now, sweetheart, but I'll call you tonight.'

And he puts the phone down. This is all going very well; even nits do not appear to faze him.

Charlie is very excited about the weekend in London with Mack, and wants to know if I think we'll get anywhere near Hamleys. I have long discussions with Mack about how helpful it will be if the first time Charlie meets Alfie and Daisy he gives them nits, but we decide that as we have used the toxic shampoo repeatedly it should be alright. I drive up on Saturday morning, with Charlie playing a long complicated game which turns the car into a spaceship. He is the captain, naturally, and keeps giving me instructions to fire lasers at the traffic, and go into warp drive on the motorway. I end up wishing the car did have lasers as it would be a brilliant way to deal with lorries.

We arrive just as Mack gets back from picking up the kids, and we decide to head off for lunch at Pizza Express. Alfie and Charlie instantly take to each other, and launch into endless chat about *Star Wars* and Pokémon. Alfie is like a mini Mack, which endears him to me instantly. Daisy is very quiet and watchful, and insists on sitting next to Mack, pushing Alfie out of the way so he falls on the floor. But otherwise lunch goes without incident, and on the way home I sit in the back of the car with the boys, and get a tiny smile of approval from Daisy. Apart from that she does her best to pretend I'm simply not there at all, which is perfectly understandable but I think this weekend will feel like at least a fortnight.

Mack has a beautiful house in Notting Hill, all stripped floors and state-of-the-art televisions. I count five separate remote controls. But it's not exactly child-friendly, and vital bits of Lego fall down the cracks between the floorboards, which amplify the sound of running children into something resembling a herd of buffalo stampeding down a canyon. The kitchen is very minimalist, and the fridge turns out to be full of Coke and beer. Decide to go shopping for supper and take the boys out with me so Daisy can have Mack to herself for a while. I get another tiny smile.

The boys trot along quite happily on the promise of an ice-cream on the way home. I spend ages wandering about and buying huge quantities of food, and then we get home to find Mack and Daisy watching videos. The boys decide the film is for girls, and demand it's replaced with something with guns. I leave Mack to sort this out while I try to fit the food into the fridge. Then we have a whispered conversation in the kitchen about the plans for tomorrow. Mack is holding out for Hamleys, while I, wanting to aim for something slightly more cerebral, am advocating the Science Museum. We end up pressed up against the kitchen door so as not to shock the small people next door.

'I'm really enjoying this.'

'Me too.'

'No, I mean having you and Charlie here.'

'Oh, yes, well, so am I. Though I'm not sure Daisy's too keen.'

'No, I hadn't realised quite how possessive she'd be. Rather sweet really.'

'Yes, but let's not push it. We can go off a bit early tomorrow, so you get some time on your own with them.'

'OK, but only after Hamleys. I've promised Charlie we'll have a look at laser guns.'

'Christ, Miss Pike won't stand a chance.'

There's a deafening crash from the living room. Alfie has managed to knock a coffee cup and a glass off the table and on to the floor in the middle of a sword fight with Charlie. There is smashed china and broken glass everywhere. Both boys look very crestfallen, and Daisy looks nervous. Mack does a bit of yelling, and then suddenly Charlie bursts into tears and says he doesn't like being shouted at, and it's not his fault, and he wants to go home, and Alfie bursts into tears and says he didn't mean it, and Daisy goes very pale and looks tearful.

Mack says, 'Oh Christ,' and doesn't seem sure what to do next, so I put my arms round Charlie for a cuddle and motion for Mack to do the same with his two. He finally gets the message and sits down on the sofa, whereupon they both sidle up to him for a hug. Peace is restored and we have a talk about how important it is to be careful with cups and glasses. Charlie offers to pay for the broken things with his pocket money, which is very sweet except he doesn't actually get pocket money, because last time we tried it there were endless arguments about why he couldn't borrow next week's money. I suggest we start making supper with Charlie and Alfie being my special helpers. They love this and begin chopping up vegetables into very odd shapes with blunt knifes I have found in the cutlery drawer: the kitchen knives are all terrifying steel things, which look like they would slice off small fingers in a second.

Supper is a success, and even Daisy says the food is all right, and then we begin baths and bedtime which goes on for hours. In the end I give up and lie down on the bed with Charlie, stroking his back until he falls asleep. I know I should be firm and simply leave him to it, but the bed in the spare room is huge and he looks tiny in it. Go back downstairs to discover Daisy is still up and Mack is looking desperate. Determined not to get drawn in, I offer to make coffee, and hear Mack insisting she goes up and tries to get to sleep. She relents and we have a peaceful half-hour drinking coffee. I decide I'll sleep with Charlie in the spare room because, apart from anything else, Alfie has managed to move into Mack's bed while nobody was looking, and is now fast asleep and will almost certainly be joined by Daisy at any moment. She's now asleep in the top bunk bed in the small bedroom which Mack has kitted out for weekends with the kids, but Mack thinks it is highly unlikely that she'll stay there.

'This is not quite what I had in mind when I asked you up here for the weekend.'

'No, but as long as they're happy I think we should go with it.'

'Yes, I suppose so, but I kind of hoped we might get some time to ourselves. I'm sorry I yelled at them earlier on. I'm not terribly good at crisis management with small children.'

'I know, I noticed.'

'My mum and dad didn't really go in for hugging much; they preferred a good slap, to be honest. I mean, don't get me wrong, they loved us, and they were no different to all the other parents round where we lived. But I'm not too sure how to handle things when it all goes pear-shaped. Laura usually took over.'

He looks anxious, which I find very endearing.

'It's fine, Mack. You're allowed to shout, it's just I think everyone was a bit nervous, you know. It was fine. They adore you, so you must be doing something right.'

Mack looks relieved, and we end up behaving disgracefully on the sofa and then we stagger off to our separate beds, full of sleeping children. I'm very pleased the weekend has not descended into hysterical tantrums yet, but can't help feeling a tiny bit overwhelmed by it all. Don't really think I'm cut out for a stepgirlfriend role, and certainly not stepmother. I'm lying in bed trying to decide exactly what I am cut out for when Charlie wakes up and bursts into tears because he's had a horrible dream where he got lost and couldn't find me. I cuddle him back to sleep and try not to read too much into his dream, as he's had similar ones in the past without the faintest hint of there being a man lurking anywhere in my life. But I'm glad I was there when he woke up.

The Science Museum is a huge hit, though personally I think it would be a much better place if you could rent energetic teenagers to charge around the exhibits with the kids, and then you wouldn't have to pretend to be interested in how engines work. We eat lunch in the café, which costs a fortune, and then race off to Hamleys where Mack spends a staggering amount of money on toys for himself and the children. We get a cab back to the house and after a quick cup of tea we leave. Charlie and Alfie part as new best friends, Daisy looks relieved, and Mack says he will ring later. It's very nice to be back with just Charlie and me, and he spends the journey home telling me that Hamleys really is the best shop in the world, and that Alfie can come to his party but not Daisy because she is stupid. When Mack rings he says he thinks the weekend was a huge success because Alfie said I cooked good spaghetti and Charlie was great, and Daisy said the spaghetti was OK. I feel ridiculously pleased. Just hope no one turns out to have caught nits.

The next morning Edna arrives early and I manage to get to the studio for the dog-food job at what feels like the crack of dawn. The dog handler turns up with four dalmatian puppies, all of whom are adorable but wildly over-excited. Then various owners start arriving with their puppies, and they're all very demanding and cannot control their dogs who run round jumping and barking. One bites the electrician who is very stoical and says, 'It's only a nip, and they don't mean no harm.' This is going to be a very long day. We now have twenty puppies, four stroppy owners and a desperate dog handler who begins to erect a puppy cage so we can try to keep all the animals in one place for more than two seconds. The cage turns out to be enormous, and it takes three of the crew an entire hour to help him get the bloody thing to stop wobbling and looking like it will decapitate any animal put inside it. When it's finished there's enough room for all the dogs and the dog handler, so he sits inside on a blanket and begins trying to calm the puppies down by singing to them. The entire crew are spellbound by this, and it does seem to be working as the puppies all lie down and stare at him in amazement. Barney arrives and says, 'What the fuck is he doing?' which doesn't really help but luckily the man doesn't hear. The set is finished, and we get ready for the first shot. The idea is a woman comes into her kitchen, puts new dried puppy food into a bowl for her dalmatian puppy and then, lo and behold, hordes of the little buggers stream in through the dog flap. Simple really, and the voiceover will say, 'Puppies love it. You'll love it. So will the neighbours. You'd better buy the big bag next time.'

Barney and John, the lighting cameraman, have a frank exchange of views, because John thinks if the camera moves too quickly following black and white puppies running over black and white tiles then the whole thing will strobe, and Barney thinks this is crap. They end up deciding to do it Barney's way, but also do a slower version in case John is

140

right. 'But if it doesn't strobe in rushes then you're in serious trouble, John.' John starts to backtrack and says he didn't say it would, only it might. While all this is going on two of the owners have got into an argument about whose puppy is most likely to win Best in Show at a forthcoming competition. This results in one of them deciding to walk out in a huff, because apparently she has never been so insulted in her life. I spot her grabbing three puppies and storming off, and try to persuade her to stay but she's adamant. When I inform Barney we now have only seventeen puppies, he says, 'Christ, why didn't you stop her?'

The puppies are quite keen on the bowls of food for a while, but then they all get full up and start lying down for little sleeps. Except for one little stalwart, who we christen Porky, who keeps shooting through the dog flap and bolting down food like crazy. We decide he's our best bet, and start to get some shots of him jumping up at his pretend owner and wagging his tail. The other puppies then wake up and join in the fun. Barney says, 'Where the fuck is Cruella de Ville when you need her?' and another owner gets the hump and threatens to leave.

We finally manage to get what we need, but it takes hours longer than we thought and we go into overtime, which cheers the crew up no end but makes Barney furious. The agency people have behaved themselves perfectly, and Paul has even managed to divert a couple of runaway puppies just before they belted out of the studio doors. The client makes a brief appearance but leaves when the puppies begin nipping people's ankles. Barney goes off muttering about bloody dogs. There's another script in for the same stuff, but this time the version is designed for bigger dogs involving a St Bernard breaking down a door to get into the kitchen and eat a bowl of food. The voiceover will say,

'Leave the door open. You know it makes sense.' I'm really not looking forward to it and half hope the client will hate this one. But I have a sinking feeling he won't and we'll all be back here before we know it, up to our necks in St Bernards.

Chapter Seven

It's My Party and I'll Cry if I Want To

C HARLIE COMES HOME FROM school clutching an invitation to a birthday party, and is already wildly excited because the birthday boy, Jack, has promised there'll be a magician and Coke and indoor fireworks. I ring Jack's mum Clare to ask for tips on a present, and tell her Charlie is thrilled about the magician and fireworks. She says, 'What magician?' and it turns out she was planning on Pass the Parcel and lots of jelly, but may be forced to reconsider now or ruin Jack's reputation entirely. We agree that small boys really are hopeless, and I promise to ring Kate to see if she knows any magicians who are likely to be available at very short notice.

By the time I ring Kate Clare has already called her, but she couldn't help. We've decided on a joint birthday party for Charlie and James this year, which is due in a couple of weeks. Kate has booked the local swimming pool for a vast fee, and the café upstairs will provide a birthday tea. We're allowed to bring our own cake, but everything else has to come from the café at hugely inflated prices. But – and this is the really fantastic bit – they do all the cleaning up afterwards, blow up all the balloons, and even provide a party helper. Marvellous. I don't care what it costs as long as I don't have to pick squashed birthday cake out of the living-room carpet.

Kate also has Phoebe's party to sort out for next month, which is proving far more tricky. The only hints Phoebe will give her are that James is not allowed to come, and if Kate won't let her wear make-up and high heels she'll die. She's on a bit of a mission about make-up at the moment, and Kate has had to start hiding her make-up bag in the back of the wardrobe to foil Phoebe's attempts to leave the house looking like Pat Butcher in *EastEnders*. I come up with the inspired suggestion that Kate books someone from a beauty salon to come round and do a full make-up for Phoebe and her friends, and then Kate can take photographs of them all. Kate rushes off to tell Phoebe and rings back ten minutes later to say sulking Phoebe has been transformed into hysterically happy Phoebe, and I'm invited to the party as guest of honour, but only if I promise not to bring Charlie.

It looks like the second dog-food job is on, and Barney has been ringing in an increasingly hysterical state because Lawrence has arranged for countless owners with St Bernard dogs to turn up at the office so Barney can see if he likes the look of them. I spend hours on the phone sorting out the studio and crew, and Mack threatens to visit the shoot with a couple of cats just to liven things up. We are due to meet up this weekend, but I tell him if he makes one more crack about cats he can stop in London.

I'm just walking in the door after picking Charlie up from school when the telephone rings. Charlie rushes to answer it, and gets there before me.

'Oh hello, Barney.'

Christ.

'Yes, I'm very well, thank you. Would you like to hear my best new joke?'

Double Christ.

'What do you call a donkey with only three legs?'

There's a long pause.

'A wonkey.'

I wave an apple at Charlie and tell him that cartoons are now on. He drops the phone and runs off clutching the apple.

'Hi, Barney.'

'I think your son and heir might have just called me a wanker.'

'Out of the mouths of babes, Barney, out of the mouths of babes.'

'He's a bit lippy for a babe, isn't he, just like his mother. Anyway, moving swiftly on, have you sorted out the crew yet?'

'Yes, I faxed the stuff through hours ago.'

'Oh good, I'll look at it when I get back to the office. Lawrence has got more bloody dogs coming in, so I've done a runner. Talk to you later.'

Poor Lawrence. I'm almost tempted to ring and warn him that Barney will not be turning up to give the dogs the once-over, but in the end decide it might be best to keep out of it. I do ring Stef and warn her, though, because Lawrence will try to take it out on her if she's not careful. Charlie wanders back in and wants to know if Barney thought his joke was good, and I say that he did, although next time he must let me answer the phone. 'Alright, Mummy, but I like talking to Barney – he's very nice, you know.' I can think of countless people who would be prepared to stand up in court on oath and swear otherwise, but decide not to disillusion him.

Jack's party day arrives, and I drop Charlie off at three pm. A lot of children are already there, and Clare looks on the point of hysteria. Jack is running round and round in small circles saying, 'I've got a magician, I've got a magician,' in an increasingly shrill voice, and snatching presents from the arriving guests. Jack's dad is wrestling them off him and saying, 'Remember we said we wouldn't open any presents until later.' It looks like there'll be a major scene at any moment, so I beat a hasty retreat before the screaming starts.

Kate comes round for a cup of tea with Phoebe, and we put on a video for her and creep off for a clandestine cigarette. We agree that we feel like naughty teenagers smoking in bus shelters. We try not to smoke in front of the kids, as apart from anything else the smug lectures are unbearable, and both admit to standing in the garden in the freezing cold with coats and hats on, simply to have a fag in peace. Pathetic really. I tell Kate that I'm feeling less nervous about Mack, but am still not entirely sure what's going on.

'I wish I could fast-forward six months and see how it all turns out.'

'Try not to think about it, and enjoy yourself while you can. It might not last six months. Oh, sorry.'

'It's alright. I'm just not very good at keeping calm and seeing how things turn out.'

'I know. Neither am I. That's why I'm crap at knitting. Anyway, what's the best thing about him? I mean, apart from the obvious.'

'He really makes me laugh.'

'Oh, that's vital. Phil never made me laugh – well, not for years anyway. Sometimes he made me snigger, but that was never on purpose.'

'How is he, by the way?'

146

'As infuriating as ever. His latest plan is to dump the baby on me for the weekend while they go off for a little break. Can you believe it? I mean, apart from anything else she's revolting. Even Phoebe was prettier than her, and she looked like a beetroot when she was born. And why on earth did they call her Saffron? You know, she had quite bad jaundice when she was born – she was bright yellow. They might as well have called her Daffodil. Phil says they want to have another one as soon as they can. God, what will they call it this time – Coriander?'

'They could go for Basil if it's a boy.'

This makes us giggle, and it's good to see Kate laughing, because last year she couldn't really laugh much at all. She had wanted to have another baby with Phil, before he announced that she had become old and boring and he was leaving her for a 20-year-old beauty called Zelda who modelled at his art class. Her real name is Sandra, but she decided to change it to Zelda when she became artistic. Apparently she thought Phil was marvellous, and understood just how important creativity was to him. Phil is an accountant, and not a very good one. He keeps losing clients because he forgets to send their forms in on time.

'But there is some good news. Apparently Zelda is getting a bit fed up with Phil already. Phoebe says last time they were there she told him to shut up twice, and said if he wanted to be creative he could cook lunch while she had a sleep. You know, I might end up actually feeling sorry for her.'

We pause for the full unexpectedness of this news to sink in, and then say, in unison, 'But not enough to have Saffron for the weekend,' and then it's time to pick the boys up.

The deafening noise of lots of over-excited children nearly knocks us over, and the magician is frantically trying to pack up his kit. Actually he looks close to tears. His rabbit is running round and round the living room pursued by lots of screaming children, and he's trying to wrestle his wand off a little girl who wants to take it home. Clare is trying to distract her with sweets but she looks very determined.

I spot Charlie and end up grabbing him by the back of his sweatshirt to get him to stop running. We're given a bag of sweets and a slice of cake by Jack's dad, who looks desperate. The journey home is fairly quiet as Charlie is busy eating his sweets. Then, without warning, he suddenly flings his piece of birthday cake out of the car window. I tell him he could have seriously injured a pedestrian with flying cake, but he is unmoved and points out that there was nobody walking along, and anyway the badgers will like it because it's well known they adore cake. So it will be a lovely treat for them for supper. Sometimes I really really wish I believed in slapping.

I try to provide a supper with no sugar content whatsoever, to counteract the party food. Charlie says he is full up and will only eat two crackers and a small piece of cheese before announcing that if he's forced to eat any more he will explode. He plays in the bath for ages, and tells me all about the magician who made a whole flagpole covered in flags come out of Jack's ear. He also produced a rabbit and lots of small packets of Smarties, and created all sorts of marvellous creatures out of balloons, which made rude noises when he let the air out. He obviously knew his target audience very well, because rude noises made by deflating balloons are a guaranteed winner with all under-tens. I agree it sounds truly marvellous and nonchalantly mention that Mack might be coming down later. Charlie seems totally uninterested in this, and wants to know if I think

Mr Smarty Pants (apparently this was the magician's name) would like to come to his swimming party. I point out that his rabbit would get wet, and this seems to do the trick.

Miraculously, he falls asleep almost immediately, and I have a peaceful half-hour trying to tidy up the house and myself before Mack arrives.

Mack looks shattered. The children have been very lively, and Alfie managed to throw up all over the back of the car on the way home. Mack's driven down the motorway with all the windows open, and says he's now so cold he's lost all feeling in his hands. I promise to do what I can to help him overcome this, and we end up on the sofa, after barricading the door shut with an armchair. We surface to make supper, and we're just drinking coffee and congratulating ourselves on our child-free evening, when Charlie starts banging on the door demanding to be let in because his tummy hurts and he's had a bad dream.

I let him in and he wants to know why the door was shut, and then starts describing his bad dream which involved Mr Smarty Pants turning up in the back garden and trying to steal Buzz and Woody. Mack seems to think Mr Smarty Pants might be Charlie's new name for him, and says he would never steal anybody's rabbits, and then I explain about the magician and he looks very relieved. I say Charlie should lie on the sofa while I go and make him some warm milk, but only for five minutes and then he must go straight back to bed. I come back to find Charlie snuggling in Mack's lap. Mack is trying to impress upon Charlie that it's vital he aims for the newspaper if he's going to be sick. Newspaper is spread over the entire living-room floor, and Charlie announces that actually his tummy doesn't hurt any more, but he still needs warm milk because he has had a fright.

He then proceeds to drink his milk as slowly as possible, and says he knows he's going to have another horrible dream, and this time it may be about vampires eating him because he had that one last week and it may come back. I run out of patience and march him back upstairs. Plonk him back into bed and issue dire warnings about not getting up again, which make him cry, so then I have to backtrack somewhat and do a bit of patting. I finally get him settled, and go back downstairs to find Mack has fallen asleep on the sofa. He wakes up with a start.

'What, oh God, he hasn't been sick, has he?'

'No, he's fast asleep. Sorry I woke you.'

'Oh it's OK, can't think why I'm so tired really. Must be all the motorway driving I seem to be doing recently.'

'Well, if you will live such a complicated life, Mr Smarty Pants.'

'I hoped you might have forgotten about that.'

'No. I think it suits you. Shall I call your PA on Monday and she can let the office know? It's a great nickname.'

'Don't you dare. Oh, and that reminds me, we've got a weekend work thing coming up at a posh hotel. Bit of corporate chat in the morning and then a dinner on Saturday, but the rest of the time is free. Would you like to come? The hotel's meant to be terrific.'

'Sounds great, but I'll have to see if Mum and Dad fancy a weekend with Charlie. It's not his birthday-party weekend, is it?'

'No, it's in August, and you can bring him if you want. I found out about it, and they do suites and have babysitters and everything.'

I'm very touched that he has checked out the childcare options. But I'm well aware that the entire weekend would be much more fun for us all if Charlie can stay at home with Nana and Grandad.

'What will I do while you're being corporate?'

'Oh, I think the wives and partners have some sort of bonding over beauty therapies or something. I'll find out if you like.'

'No thank you very much. I can't think of anything worse than being stuck with a load of corporate wives having beauty treatments; I'm not really cut out for pretending to be a Stepford wife. I just can't see me spending all weekend talking about private schools or the best places to go skiing while you sit in the bar and talk business.'

'As if. And they are not Stepford wives. Well, a couple of them are, but the others are perfectly normal, or they looked like they were at the last do I went to.'

'Hmm, well, we'll see. Anyway I've got Charlie's party to worry about first – have you decided what you want to do yet?' I'm secretly hoping he will decide not to come, as that way I can concentrate totally on the birthday boy. It turns out he has to spend the weekend with Daisy and Alfie as he won't see them for a fortnight after that, because Laura is taking them to see her mother. We start talking about the possibility of us booking a week away together in August, with all the children, but the potential for disaster and our attempts to find a suitable date defeat us entirely. We go to bed both half-asleep, but wake up in the middle of the night and discover we are feeling much more energetic.

I spend Sunday trying to build up my strength for the week ahead, and persuading Charlie that we don't want to go for a walk in the rain because jumping in puddles and filling your wellies with water is not something grown-ups really count as fun. Mack leaves just after tea, amidst howls of protest from Charlie who wants him to stay and play

Junior Scrabble. I end up having to offer to play instead, and Mack drives off with a big grin on his face at his lucky escape.

The St Bernard shoot turns out to be far worse than I could possibly have imagined. The dog trainer does not attempt to sing this time, but merely tries to stop the owners arguing. The owners all look like their dogs, with extraordinary hair and grumpy faces. We have five huge dogs, and they all smell awful. Two of them hate each other on sight, and begin growling in a very ominous way. Their owners have to sit at different ends of the studio. And the dogs slobber an amazing amount. The make-up woman refuses to go anywhere near them.

'I'm not here to wipe spit off dogs' chins. I've got a diploma, you know, I've worked with some really famous people.'

I manage to restrain Barney from sacking her on the spot, because we still need make-up for the actress who will be the pet owner and pour food into a bowl before getting leapt on by her dog. She's very game, and doesn't seem to mind the dogs jumping all over her, which is a relief really because we couldn't stop them even if we wanted to. The entire crew refuse to go anywhere near the dogs, so I end up wiping up dog dribble in between takes. The dogs get very hot under all the lights and have to be taken out for walks. One makes a break for it in the car park, nearly flattening the client who is just arriving. He's not pleased and wants to know where the animal trainer is, and why there are dogs all over the car park.

We eventually get enough shots of the dogs rushing across the kitchen floor, and move on to the bit where they knock the kitchen door down. The dogs don't want to jump up at the door, and then they finally get the hang of it and won't stop. Everyone gets very hot, and the dogs get niggly. And being stuck in a small airless studio with lights and wires all over the place, and five niggly St Bernards, is not much fun. In the end we get as much as we are going to get without killing the dogs and stuffing them, which we think the owners might spot, so we call it a day. Barney says in a very loud voice as he's leaving, 'Annie, write this down: if we ever get stuck in an avalanche and have to call for help, I don't want to be rescued by a fucking St Bernard.'

The crew fall about laughing, and all the owners descend on me in a fury. Then the two dogs who have been threatening to kill each other all day finally spot a window of opportunity to shake off their owners and get down to business. There's a tremendous sound of growling from the far end of the studio, and then the two dogs merge into a blur of flying fur. The owners rush to try to separate them, and a helpful carpenter throws a bucket of water on them, which stops them for a split second, just long enough for their owners to grab them and start dragging them apart. It turns out that soaking-wet St Bernards are even worse than dry ones, and it feels like we'll never get home, but one by one the owners depart and we start to pack up. Suddenly there is another commotion, and one of the electricians yells, 'Fucking dogs. One's had a crap in my toolbox.'

We all agree that we will never, ever, work with animals again.

The day of our joint birthday party arrives, and Charlie is up at six am and insists on wearing his swimming trunks to eat breakfast. Kate rings and says James is doing exactly the same, so I invite them round for lunch because Mum and Dad and Lizzie and Matt are coming, and at least it will fill in a bit of time before the party starts at three. Charlie thinks this is an excellent plan, and starts running up and down hopping. I persuade him to help me make salads for lunch, and he enthusiastically cuts up tomatoes until they are reduced to a pulp. I move him on to lettuce, but then spot him squirting vast amounts of Fairy Liquid into a bowl of water to make sure the leaves get really clean, so we have to start all over again. I'm roasting a chicken, and Kate has promised to bring round lots of cold ham to add to the meal. The oven makes the kitchen boiling hot, and then Charlie burns his hand on the oven door, and becomes hysterical.

The burn is tiny, but I hold his hand in cold water to make sure it doesn't get any worse, and then go upstairs to the bathroom in search of antiseptic ointment. Charlie follows me, moaning, and manages to walk straight into the bathroom door and cut his lip. He begins to sob, blood dribbles down his chin and he sobs even louder.

'I won't be able to go to my party.'

'Yes you will, darling, it's only a tiny little cut. It'll stop bleeding in no time.'

Give him a cuddle, but the tears are still falling and he's feeling very sorry for himself.

'I think I might need a tournament, Mummy.'

Can quite understand how a couple of medieval knights jousting on the front lawn might take his mind off things.

'What do you mean, darling?'

'You know, one of them bandage things you put on, like on *999 Ready for Action*.'

Didn't realise he had watched *999*, or any other first-aid programmes, come to that. But I know Edna adores them, which might explain it.

'I think you might mean a tourniquet, Charlie. That's a

154

kind of bandage you put on very big cuts, but not on tiny cuts on lips.'

Although if he carries on moaning I might give it a try.

'Yes, but have you got one, Mummy? I might lose all my blood out my lip and then I won't be able to swim at my party.'

He begins to sob again. I dab ointment on his hand, and then we hear Kate arriving with Phoebe and James, and he rushes downstairs with his injuries miraculously healed.

Mum and Dad turn up with an enormous Lego set for Charlie, who is thrilled and thanks them very nicely before charging upstairs with James to begin building. Lizzie and Matt bring another huge box of Lego which goes with the fort Mum and Dad have brought, and also a hideous gun that makes an appalling squealing noise. Lizzie apologises but said Matt was sure Charlie would adore it. He does. I have to take the batteries out so we can eat lunch in peace. Mum and Lizzie have made an enormous cake: it takes two of them to carry it out of the car. It has 'Happy Birthday, Charlie and James' on it in blue icing, and weighs a ton. Which is a good job because at the last count there are forty children coming to the party, with assorted parents and grandparents.

Thankfully we don't have to worry about party bags because no one does them round here: a slice of cake and a bag of sweets is the usual drill. Lizzie is most impressed and says her friends in London spend a fortune on party bags for children's parties, and get quite competitive about the contents. Everything is looking good and we set off in three cars, but for some reason Dad turns out to be driving the car at the front of our little convoy and he's the only one who doesn't know the way to the pool. Very complicated man-oeuvres in narrow country lanes follow, but finally Kate gets in front in her car and leads the way.

We arrive and round up the party guests and receive their presents, which we have to grab off the boys to stop them opening them in the car park. The party helper turns out to be a small teenage girl who looks about twelve, which does not bode well. But she does a very impressive line in yelling, and soon has them standing in two straight lines, telling her what they want to eat for tea. She marches them off to the changing rooms, and before we know it we're all in the pool jumping off the slide on the special inflatable island. Mum and Dad sit in the visitors' gallery and take loads of pictures. There are four lifeguards, and they stand at each corner of the pool watching very closely to make sure that the children who shoot down the slide at the end of the island come back up again. They all have long poles to poke at anyone who appears to be drowning, and I'm generally very impressed by how attentive they are. Kate is too, and we are just congratulating ourselves on how well everything is going, when we see a small red-faced boy being pulled out of the pool clinging on to a pole and coughing and spluttering, looking like he's swallowed ten gallons of water.

We rush over to see if he's alright, but he seems perfectly happy once he's got his breath back. The lifeguard looks very pale, though, and says that there's always one at every party, and at least this one wasn't sick. Quite. The pool staff have obviously had lots of experience of getting over-excited children out of the water, because they simply deflate the inflatables and shout, 'Time to get out.' The children all groan but do as they're told, and then the helper reappears and marches them off to get changed. This proves as tricky as we thought it would be, but finally all the children are reunited with their clothes and are sitting upstairs eating chips and wearing party hats. The cake is a big success, and both Charlie and James go very pink while 'Happy Birthday' is sung.

Phil appears halfway through tea, carrying baby Saffron. He's late and Kate is furious. Saffron starts to cry and Phil tries to hand her to somebody else to hold, but no one is daft enough to fall for this so in the end he says he'd better go, but will come round later tonight to see James properly. James seems fine about this but Kate's upset and says she doesn't know why he bothered to turn up at all, but then she calms down and says well at least he did turn up, which is what really matters as far as James is concerned. I suppose it is really, but it does seem just a tiny bit thoughtless. Especially as Kate has organised the whole thing and all he needed to do was get here on time.

Parents start arriving to collect their slightly damp, over-excited children, who all say they have had a lovely after-noon. I drive home feeling totally exhausted but relieved that it's all gone so well, and there were no tantrums. Kate is taking James and Phoebe straight home; James has already opened a couple of presents by the time she gets him into the car. Charlie opens all of his as soon as we get home, and is delighted with each and every one. I can't help noticing that in most cases the poorest parents have provided the most expensive gifts. I've noticed this before, and always find it strangely moving. Mum says it was the same when I was little, and one very rich mother dispatched her daughter to one of my parties with a packet of Smarties and a balloon wrapped up in posh paper. Whereas Ivy, who had no money at all and did three cleaning jobs to try to make ends meet, sent her little girl along with a brand-new Cindy doll and an outfit she had made for it out of sparkly chiffon. I remember the chiffon outfit, and we go off into a reverie about long-lost dolls and their clothes until Dad says, 'For God's sake, what does a man have to do round here to get a cup of tea?' Am tempted to answer, 'Put the kettle on,' but resist.

I spend the rest of the weekend helping Charlie recover from the excitement of the party. Mack rings and is regaled with how brilliant it was by Charlie. Then he talks to me, and says his friend Graham is having a dinner party next Friday and would like to meet me. Which is nice, but it's the night of the school barbecue.

'You're not seriously trying to tell me that you would rather go to a school barbecue than come to an extremely smart dinner party with me, are you?'

'Well, yes, actually.'

'Darling, I really want you to come.'

'Yes, I know, but Charlie really wants to go to the school thing. There's going to be a tug-of-war and we've been practising. Last year the men won the Men versus Women competition, so it's vital we win this year.'

'Oh well, that's different. If there's a tug-of-war I can quite see the attraction. How exactly do you practise for a tug-of-war, if you don't mind me asking?'

'Oh, Kate has tied a rope to an old tree stump in her garden, and we've been trying to pull it out. I just keep falling over, but I think I've got a bit stronger.'

'I've never met a woman who tries to pull out tree stumps before. It's a whole new world for me. What a busy life you lead.'

'Shut up. Anyway, I hate dinner parties. There's only so much fennel coulis a girl can take, you know. And this thing is an official PTA event, so if I don't turn up they'll put me on the Absent Without Leave list and I'll be on the lost-property rota for months. I'll have to spend hours sorting through dirty socks.'

158

'Alright, alright. You do the barbecue and I'll do the fennel thing.'

But I can tell he's not happy, and is not used to having his plans altered. Still, he'll have to get used to it because I really do hate dinner parties. I redeem myself by saying that Charlie has got all his Pokémon cards sorted out, and has kept all his spares for Alfie. Mack is very pleased, and says he's already spent a small fortune on cards and any new supplies which don't involve him shelling out hard cash are extremely welcome.

On the last day of term I turn up in the afternoon to collect a huge array of PE kit, painting shirts and piles of drawings and paintings. Also Charlie's school report, which turns out to be hilarious. Good old Miss Pike obviously has a bit of a soft spot for him and has tried to be as positive as she can. Apparently he's a lovely reader, is in the top group for maths, tries hard but is easily distracted, and never really got the hang of knitting but made a lovely clay boat. Mrs Taylor has written 'Keep up the good work' at the bottom, but it turns out she's put this on nearly every single report so maybe she was just trying to keep a positive theme flowing and cut down on her workload at the same time, which seems entirely sensible to me.

I arrange with Kate that she'll pick us up in her car later, and we'll all go back to school for the barbecue. Thankfully it's not raining, and the weather has been hot and sunny all day so we won't need wet-weather gear like we did last year. I give Charlie a normal tea, because he's starving and he'll be far too busy running around with his friends to eat later. I've managed to avoid having to make any food this year, by a nifty bit of manoeuvring at the school gates, but have promised to bring some wine and sausages as our contribu-

159

tion to the evening. We arrive and I deposit the food, and then we spread out the picnic blankets on the playing field while the children eat crisps. Sally and Roger turn up, with William and Rosie, and we settle down with bottles of wine and Coke. The barbecue is lit, and the playground fills with smoke. Music blares out from two loudspeakers, and the teachers try to organise the children into teams for races. The school abandoned sports day some time ago in favour of a combined evening event with the PTA, and everyone agrees this is much better than sitting in the boiling sun watching small children get very hot in their PE kits.

The races start, and Charlie comes last in nearly every single one. He's standing chatting to James for at least a minute before they even realise the egg-and-spoon race has actually started, and Miss Pike has to rush up and urge them both on. But they don't seem to care. William is more successful, winning one race and coming second in another. Charlie and James turn out to be rather good at the three-legged race, partly because they don't even attempt to run, but simply saunter up the course and thereby beat nearly all the others who shoot off at a tremendous pace and promptly fall over. The teachers manage to contrive things so that each child wins something, which is very clever of them really as most of the reception class run in completely the wrong direction in their race, or refuse to run at all.

Once the medals have been doled out, the tug-of-war is announced, and the first competition is the Men versus Women, like last year. It turns out we have a secret weapon in a new mother of three, who's built like a small tank and is brilliant at hanging on and not moving an inch. We all take our shoes off, and roll up our trousers or tuck skirt hems into our knickers, to show we mean business, and try to grip the rope as hard as we can. The other women cheer us on, and shout abuse at the men. I feel positively gladiatorial. Kate is behind me and Sally is in front. Roger risks a little shout of encouragement, and is glared at by all the men.

We win the first round, the men win the second, and then things get very tense for the third and final round. We all cling on desperately and then Tank Woman gives an almighty pull and all the men fall over. We do too, but only after we have yanked the rope far enough to be declared the winners. Marvellous. We run about yelling and congratulating ourselves, saving all the special praise for our new team mate who goes bright pink at all the compliments. The children look very embarrassed, and turn away from the spectacle of their mothers making total fools of themselves. Some of the men are sulking and demanding a rematch, but we are jubilant and will have none of it. Out of the corner of my eye I spot a familiar car, parked at the edge of the field, a huge BMW which I'm sure is the same as Mack's. Walk over to take a closer look and, sure enough, the door opens and Mack gets out.

He gives me a blistering kiss hello, which causes ripples of comment to spread round the entire playing field. I can see I'll have some explaining to do in the village shop next time I pop in for a pint of milk.

'I couldn't resist – the tug-of-war, it just sounded so enticing. I've been sitting here watching you and the girls and I must say it was most diverting. Are you going to leave your skirt tucked up like that? It's very fetching, but you might get cold.'

'Shut up. You're just in time for the Villagers and New-comers contest. Anyone who hasn't lived in the village for more than five years gets dragged round the field by the locals. Come on, you'll love it.'

'Oh no, I couldn't possibly. I'm trained to kill, you know,

161

Moneypenny, and things might get ugly. Look, there's another woman with her skirt tucked into her knickers – she seems to know you.'

'Yes, that's Kate.' Kate comes over and looks at Mack and I introduce them. I notice she smoothes out her skirt while she's saying hello, and I do the same because, apart from anything else, it is getting a bit chilly. We invite Mack to come and sit on our blanket and join in the fun.

He's brought a very stylish wicker picnic hamper, packed by someone with far better taste than us, full of gorgeous little pies and cakes and a bottle of champagne, with real glasses and a posh waterproof blanket.

'I didn't know if this was a bring-your-own sort of thing, I hope it's alright.'

'Alright? It's fantastic. But I must go and buy some stuff from the PTA stall or people will sulk.'

I leave Kate chatting to Mack and go up to the salad stall to be confronted by a row of very tense women, standing behind their bowls of salad. I do the right thing and ask each of them for a portion, and compliment them on how delicious it all looks. If the local WI did a course on competitive salad making, this lot would sign up tomorrow. Mrs Harrison-Black is overseeing the barbecue, by occasionally shouting at the two men who are doing a perfectly good job without her. I buy some sausages and then, duty done, I go back to our picnic spot, to find Mack is now sharing out extremely expensive-looking cakes between Charlie, James and William, who are chomping away as if their lives depended on it. Charlie doesn't seem at all surprised to see Mack, and shows him his newly acquired medal before running off to play. Kate gives me the thumbs-up sign while Mack is putting the hamper back into the car.

'You didn't tell me he was so gorgeous.'

162

'Well, you know, a girl doesn't like to boast.'

'Well, I bloody would. The entire field is lusting after him. Well done you.'

Sally joins in, 'Oh yes, he's lovely,' and Roger says, 'He seems a decent-enough chap,' which makes us all laugh, and then Kate says, 'Oh, watch out, he's coming back.'

Music starts blaring out from the loudspeakers again and people start dancing. There are strings of fairy lights strung all over the playground, and people drink far too much wine and think they can Twist Again, Like They Did Last Summer. It turns out they can't, but they don't seem to mind. Children start falling asleep as the sun goes down, and are tucked into the backs of cars by parents who want one more dance before they go home. Miss Pike has drunk quite a lot of wine, and is doing a version of the hokey-cokey all by herself, but she seems happy enough so we don't like to interrupt her. Some of the dads organise a twilight game of football, which turns out to be hilarious because most of them are a bit tipsy and keep falling over. The children who are still awake, including Charlie and James, have a lovely time scoring countless goals against Roger, who only agreed to be in goal because he thought he might be able to sit down for a bit. Mack says he is crap at football, and anyway he isn't wearing the right trousers. This makes me laugh so much I have to apologise and say I'm a bit drunk, and he says he noticed, and pretends to sulk and then suddenly kisses me, which is very nice but does not go unnoticed by Mrs Harrison-Black.

Suddenly the music changes to slow smoochy numbers and Mack asks me if I want to dance. Actually I'd prefer to lie on the blanket and have a nice little sleep but since he's come all this way I feel I should at least agree to dance with him. We walk over to the playground and the fairy lights, and begin to dance. I'm just getting into the swing of things, and enjoying myself immensely, when Mrs Harrison-Black barges over, taps Mack firmly on the shoulder and says, 'I don't think we've met.' Mack looks at her with utter contempt, says, 'No, that's right. We haven't,' and then does a sharp twirl and leads us off to the other side of the playground. I'm so delighted I can hardly speak, and give him a kiss which turns out to be rather more passionate than I'd intended, and then the music stops. We walk back across to our blanket, and find Kate cuddling both James and Charlie who are almost asleep. Mack puts Charlie into the back of his car, while I tell everyone about his marvellous first encounter with Mrs Harrison-Black. We decide to leave before she comes over for Round Two. Mack drives us home and I stick Charlie straight into bed, and then Mack challenges me to another tug-of-war contest, this time with the duvet. I win again. The perfect end to a perfect day.

Chapter Eight

Yes, We Do Like to Be Beside the Seaside

THE WEATHER HAS TURNED extraordinarily hot, and the combination of heat and trying to keep Charlie amused is totally exhausting. I decide, not for the first time, that I simply do not have what it takes to cope with the school holidays. I'm already totally fed up with spending ages filling up the paddling pool and arranging a selection of toys in the back garden, only for Charlie to chuck mud and grass in the pool and then announce he wants to watch a video. We try some painting outdoors with poster paints and sponges. The paint goes everywhere, and Buzz and Woody end up multicoloured. I can't even justify going into the office to get a bit of peace and quiet because Barney has gone off to his villa in France.

Lawrence is taking the opportunity to change the filing system in the office so nobody will be able to find anything in September, and will have to ask him where things are, which he will adore. He's also moving all the desks around and trying out new combinations of furniture. Whatever he finally comes up with, I'm sure I will still have the collapsing chair. I've taken the precaution of removing all my files and notebooks and bringing them home, so he can't lose them during the move. He's still very annoyed about this.

I decide to renovate our garden pond, and spend hours and a small fortune at the garden centre buying a pump and cable. Vital bits of the pump keep falling off and disappearing into the mud at the bottom of the pond. Charlie thinks the whole project is enormous fun and helps out by filling buckets with pond water and sloshing them over the entire garden. I balance on the edge of the pond trying to sort out the waterfall, which is made up of boulders and small pebbles. I fall in twice and get totally soaked. Switch on the power via a socket in the garage and rush out to see the full effect. Unfortunately the pump is more powerful than I thought and the waterfall dislodges all the boulders and plants, and the fountain's about thirty foot high. After hours of trotting backwards and forwards, I finally get it right, and I sit with Charlie watching the fish enjoying the unusually clean water, and listening to the gentle sound of the splashing fountain.

I'm just starting to relax when the pump reasserts itself and goes into overdrive. Charlie and I get soaked, and the waterfall dislodges all the plants again. Charlie runs around screaming with delight while I lose my temper and remove the pump and bash it against the garden wall for a bit. This seems to do the trick and it functions perfectly from then on, with no more Niagara impressions. I invite Kate round to applaud my handiwork and she's suitably impressed. She's off on holiday tomorrow, to stay in her Aunt Stella's cottage in Dorset. We're going down to join her for a long weekend. We've had trips to the cottage before, and the children are very excited about revisiting old haunts. I just hope I manage to get there without my usual three-hour detour getting lost. Kate has written out very detailed directions.

166

'I still can't work out how you ended up in Portsmouth. Anyway, here's the route door to door, you really can't go wrong. Do you think you might arrive before dark this time?'

'It's possible, but I'm not promising anything.'

We arrive at the cottage after dark, again. I lost Kate's instructions somewhere in a motorway service station, and had to rely on my map-reading skills. I'm getting the hang of Portsmouth now, and avoided getting stuck in the ferry queue this time. Charlie and James begin crashing about unpacking toys and Kate cooks supper while I unload the car. Then we sit and watch videos with the children, and drink too much gin. I'd never realised before just how witty *Mary Poppins* is. We finally give up trying to put the children to bed and all go upstairs together. Charlie and I are sharing the spare bed, an old-fashioned huge brass thing, which makes an incredible racket and sways slightly from side to side. Charlie adores it. The mattress has an enormous dip in the middle, which Charlie settles into and says it's just like a nest. I cling on to the side and try not to rattle the bedstead for fear the sounds of clanking brass will disturb the entire neighbourhood. I wake up countless times during the night being smothered by Charlie as I drift into the dip. Try to climb back out but the bed makes so much noise I end up getting up and going downstairs for a little rest.

I find Kate sitting in the kitchen having a cup of tea. Apparently her bed also has a dip, and she'd ended up with both children draped across her and thought she'd suffocate if she didn't get up. She makes more tea and we wander. The garden looks very beautiful, and we sit drinking tea outside in our dressing gowns.

'So what do you fancy doing today then? Beach and then lunch back here, or shall we make a picnic?'

'I'm already fed up to the back teeth with picnics, and it's only the second week of the holidays.'

'Me too. OK, what about beach and then a pub lunch?'

'Now you're talking.'

We spend hours on the beach, with the children running in and out of the sea and making sandcastles. We head off to a pub for lunch and eat crab sandwiches and the children drink lemonade.

'Mummy.'

'Yes, Charlie.'

'Next time we should have ginger beer and then it'll be like the Famous Five. Because there are five of us, you know.'

We are all enchanted by this, and plan Famous Five-type adventures for tomorrow. We'll have a treasure hunt in the garden, and a mystery walk where we pretend we're lost and the children have to find the way home. It starts to rain, so we go back to the cottage and begin an epic game of Monopoly which gets very fraught when we discover that both James and Charlie refuse to pay up when they land on somebody else's hotel, and Phoebe has hidden half of James's money under the board while he wasn't looking.

The treasure hunt in the morning is a big success, which is mostly down to Kate's clever idea of writing all the clues in code, which they have to translate with the help of a codebook James has brought with him. The boys put on treasure hunts all afternoon, hiding toys and then giving each other cryptic clues like 'It's under the sofa'. We decide to go crab fishing after tea, so we buy bacon for bait and three plastic reels from the village shop and then stand for hours balancing on a bridge over the small creek that runs into the sea. We catch five tiny little brown crabs, and one much larger black one, which sit in a bucket between James and Charlie and are much admired by passing children. We release the crabs and then go for a fish-and-chips supper at a brilliant place on the beach which Kate has known since her childhood.

It might not be the most glamorous holiday, but we're all enjoying ourselves apart from the sheer hard slog of cooking and washing-up and planning food for three children who can eat their own bodyweight in food at every mealtime. The children play on the beach after supper, while Kate and I drink coffee. Kate confesses that she always hated holidays with Phil, which she says usually turned into a lethal mixture of blazing rows and late-night attempts by Phil to make everything all right by practically jumping on top of her when she had almost dropped off to sleep. It sounds absolutely charming.

'So, how's Mack?'

'Great. But it does make life much more complicated.'

'You know, I never thought I'd say this, but I actually really like being on my own with the kids. It's so much more fun than living with Phil.'

'I know what you mean. Don't get me wrong, I don't want to lose Mack. Actually, it seems like a miracle that I've found him in the first place. But I just don't know if I can handle the full monty. Living together, the whole routine, I just can't see it.'

'Has he said anything then?'

'No, thank God. And it's still early days. But I can't help thinking that if we ever get to that stage I really don't know what I'll do. Apart from anything else, I can't see him living in the country with me, and I don't want to live in London.'

'You could do a bit of both.'

'I suppose so. I could handle that, I think. Anyway, I don't want to lose him, that's for sure.'

'You really like him, don't you?'

'Yes, he's wonderful.'

Kate makes pretend being-sick noises.

'Anyway, we've got to get through our family holiday together first. Mack's booked a hotel in Cornwall. We've got a suite with three bedrooms, videos, satellite, the full works. It's got two pools, an adventure playground, and hordes of children's entertainers. But I can't help thinking it might turn out to be rather more like hard work than Mack seems to think. Bedtimes are going to be a nightmare. I reckon Alfie and Charlie will be OK, but I'm not too sure about Daisy.'

'Do you want some girl-handling tips?'

'Yes please.'

'Bribe her. It's just like boys, really, only with nail varnish and make-up. She may despise you for it, but she'll behave at mealtimes, believe me.'

Oh God, I feel even more nervous now. I try to explain this to Mack when I talk to him the next day, but he says, 'Oh, don't be ridiculous, it'll be fine. The kids all like each other – the only person you need to worry about is me; I tend to get a bit restless on holiday. I'm not very good at lounging about doing nothing. Still, I'm sure you've got lots of novel ideas on how to keep me entertained, haven't you, Moneypenny?'

'No I have not, not unless you like treasure hunts.'

'I love treasure hunts.'

But he says this in entirely the wrong tone of voice, which suggests he's thinking about some erotic game where one of you wears a white silk blindfold, instead of grubbing about in the hotel shrubbery looking for a packet of Smarties and a small box of crayons.

'Mack, I'm serious. We should make sure we bring some games and stuff to keep the kids entertained.'

'Darling, this hotel costs a bloody fortune precisely because they guarantee to take the kids off your hands for the entire duration. My PA has set them up with an itinerary that would make even the most hyperactive kid knackered by teatime.'

'Look, don't get me wrong, I'm all for some child-free time; in fact I can't think of anything nicer. But don't you think it's a bit much to take them on holiday and then park them with strangers for the entire week?'

'No, I do not. Not at the prices they charge. Peter and Georgia went there last year and he said they never saw the kids for the entire week.'

Peter is one of the big noises at Mack's agency, and his wife Georgia is a loathsome Sloane, according to Mack, who whines and moans constantly and is always under-mining Peter in public and then getting embarrassingly drunk.

'You said Peter was a prat and Georgia was the kind of woman who should have been sterilised at birth.'

'Well, yes, I suppose I did. God, you are annoying sometimes. Anyway, you can meet them next weekend and ask them all about it. It's all booked, by the way, and I think we should go down on Friday night if that's OK with you. There's some session in the evening where I'm supposed to say a few words.'

'That should be fine. Mum and Dad are coming down on Friday anyway, so I can meet you in town if you like.'

'Brilliant.'

'What clothes do I need for this weekend? I've never been to a corporate-strategy do before. Barney doesn't really go in for that kind of thing.'

'Well, bring your velvet dress for a start. In fact, bring all your posh frocks.'

'Mack, I've only got two. And one of them is so tight I can't sit down in it. Will there be lots of buffets?'

He laughs. 'Bring them both, and that new shirt. I love that shirt.'

The shirt is a sheer black chiffon number, a present from Leila. I showed it to Mack last time he came down for the weekend and asked him if it was too rude to wear outside the house. Leila swears you wear them with just a black bra underneath, and no one thinks you're auditioning for a role in a porn film, but I wasn't convinced and wanted a second opinion. Mack's reaction guaranteed I will not be wearing it to any PTA functions without a vest, and probably a cardigan on top just in case.

I return home from Dorset to face a huge pile of washing, and Charlie getting very bored because he doesn't have James on hand to play with for every waking moment. I'm trying to pack for my weekend away, and Charlie is longing for Nana and Grandad to arrive. I end up having to play Pirates instead of packing, and get smacked in the eye with a plastic cutlass. Charlie is distraught at the unintentional injury, so I end up comforting him clutching a cold flannel to my eye. I hope I don't end up at the posh strategy weekend with a black eye. Mack thinks it's very funny and suggests I wear an eye patch, which will look very mysterious and sexy. Sometimes I think he's totally mad.

I meet him at the office as arranged, thankfully minus an eye patch, after a long lunch with Leila. She's insisted on inspecting the contents of my bags and promptly rushed me round the shops for some emergency purchasing. I now own a beaded cardigan and a lace vest. We spent most of lunch talking about the state of play with James, who seems to be making noises about them living together. Leila can't decide what she thinks about this, as she half wants to hold out for the ring-on-my-finger moment, and half wants a practice run to see if he drives her crazy when they're actually sharing the same house. They're off for a fortnight in the South of France and she says she'll try to make her mind up then, so I should stand by for emergency telephone calls and must carry my mobile with me at all times.

Mack drives very fast down to the posh hotel, which turns out to be very posh indeed. It's a beautiful old manor house surrounded by acres of parkland, and is very designerly with lots of old oak floors and modern furniture. There's a fabulous mixture of chintz and leather, and the bedrooms are fantastic, with miles of white linen and enormous baths. We dump our bags and go for a walk. The outdoor swimming pool is beautiful, edged with grey slate and surrounded by pale wood with the water heated to the perfect temperature so a faint haze of steam rises above the surface. An anorexic-looking woman is just climbing out as we walk by; she looks like a famous model whose name I can't remember. She also looks like she could do with steak and chips, but doubt this is on her agenda. The car park is full of Porsches and Mercs, with an entire fleet of BMWs just like Mack's. Other company personnel have obviously arrived.

We wander back and find ourselves in the middle of the company drinks party. Suddenly the sound of a helicopter overhead draws everyone to the windows, and the helicopter lands in a nearby paddock. Three men emerge and walk up the drive, very, very pleased with themselves for arriving in such a glamorous manner. Inevitably they're from the agency, and saunter over and start chatting to Mack about how handy Battersea heliport is. 'Jump in the old chopper and Bob's your uncle.' Bob's your sickbag, more like, if my brief exposure to helicopters is anything to go by. Barney made me spend two days stuck in one a few years ago, filming a horrendous job for wallpaper paste in Miami.

Mack introduces me, and then one of the Helicopter Boys says, 'So, Annie, had much experience with choppers, have you?' and the other two guffaw.

'Only a little; I did a job using helicopters a few years ago. But they were much bigger, and the pilots were Vietnam vets, mad as snakes. It was a bit like being stuck in a tumble drier for two days. I'll never forget it.'

Mack is delighted with this, and so are half the people standing nearby, who all snigger and look away. The Helicopter Boys are not pleased.

We rush back up to our room so that Mack can collect some folders and papers and we can get changed for dinner. There's a knock on the door and a bossy woman from the agency bustles in with an itinerary. It turns out that Mack's idea of a relaxed weekend is not exactly what the agency has in mind. He has ten minutes before the first meeting starts.

'Fuck. I said I wasn't going to do any of this and the bastards have put me down to lead the meeting. Look, I'd better go down and sort this out. Will you be all right?'

'As long as I can have room service and a bath, I'll be in bliss.'

'OK. See you downstairs for dinner at half past nine.'

The bath turns out to be so huge I nearly go under twice. Then I hit the Jacuzzi button with my elbow, and a mountain of bubbles is produced. The bubbles rise over my head. It's like something from an early episode of *Dr Who*. I fight my way out, and then spend ages mopping up with towels, and have to get dressed in a frantic hurry. Decide to give my new beaded cardigan a try, and the black lace vest, with my smartest black trousers. The cardigan has lots of tiny black jet buttons which take ages to do up. I get downstairs ten minutes late, to find a huge throng of people in the bar. All the women are wearing serious frocks. Just as I spot Mack hidden in the farthest corner of the room, everyone starts moving off into dinner. There's a seating plan, and Mack has been put miles away with the top brass.

I spend what seems like hours making small talk with a very irritating woman called Sophie. She seems remarkably well informed and gives me the job title and short career résumé of everyone seated at the table. She then moves on to talking about private schools. I drink too much and find sitting and nodding becomes much easier as the evening progresses. Finally the dinner finishes and Mack comes over looking very pleased with himself.

'Just had a fascinating chat with old Bates.'

'Oh, and that's a good thing, I take it.'

'Yes. He's the chairman. I must say that cardigan is very fetching.'

'Thank you.'

'I especially like that lace thing. One small point, though: promise you won't sit next to the old man. You'll give him another heart attack.'

I glance down and see that my cardigan has unbuttoned itself and my lace vest is now barely concealing my chest.

'Oh fuck.'

I frantically start doing up buttons, and Mack laughs and whispers, 'Let's go for a swim. That is unless you want to stay and flash your bits about for a while.'

'No, thank you very much.'

We sneak off, grab our swimsuits and find the pool is floodlit and billowing wafts of steam into the darkness. I'm not sure swimming whilst drunk is entirely a good idea, but it turns out to be great. We end up kissing in the deep end, and look up during one particularly passionate moment to see that we are being watched by about twenty people from dinner who've wandered out on to the terrace overlooking the pool. They pretend they haven't noticed us, so Mack shouts hello and invites them in for a swim. One or two of the men seem keen, but the women are having none of it. Mack thinks this is very funny, but I can't help feeling I have somehow been judged and found wanting by the proper wives and partners.

This impression turns out to be correct when I'm given lots of cold stares at coffee the next morning. There's another round of meetings scheduled, and all sorts of hideous beauty therapies have been booked for 'partners'. Most of the women are in very smart Lycra leisure gear, and look like they are planning serious sessions in the gym. I am in a white shirt and baggy linen trousers, with sunglasses for my hangover, and look like I'm planning a nice little lie-down. It seems we missed breakfast, which was another corporate meal affair, and Mack has already missed two meetings. He doesn't seem to care in the slightest, and tells a very keen young man who offers to give him the notes from the early-morning sessions to fuck off and get a life. I'm not sure those Panadol have really kicked in yet.

I stagger back upstairs to sleep and then crawl back downstairs at lunchtime in search of tea and newspapers. I discover a small group of women sitting in the library smoking and laughing. My kind of girls. It turns out that they're also on the wives and partners list, but have been to this kind of thing before and tend to keep a low profile, preferably by the nearest bar. I have a lovely afternoon sitting in the bar chatting. Drink far too much, and then Mack wanders in with a couple of men, just as we are all screaming with laughter at one woman's description of her mother-in-law. They all look faintly startled to find us there, and announce that the meetings have now finished and we're free until dinner. We carry on talking for a bit, but the conversation is much less amusing now the men have turned up.

'I hope you weren't telling that lot dirty jokes.'

'Why not?'

'Well, one of them was the chairman's wife, for a start. Trust you to get in with the renegade bunch.'

Dinner is far more relaxed as the seating plan has mysteriously disappeared, and Mack and I sit with my newly discovered friends and their partners. I meet Peter and Georgia during the pre-dinner drinks and discover that Georgia really is as bad as I've been led to believe. She tells me all about the hotel we're going to, and says, 'Rarely, we hardly saw the children for the entire week. Of course we took Nanny, but we hardly needed her which was super.' Quite. Mack drags me off before she can launch into a monologue about Tuscany, where they're going this year, thank God. I almost feel like ringing the Italian Tourist Board to warn them.

We end up in the bar until the small hours, playing a game invented by the chairman's wife Helen, a sort of rude version of I Spy. Most diverting. Mack turns out to be very good at charades, and Helen and I win a bottle of brandy in a weird version of Twenty Questions about recent ad campaigns. Mack lodges an appeal because two of the ads in question are ones I actually shot with Barney, but he's overruled and has to pay a forfeit for being a bad loser. We adjourn to the swimming pool, and Mack swims an entire length fully dressed, quite cheerfully as it happens. I can only hope he will still be so cheerful in the morning.

We spend most of Sunday in bed, reading the papers, and I talk to Charlie who says Nana has made a tragic mistake with the breakfast cereal again – this time the culprit is Cheerios – but apart from that he's having a brilliant weekend. We have lunch in bed, and then spend most of the afternoon in the bath soaking the bathroom floor. We leave just after tea, bidding fond farewells to our new friends. We manage to escape just as Georgia is heard in the distance barking at Peter to hurry up. I sleep during most of the journey back to London, and Mack helps me retrieve my car from the agency car park with the help of his special card which opens all the gates.

'Thanks for a lovely weekend.'

'My pleasure, Moneypenny. My pleasure. I'll pick you up next Friday ready for the off, then, shall I? Kids, cases and Valium. Got that?'

'Yup. And buckets and spades and fishing nets. Charlie won't go anywhere without his fishing net now. It's really tricky in Safeway's.'

I get home to discover that Charlie has made a camp in the garden, and slept in it last night. Mum and Dad were up half the night peering out the window and checking he was alright. In the end Dad slept out there with him, and now has a terrible crick in his neck so he has to talk with his head on one side, a bit like a parrot. Mum's done all the ironing and given the house a good tidy. I must go away more often. They depart, with much kissing and waving, and Charlie runs down the lane after them. Then he saunters back and says, 'I'm starving.' I make bacon and eggs, which we eat inside the tent in the garden. I stupidly put the pond pump on and it goes into hyperdrive and nearly flattens the tent with a torrent of water. Charlie is outraged and we have to spend ages restoring his camp to its former glory.

Packing for our holiday with Mack turns out to be something of a challenge. Charlie wants to take all his toys, but finally settles for one rucksackful, and his fishing net. But the combination of clothes and other vital supplies fills up an enormous suitcase, and then I spend the entire journey remembering things I forgot to pack. The children all sit fairly happily in the back of Mack's car, which is enormous and has three seats and three seatbelts, and listen to different story tapes on their Walkmans, in between falling asleep and having the occasional light bicker. But nobody is sick, and we only stop twice. The motorway service stations are hideous as usual, and Mack spends ages in a video arcade on a ski-simulator game, hurling himself down mountains while the children stand and watch him and yell useful hints like 'You idiot, you've just skied into that cliff'. Then they all insist on having a go, and all score higher than Mack.

We arrive at the hotel just in time for tea, and are ushered up to a palatial suite by a very obsequious man who turns out to be the assistant manager. He keeps calling me madam, and insists on showing me how to operate all the remote controls. One is dedicated entirely to opening and closing the curtains. The children run about yelling, and then discover the balcony, spot the pool, and beg to go for a swim. As if by magic there's a knock on the door and a woman announces she's come to take the children for their first swimming lesson. I can't help but be impressed by Mack's arrangements. The phone rings, and Mack's PA says she's just ringing to check we've arrived safely, and to let us know she's faxing through the itinerary as she knew Mack would lose it, and reception are bringing it up now. Do we want fax in our room, since this can easily be set up? Christ. I realise what I've needed all these years is a really good PA.

I study the itinerary over tea, and it turns out we have half an hour a day with the children, if that. But a window of family time has been scheduled for the last day, with an alternative activity pencilled in just in case this proves too much for us. I suggest we talk to the children over supper and see what they'd like to do. Mack thinks this is a very bad idea, but eventually relents. The children come back from swimming, and we get them changed and go down for supper. The dining room is enormous and full of families who are clearly not used to eating together. There are high chairs everywhere, and lots of toddlers hurling food about. One man looks like he's gone into shock, and sits staring into the distance while a small girl sorts through the food on his plate and helps herself to anything she likes the look of. The family on the table next to us are in the midst of a bitter dispute about broccoli: their small boy is sitting looking very determined with his arms crossed and his lips tight shut.

It turns out this is children's supper time, and the Adults Only meal is available later. This sounds like the food will be cut into rude shapes or something, which makes me laugh. I share the joke with the children who all adore it, but

Mack is less pleased and says please can we get on, because all the noise is giving him a terrible headache. We eat pizza and ice-cream and study the timetable for the next few days. The children are keen to do all the activities on offer, and we promise a few trips to the beach as well. God knows what all this is costing; I've offered to contribute but Mack won't hear of it. Which is a good thing really, as I suspect the bills here would make me faint.

The children spend their days rushing from activity to activity, and we meet up for lunch before they depart for afternoons of swimming and games. I go along to a couple of the sessions to check them out and they look well organised. Charlie and Alfie learn to dive, sort of, and are having a marvellous time. Daisy is less enthusiastic, and would clearly be much happier if I went home, and took the boys with me. We spend an afternoon on the beach, as promised, and Mack gets deeply involved in building an enormous sandcastle with Charlie, while Alfie runs backwards and forwards to the sea bringing water to fill up the moat. I'm lying on a blanket with Daisy when she says, 'You've got a very big bottom, haven't you, Annie?'

'Um, yes, I suppose I have.'

'My mummy is much thinner than you, actually.'

I'm torn between horror that she's already part of the It is Vital to be Thin conspiracy, and outrage at her being quite so cheeky. I'm also a bit miffed to hear that I am Bessie Bunter to Laura's sylph-like form.

'That's nice for her, isn't it? Do you miss her a bit?'

'Yes. A lot actually.' She bites her lip and looks at her sandals.

'I'm sure you do. What about ringing her when we get back to our room? And then maybe we could dress up for supper tonight, and you could borrow some of my nail varnish.'

A look of pure delight flashes across her face, which she quickly masks. Thank God Kate gave me her girl-handling tips.

Supper turns out to be a bit of a disaster. Mack has been getting increasingly bored over the last few days. We've had a perfectly nice time, and lots of clandestine sex, which has been brilliant, but I can sense he's had enough of Being On Holiday With The Children. He's taken to ringing the office every morning and shouting at people for a bit, which seems to cheer him up, but it wears off by teatime. We wander down to supper with the children as we ate on our own last night. Daisy has new silver nail varnish on, but Mack hasn't spotted it. She's made me promise not to tell him, but I know she secretly hopes he'll notice and be dazzled. I try to whisper to him a few times but he keeps wandering off. The restaurant is swarming with children, and Mack is clearly thrilled to be sitting surrounded by such chaos. He starts moaning about the limited choice on the menu, and then throws a fit when the melon turns up and is freezing cold. It's obviously been in the fridge for hours, and is very icy. He sends it back, despite the fact that Alfie has already eaten nearly all of his.

Then the main course arrives – pasta, but it's overcooked – and Mack discovers his glass has smudge marks on it. He summons the waiter, a teenage boy obviously only working for the summer and not destined for a career in the service industry.

'I'm sorry about the pasta but there's nothing I can do about it now, is there? Do you want me to bring you a new glass?'

Mack narrows his eyes, and says in a terrifying voice, 'No, just get me the manager. Now.'

The manager appears and Mack launches into a blistering tirade which silences the entire room. The manager ends up practically crawling backwards in an effort to placate him. Fresh pasta is promised, a bottle of champagne is produced, and clean glasses. And is there anything else sir can think of which the manager can reasonably acquire without breaking the law?

The dining room settles back down, and Mack is triumphant. I can't help feeling he's enjoyed himself enormously, which annoys me intensely.

'That wasn't very 007, was it, James? Shaken but not stirred and all that.'

'Oh don't you fucking start.'

There's an audible gasp from Charlie, and Daisy and Alfie slump down a bit further in their chairs and look at their feet.

'I beg your pardon?'

'You heard me. These people have got to be told.'

His eyes are flashing and he looks more animated than I've seen him for almost the entire holiday.

'Look. If you want to get your kicks by bullying waiters, then fine, go ahead. But count me out. I mean, it's not exactly laudable behaviour, is it; they can't really turn round and tell you to fuck off, can they? Much as they'd like to. So you know what, I'll do it for them. Fuck off, Mack. You've half terrified the children and ruined their evening. I think Charlie and I will have our supper upstairs, and you can sit and rant down here. Oh, and by the way, you might want to take a closer look at Daisy. She's spent hours doing her nails. I'm sorry, Daisy, but I just don't think he's going to notice, do you, darling? They look lovely, by the way, but Daddy is too busy bullying people to notice.'

Mack stares at me with his mouth slightly open. He's about to launch into a counter-attack but he misses his moment because I storm out of the restaurant, holding Charlie's hand, which slows me down a bit. The waiters all throw me looks of undying devotion, and the manager gives me a beaming smile. He's been hovering by the door listening intently.

'Supper in your room perhaps, madam? I'll take care of it, on the house; it will be our pleasure. Just go right on up and we'll be with you in a moment.' And then he bows.

Christ. I've really done it now. I settle Charlie down, and explain that grown-ups argue sometimes and everything is fine. And no, he cannot use the F-word just because I did. He seems to accept this but still looks worried until the supper turns up, and he spots the puddings: huge ice-creams. There is also Coke to drink, and an enormous bowl of chips. He launches into the food as if he's not eaten for days, and seems perfectly happy. I have a large gin and tonic, and then give him a bath and lie in his bed reading him stories. Mack seems to be taking a very long time, and I can't work out what I'll actually say to him when he does turn up. I lie on the bed trying to read to Charlie and think of possible conversations with Mack at the same time, which affects my reading ability rather badly and Charlie complains so I have to concentrate harder. I end up falling asleep, and I'm woken by Mack gently shaking my arm.

I follow him out on to the balcony. Alfie and Daisy are asleep: Mack says he wanted to get them settled before he woke me up. It's nearly midnight and he looks exhausted.

'I'm sorry, Annie.'

'So you should be.'

'I'm not very good at apologies.'

'So I noticed. Anyway, there is some good news. If you let me do the ordering from now on I think you'll find the hotel staff have adopted me as their favourite guest. The manager nearly kissed me when I stormed out earlier. Were the kids OK?'

'Well, yes, after a bit. Oh, and by the way, what on earth possessed you to let Daisy paint her nails? They look awful.'

'Yes I know. But it's part of my bribery and corruption plan to get her to stop telling me that my bottom is much bigger than Laura's.'

'Oh, right.'

'Don't worry, it'll come off. I'll make sure she isn't wearing full make-up and heels when you take her home.'

'That might be best. Laura is pretty fierce about that kind of thing. Do they do homoeopathic nail varnish by any chance?'

'I don't think so. But it's a bloody good idea. It'd sell like hot cakes in Harvey Nichols.'

'Anyway, I am sorry. I just get a bit jumpy sitting about for days on end with nothing to do.'

'I've noticed. But you can't take it out on other people, you know, especially not your own children.'

'I know. Look, can we stop talking about my faults now; I'm not really enjoying it, to be honest. Let's talk about your big bottom instead.'

Mack behaves perfectly for the rest of the holiday. The hotel staff tend to tiptoe round him as if they're close to some sort of unexploded bomb, and the manager continues to treat me like a long-lost friend, rushing over to greet me every time we walk through reception. Daisy continues to wear silver nail polish, and moves on to purple for the last day. I have to spend ages getting it off before the journey

185

home, but she accepts this quite happily. Alfie and Charlie become best friends and spend hours stalking round the hotel grounds with their fishing nets trying to collect insects. Charlie confides to me as we are packing that he'd quite like to take Alfie home with us, and Mack can come too, for a bit, but not that Daisy because she's a girl.

I'm very glad to get home. The holiday has been lovely, apart from the blazing-row episode which I could really have done without. I confide in Leila that although Mack is delightful, apart from the occasional outbursts, it was a bit of a strain spending so much time with him and all the children, and somehow I wish we were still at the stage of an occasional night in town. Leila points out that the first few dates are always the best, but real life is not like that, and anyway Mack is perfect for me. Apparently everyone has hideous rows on holiday, and the added bonus of children is bound to cause tension. She and James had a huge fight at a monastery in the middle of nowhere, and Leila drove off in the hire car and left him because he was annoying her, and then got back to the villa and calmed down. Then she went all the way back to collect him only to find that he'd called a taxi and spent a small fortune getting back to the villa. According to Leila, he sulked for three days. We agree that holidays are actually quite hard work, and really we should all try to remember this when we start packing the factor 20.

I sort out Charlie's school uniform ready for next week, and the start of the new term. He no longer fits into half of it, and I search in countless shops but they've all sold out. Marks and Spencer only have trousers for four year olds, and one jumper, in the wrong colour. Apparently all the organised mothers bought up everything weeks ago, and it hasn't occurred to M&S that less-organised parents might want to purchase school uniform during the week before term starts. Bastards. I finally track down two pairs of trousers, and get the sweatshirts with the school logo on from the poor woman who volunteered to do the uniform for the PTA and now has a house full of sweatshirts and PE kit.

I make a huge mistake and tell Mum about my recent shopping difficulties. Two days later a large parcel arrives with a pair of enormous school trousers made out of some special indestructible material. She bought them in the same shop where she used to buy uniform for Lizzie and me, and says that she got them nice and big so he'd have room to grow into them. I spent years at school in dresses that were three sizes too large, so there would be room to grow, and am determined Charlie will not suffer the same fate, and have to wear trousers which flap round his knees, so I hide them. I ring her up to thank her, and it turns out there's even worse news: she's found some lovely navy wool and is knitting him a school cardigan. I explain that I tried to get him to wear a cardigan last winter, because I found a fleece one and thought it would be warm as the school heating had packed in and the children were wearing hats and coats in class. But he refused point blank to even consider it, and announced very gravely that boys do not wear cardigans.

Mum takes this news surprisingly well and says she's only done one sleeve, and can easily turn it into a jumper. So that's alright, and lucky I called, really. Do I want a V-neck or round neck? I settle for a V-neck because the tiny round-neck jumpers she made for him when he was a baby were so tight I practically had to give him a local anaesthetic to get them on. It's very kind of her really, and a knee-length jumper with arms three foot too long will no doubt come in very handy if it snows. She moves on to telling me, in graphic detail, about the latest operation on the man next door, which sounds appalling until I realise it was actually an operation on his dog. I agree with her that it's amazing how quickly animals heal, and then get off the phone before she can launch into an update on the woman opposite and her recent hysterectomy. I already know far more about it than I ever wanted to.

Chapter Nine

The Heart of Darkness

A UTUMN HAS DEFINITELY ARRIVED. The weather has bypassed the season-of-mists-and-mellow-fruitfulness stage and gone into freezing mornings and evenings, with rain during the day. Mack is in Tokyo, pitching for an intergalactic car campaign. He's dreading it because he says the potential clients tend to disappear into huddles and rattle off torrents of Japanese while you stand there like an idiot. And he never knows when to stop bowing – apparently it's vital that you stop at the right moment or it can go on for hours.

Leila is in New York trying to land a big American client and Kate is trying to cope with both James and Phoebe having rotten colds. They've taken to lying on the sofa shouting requests for drinks and titbits. I feel shivery and very bad-tempered, which is always a sign that I'm about to get a mammoth cold which Charlie will catch, just when I can least cope, and I'll be forced to rise from my sickbed and tend to him. Great.

Charlie develops his version of the cold overnight, so I keep him off school and he spends the day draped on the sofa moaning and watching videos. He spends the night in my bed, kicking the duvet off every ten minutes and occasionally surfacing to demand a drink – but not just any drink; only warm juice will do, apparently. So I get up, make warm juice and by the time I get back to bed he's fast asleep again. I end up stamping round the kitchen in frustration. He's no better the next morning, so we go to see the GP at the surgery in the next village. He makes the usual speech: it's a virus, keep up the fluids, give him Calpol, there's no point in having antibiotics, and please bugger off now as I have thirty-eight OAPs in the waiting-room and want to get home before dark. Charlie sleeps, fusses and whines and generally irritates the hell out of me. I am not cut out for this nursing lark, and spend ages on the phone with Kate who agrees that children with colds are unbearable.

The next day he's still not well, and is very hot and sleepy. He doesn't even complain when I give him Calpol – which he usually manages to turn into his version of the suffragettes being forcibly fed in Holloway. I have a long and heated discussion with the GP's receptionist and she finally agrees to book a home visit if I promise not to ring her ever again. The GP arrives mid-morning, and I explain that Charlie seems really unwell. He pokes him about a bit and then gives me a short lecture about how being a parent includes looking after ill children and I just have to get on with it. I thank him profusely for being so understanding; he looks at me like I am mad, and then rushes off muttering about home visits being for emergencies, not children with perfectly ordinary colds. I wish with all my heart that Charlie had been able to muster a bit of projectile vomiting all over the GP when he was poking him, but the poor little thing just lay there being pathetic.

By lunchtime Charlie is still sleeping on the sofa, but he now looks a pale-grey colour. I keep poking him to see if he's all right, a technique I developed when he was a baby. During one of my prodding sessions I see what look like two tiny dots of purple Biro on his neck and I'm gripped by a terrible panic. I keep trying to convince myself that they're paint or felt-pen marks, but deep down I know they are not. I have a strong desire to simply pretend I haven't seen them. It's almost like a physical pain; the minutes are ticking away and I'm gripped by a blind panic and can't decide what to do. It feels like I've been hit by a huge invisible object. Finally I decide that I must call the doctor and need to hold Charlie close, so I put my arms round him to move him on to my knee and he throws up all over the sofa, but doesn't wake up. This really terrifies me: he normally makes a tremendous fuss about being sick.

I stagger to the phone, half dragging Charlie as I don't want to let go of him. He still doesn't wake up, and I realise he's semi-conscious, maybe even in a coma. I have visions of sitting by his bedside playing *Lion King* tapes for the rest of my life, willing him to wake up. I telephone the surgery, but the receptionist is not interested until I begin shouting. Then she puts the phone down. I ring back and say as calmly as I can that I think Charlie is unconscious and if she doesn't put me through to a doctor in the next five seconds I will drive over there and slap her. Hard. This does the trick and she puts me straight through to the doctor.

Luckily it's the same one who came out this morning, and I tell him Charlie now appears to be unconscious; this panics him and he says he'll come right away. It's only about a ten-minute drive, but I keep thinking I should be doing something, some vital piece of first aid that I can't remember. So I sit on the floor holding Charlie and enter a kind of chasm of fear and pain, like a huge black blanket smothering us both. The doctor arrives, takes one look at

Charlie and the two purple dots and gives him the biggest injection of penicillin that I've ever seen. It's like an injection from a comedy sketch: he uses a huge needle and syringe, full of pale liquid. He sticks the needle straight into Charlie's thigh, and pushes really hard, but Charlie doesn't even stir. He begins rummaging around in his bag, finds his mobile phone and calls for an ambulance, stressing that this is a GP referral, an emergency, and then he gives very detailed directions on how to get here. Hearing him give our address is really strange. His voice sounds scared, and I notice his hands are shaking.

We sit on the floor, me clutching Charlie and rocking him backwards and forwards, and the doctor holding Charlie's hand and trying surreptitiously to check his pulse. I ask him if he thinks it's meningitis, which is the word that's been lurking in the back of my brain although I've been too frightened to realise this until I actually hear myself saying it. He nods and looks at me, and I can see the fear in his eyes. We don't speak after that. Charlie's still in his pyjamas, pale blue with white stripes, and I count the stripes again and again as we sit in silence for what seems like hours until we hear the ambulance siren. There are seventeen white stripes, and sixteen pale-blue ones. The ambulance arrives, and the driver and the doctor begin a whispered conversation. I carry Charlie down the drive. He's so heavy I can hardly manage but I don't want anyone else to hold him.

Sitting in the ambulance is really strange. The ambulance man doesn't touch Charlie but gives me an oxygen mask to hold close to his face, so I sit with him in my arms and try to avoid falling on the floor each time we go round a corner. No one speaks: just blank faces and silence. Maybe there's nothing he can do, maybe he's just a crap ambulance man, but I really wish he'd say something reassuring. We turn off the main road into the hospital and head towards Casualty, and I expect to see an expert team jogging on the spot waiting for us to arrive, but instead the doors are shut and the place looks deserted. They stick Charlie on a trolley and park it in a corridor. A nurse eventually wanders over and says Cubicle Three, but when we open the curtains a man's lying on the bed. He glares at us. I glare back, and we stand in the corridor again while the nurse dithers about. Minutes are ticking away, and Charlie looks even worse than he did at home.

I can't believe this is really happening, but finally realise I have to do something and somehow summon up the energy to throw another fit, and threaten to sue the hospital unless someone calls the paediatric consultant immediately. I grab hold of a doctor who's walking past and demand he does something, and he agrees to have a quick look, obviously thinking I'm being very difficult and hoping I'll let go of his tie in a moment or two. I tell him I think it's meningitis, and suddenly things start moving. The nurse mutters that it's not her fault, nobody told her, and gives me a furious look. I'm about to start screaming when a man appears at the end of the corridor. He's causing a huge fuss by shouting at the nurses and generally behaving as if he owns the place, and I realise this must be the consultant. Or a very smartly dressed drunk.

It's the consultant, and he takes one look at Charlie and starts yelling even louder. We move into the resuscitation room, and senior nurses in dark-blue uniforms start to appear out of nowhere with bits of equipment. They can't find a really tall drip stand and the consultant, who's introduced himself as Mr O'Brien, wants one, so I have to stand holding a bag of fluid above my head squeezing it as tight as I can while Mr O'Brien yells out orders. Terrifying reddish-purple bruise-like marks are appearing by the second all over Charlie's chest and legs, and the rest of him is now a very pale grey. They have cut his pyjamas off, and he's lying naked on a white sheet, making moaning noises but nothing recognisable even when they're jabbing him trying to get needles in. This is so horrible I can hardly breathe.

Various nurses keep trying to get me to go and sit in the relatives' room, but I've seen too many television programmes to fall for that one: I know if I go in there something terrible will happen. So I refuse, and get a nurse to ring Mum and Dad, and stand holding Charlie's hand, willing him to wake up. Mr O'Brien disappears briefly and returns saying he's called in the specialist team from Guy's Hospital in London as these kind of cases are very rare and need expert handling. They're on their way by helicopter.

We stand and wait in silence. Charlie's now covered in appalling bruises, and looks like he's been in some sort of hideous accident. Suddenly the doors burst open and in marches the smallest doctor I've ever seen, wearing a bright-orange flying suit. He's followed by two nurses, also in orange suits, carrying countless orange nylon bags. Everything seems to be fastened with Velcro so there's a tremendous ripping noise as all the bags are opened, and then they begin swapping needles and drugs and start filling in charts and asking me questions.

All the other doctors and nurses stand back and watch in respectful silence, and the air of panic gradually seeps away. The chief of the hospital turns up, introduces himself, and joins the audience. Finally, when the new guy is satisfied he's got things under control, he talks to me, sounding like he's made this speech before to a variety of traumatised parents. He says his name is Steve Johnson, and he's going to take Charlie to the paediatric intensive-care unit at Guy's, by ambulance which will be less stressful than the helicopter. At the moment he's stable, but things may deteriorate very rapidly, and he might need to be put on a breathing machine. The marks are septicaemia, which is a kind of blood poisoning, and they see it all the time with these kind of cases. The next twelve hours will be crucial.

I'm not allowed to go in the ambulance with Charlie, because there won't be room. So he suggests I start making my way up to Guy's and they'll meet me there. He ends by repeating that I must not panic if the next time I see Charlie he's on a breathing machine; it's just a little tube and they can easily remove it. He smiles, trying to be reassuring, and then turns his attention back to Charlie. I nod to all of this. What I really want to say is *Don't fucking panic, are you kidding?* I can do screaming sobbing panic, or quiet hysterics in the corner, but there's absolutely no way on earth that I can do no panic at all. Let's stick a tube down *your* throat and cover *you* in horrible bruises and you cannot panic and me and Charlie will go home. And could all these people staring at my naked baby please fuck off and leave us alone. I really feel like punching somebody, or smashing something. I want to make a huge scene. Don't these people realise what's going on? How can they be so calm? I feel completely overwhelmed with terror and rage.

I'm desperate to walk out of the room and just keep on walking until I get somewhere where I can collapse in a heap. But I can't leave Charlie; I just know he can hear me endlessly repeating his name. I keep saying, 'I'm here, Mummy's here, it's alright, Mummy's here, it's alright,' again and again until even I'm sick of it. I want to insist that I go in the ambulance, but part of me just wants to run away which makes me really guilty and selfish. I also have a horrible feeling that they don't want parents in the ambulance in case they have to do some hideous procedure on the journey. I don't want to think what this might involve.

Mum and Dad have arrived, and I can tell Mum's been crying, and Dad appears to have shrunk and looks very pale and frightened. I don't think I've ever seen him look frightened before, except for the time when I rode my bike into the river. He stands in the middle of the room saying, 'Poor little thing,' over and over in almost a whisper, and Mum stands next to him looking desperate, shredding tissues and staring at Charlie. The doctor comes over and talks to Dad and they seem to agree that we should leave now in Dad's car and drive to Guy's so we are there to meet the ambulance when it arrives. I also suspect Dad knows that I will not be able to watch them wheel Charlie out of the room.

I can't leave Charlie without saying something, and don't want to say goodbye, so in the end I ramble on about going with Grandad and we'll see him at the hospital and it will all be alright. I'm about to lose it completely when Dad grabs my hand and practically drags me out of the room. Mum is staying with Charlie until the ambulance is ready, and then she's going home to get things. I'm not sure what things, and neither is she. But it doesn't matter. I couldn't have left him there if Mum wasn't staying with him. She's gathered up the remnants of his pyjamas and is standing there folding and refolding them and whispering to him as we leave.

The drive to Guy's is a nightmare: the traffic is horrendous and then we get badly lost. The desire to hit other drivers who don't move out of the way and let us through is overwhelming, and Dad drives even more aggressively than usual, cutting up two taxis and a double-decker bus with manoeuvres which leave us all breathless. I feel an increasing sense of panic as I realise I can't bear to be so far away from Charlie, and my mind fills with terrible images of what's happening to him while I sit in traffic jams. I find my mobile phone in my bag, which I don't remember picking up. Maybe the doctor gave it to the ambulance man.

I ring the hospital and they say Charlie is on his way to Guy's in the ambulance, and was stable when he left. Then I ring Leila's office and tell them to get a message to her, and I also ring Kate, who bursts into tears. I can't work out what time it is in Tokyo, and anyway I can't face making any more calls, so I sit in silence as Dad battles through the traffic. We finally find the hospital, but have to park miles away. It's dark now, and very cold. Dad gives me his jacket to wear, and I notice that he's shivering but he pretends he's hot and refuses to take his jacket back. We look a sorry pair stumbling along the streets trying to find the entrance and then follow the arrows to paediatric intensive care. Finally we arrive, but there's no sign of Charlie. I have visions of desperate roadside surgery somewhere on the motorway, but then the ward doors swing open and Charlie's wheeled in on a huge bed, attached to all sorts of wires and drips but thankfully no breathing machine.

A large number of doctors and nurses surround him, and start adjusting the machines and drips and filling in charts. We stand to one side, thankful that so many people are focusing totally on our boy. The marks all over him seem slightly smaller now, but the shock of seeing him looking so tiny and ill is just too awful and Dad suddenly rushes off saying he's going to get some tea but I think he's actually crying. I can't bear this, somehow Dad crying is the last straw, and I begin to weep silently while I stand holding Charlie's hand. Dr Johnson notices this and puts his hand on my shoulder. He says that things are going well, the bruising is getting smaller – they are measuring it, apparently – and all in all we just have to sit and wait.

Lizzie and Matt arrive, and Dad says he should go and get Mum. He promises to ring later and puts his arms around Lizzie and me before abruptly breaking away and almost running down the corridor. Lizzie was there when Charlie was born. She was the first person to hold him after the midwife. She looks terrified. We don't speak; we just sit staring at Charlie. He surfaces at one point, and says, 'Mummy,' but he's looking right at me when he says this, which freaks us all out and starts a dreadful train of thought about how I'll cope if he wakes up and is blind. The short answer is I won't. I make all sorts of vows and pacts with God, promise to be a better person, anything, if Charlie can just be allowed to survive. It's ridiculous really, as I have to start each pledge by admitting that I'm not actually a believer, but could he please not hold this against Charlie who really didn't mean it when he said he was a pagan. Then I realise this might be rather annoying if there actually is a God, so I promise that anything can happen to me as long as Charlie is alright, and it's not his fault he's been brought up by a heathen mother. If this goes on much longer I think I'll lose my mind completely.

A man in a suit appears and says he's the hospital administrator, and has had a call from someone called Leila in New York, who has told him that no expense is to be spared to get her godson better. He says he thanked her but explained that there are no private intensive-care facilities, and that Charlie is with one of the best teams in the world. Leila has left a message saying she's sitting by her mobile phone and will I please ring her because she's going out of her mind, and he gives me a piece of paper with the number on. Lizzie goes off to track down a phone that can be wheeled to the bed, because mobiles aren't allowed as they affect the machines. When I get through to Leila she bursts into tears and sobs down the phone that she's coming home straight away. I finally manage to calm her down, and say she is to do no such thing because there's nothing she can do, and promise to call her as soon as I have any news. I ask her to track down Mack in Tokyo and she promises she will. She says she's due back tomorrow night anyway and will call as soon as she gets home, and then she starts crying again.

Charlie has his own nurse now, who sits on a stool at the end of the bed and watches him constantly. She keeps checking his hands and feet, and finally I can bear this no longer and ask her why. She says that in some cases the blood supply to the extremities can be compromised and there can be complications. Lizzie makes a weird noise at this point and Matt grips the metal on the side of the bed so hard his knuckles go white. I dimly remember reading about some poor woman who lost her fingers and toes after having meningitis, and feel a whole new wave of shock come racing towards me, like an avalanche. I spend the next hour massaging Charlie's feet.

Dr Johnson comes round again and seems pleased with Charlie's progress. He strokes Charlie's arm all the time he talks to us. He says that usually if things are going to get really bad they would have done so by now, and that the prognosis is excellent. I do not want to think about what he means by really bad. This is as bad as I can take. The next few hours are still crucial, but he would be very surprised if things weren't looking a lot more cheerful come morning. He looks totally exhausted, and I want to say something to him, but I can't think of the words.

Lizzie suggests I might like to go for a coffee while she and Matt stay with Charlie.

I wander off and find the parents' room, which has a kettle and an odd collection of mugs and instant-coffee jars. I guess people are in here long enough to buy a jar of coffee, but not long enough to finish it. For some reason this frightens me, and I don't want to use the coffee or the mugs, as if they might somehow be contaminated. There are a couple of other parents in here, looking shattered, and a woman is sitting on a chair in the corner crying in a desperate quiet kind of way, as if she's been weeping for hours. I cannot face this, I don't want to know what's the matter with their children, and feel overwhelmed by selfish instincts. All I want is to sit in silence, drink a cup of coffee and think about Charlie. I leave and find a coffee machine and a room where I can smoke a cigarette.

Sitting there in the foul little smoking room staring at my feet, I realise a young nurse has come in, and is sitting smoking frantically looking shattered. It seems really rude to just sit there, so I say it must be really tough working with children who are so ill. This is a big mistake. She launches into a traumatised speech about having to carry a dead baby girl down to the mortuary on Christmas morning last year, and how the mum ran along the corridor with a special pink blanket for the baby, because she didn't want her to get cold. 'It's weird,' she says, 'they often do that, the parents. They don't want them to get cold.' I feel my heart shrink, and rush back to the ward. Lizzie and Matt are sitting either side of Charlie's bed, holding his hands. I take Matt's place, but don't share the story about the dead baby with them.

At some point a nurse comes over and says there's a call for me on the ward phone. It's Mack. He sounds like he's a million miles away, and there's a weird echoing tone on the line so it feels like we're talking in a cave. Mack says he got a message that his little boy was ill and he was to ring a number in New York. He finally managed to get hold of Leila who explained it was not Alfie but Charlie. He doesn't say anything, but I can tell he feels guilty about feeling relieved it wasn't Alfie. He says he'll fly home if I want him to, and his voice goes all shaky, and I tell him they seem to think Charlie is doing OK, but that it's the most terrifying thing, and yes, I do want him to come home except that there's nothing he can do, and actually all I want is to sit with Charlie until he wakes up. I promise to call him with news as soon as I have some, and then he says he'll let me get back to Charlie, and we say goodbye. I sit thinking that he's bound to feel guilty about being a tiny bit glad when he heard it was Charlie not Alfie, and I must make it clear to him that I totally understand. I suddenly realise I wish it *was* Alfie, and feel shocked at how easily I would trade Alfie for my baby.

The nurses are changing shifts, and our new one, Karen, very gently suggests it might be best if Lizzie and Matt went home and got some sleep, which they do. We don't say goodbye; we just sort of nod. I lie on the little camp bed they've put next to Charlie's bed, but he keeps making little moaning sounds so I decide to hold him; this sets off the alarms on the machines and in the end Karen switches them off. She says she'll keep an eye on him, and he seems more settled when I hold him. I don't want to get on to the hospital bed with him as somehow this seems wrong, so I end up with him in the camp bed with me, which is really stupid since it's tiny, deeply uncomfortable and not very stable. But at least I can hold him. Karen goes off to get me a cup of tea and some toast at about three am, and I eat this lying next to him, dropping crumbs on his head and watching him breathe. The last time I had tea and toast in hospital was the night he was born. I'd like to sleep but I'm too frightened to close my eyes.

Very early in the morning the doctors appear doing their rounds. They all say Charlie has made an extraordinary recovery and we can now move to a side room where they'll keep him under observation. If he stays stable we can go back to the local hospital in a few days' time. They're all terribly pleased, and keep touching his feet and smiling. The faint bruise marks are barely visible now, and he's almost surfaced a couple of times. I wish they would all go away as waves of relief seem about to overwhelm me and I really want to cry.

I mutter my thanks at them and then stare hard at Charlie, but they don't seem at all offended and each of them touches my arm before they move off down the ward. Karen smiles at me, and then Charlie opens his eyes and says, 'Why is Peter Pan on the ceiling?' I feel sure this is some sign of brain damage, but when I look up I see a painting of Peter Pan, along with Wendy and Captain Hook. In fact the whole room has paintings on the walls and ceiling, but I hadn't noticed them before. Charlie has gone back to sleep, but he has a tiny smile on his face. I sit and cry quietly, until Lizzie turns up. I tell Lizzie he's woken up and spotted Peter Pan, and she starts to cry as well.

We move to the side room, and it's lovely to have a door to shut the rest of the hospital out. We also have a telly and a bathroom, and Lizzie has arranged for a phone. We need bucketloads of change, which she magically produces from a carrier bag, which also contains smoked-salmon bagels and a flask of coffee. Charlie wakes up properly for a bit, weak but determined to sit up. It's heartbreaking how much

202

this exhausts him, and he falls asleep again almost immediately but looks a much more normal colour. The door opens and a nurse ushers in a motorbike messenger. He has a package from Leila and is under strict instructions to deliver it into my hands only, or she will have him killed. The huge parcel contains two big bottles of mineral water, posh chocolates, a pale-lilac pashmina, miniature bottles of vodka and gin, a water pistol shaped like a dinosaur, a toy machine gun and two packets of chocolate biscuits. Perfect, and I drink the vodka whilst trying out the machine gun. Lizzie goes off to work, but promises to return later.

Another messenger arrives, this time with an enormous grey velvet donkey, with a card from the office sending all their love. The donkey has a name tag round his neck on which Barney has written 'I am called Wonkey'. I can't believe he's remembered Charlie's favourite joke, and burst into tears. I ring him and discover that Leila tracked him down, and he's been calling every couple of hours and checking how things were going, but said he didn't want to bother me. I find myself crying down the phone, which he copes with brilliantly. He says I'm bound to be in shock, but that we're over the worst and must just get lots of rest. I dimly remember one of his children had some sort of serious illness years ago, which turned into pneumonia and took weeks to sort out. He's very calm and reassuring, which is just what I need, and says that even Lawrence is upset and offered to go and buy the donkey. And do I realise how many shops you have to go to before you can find a perfectly ordinary toy donkey? I feel much better after talking to him.

I ring Leila's office and say I can't work out the time in New York but suspect it's the middle of the night, so can they call her at a reasonable hour and tell her how well things are going, and thank her for the parcel, and they promise they will. I try to get hold of Mack but his hotel can't track him down, so I leave a message. Charlie wakes up, and says he wants a drink. I now have nice water to offer him instead of the stale lukewarm tap water in the plastic jug by the bed, and he drinks cup after cup before he spots the machine gun. He's in bliss with this, and discovers it makes a hideous noise, and then he sees the water pistol, demands it's filled up and soaks the entire room. He also soaks the nurse who pops her head round the door to see how things are going. He falls asleep clutching the water pistol tightly in one hand, and the machine gun in the other.

Mum and Dad turn up, and Dad is carrying an enormous basket of fruit so we can only see his hands and feet as he staggers in through the door. Mum has brought enough food to feed the whole hospital, and has also purchased the entire nightwear range from M&S. Charlie is thrilled with his new Bart Simpson pyjamas but rejects the tasteful towelling ones as boring. They start to campaign for me to go off and have a break, go for a walk, buy a new car, anything to get me out of there. It suddenly dawns on me that this has been a double trauma for them – not just their grandson but their daughter in trouble – and that it will only be alright when we're both home and back to normal. They both look totally shattered.

I eventually agree to go out with Dad and get a coffee and some fresh air, while Mum sits with Charlie and he squirts her with his new water pistol. I feel fine until we walk out of the hospital gates and then suddenly I'm overwhelmed. There are so many people rushing about, and I feel a strong desire to start telling them how lucky they are, which thankfully I manage to overcome. I realise now just how easy it is to become one of those people who wander up and down the streets muttering. I want to run back to Charlie, but Dad makes me sit down and eat a sandwich and drink some coffee. Suddenly I find there are tears rolling down my cheeks. It's almost as if it were happening to someone else. I'm just sitting there, drinking my coffee, but the tears won't stop. Dad strokes my hand and says, 'It's alright, darling, just eat your sandwich,' and I do, and the tears gradually subside. Then we go back and find Charlie is asleep again.

He's much better in the afternoon, and his colour's almost back to normal, although he's still very weak and falls asleep after the slightest exertion. He's got a drip in his hand for them to inject his drugs into every couple of hours, and it keeps blocking which means it's agony when they push the stuff into it. Holding him down screaming while they do the injections will haunt me for ever. The nurses who pop in every now and again are from the general ward rather than intensive care, and they're a pretty sour bunch. They rarely bother to speak to Charlie at all, and treat me like a nuisance. Which is odd because the nurses in intensive care seemed positively delighted with parents who sat by the bedside for hours on end, and encouraged them to chat and read stories even if their child appeared to be totally un-conscious.

In the evening an agency nurse appears, in a different uniform to the usual ones, and refuses to do the drugs if the drip hurts so much. She says, 'Never you mind, pet, we'll get it sorted,' and calls a doctor who uses an anaesthetic, repositions the drip and the drugs go in fine. I thank her, and Charlie says she can be his nurse for ever. I'm furious that the other nurses didn't get it sorted out earlier, and even more furious that I didn't make them. I can only hope that one day very soon someone gives them a huge amount of drugs through a blocked drip and ignores them when they scream.

Charlie's asleep again. I ring Kate and bring her up to date. She says everyone at school is terribly upset, and Miss Pike is getting all the children to make special pictures for Charlie. She offers to drive up with anything we need, but I tell her we should be back at the local hospital soon and anyway I don't know how infectious this is. She tells me that the area health people have said that one case is not enough to warrant coming into school and giving everybody mega-antibiotics, and that the inoculations don't work for the worst kind of meningitis anyway, and have no impact at all on septicaemia. So everyone must just stay calm and watch their children carefully. Which, as Kate says, is so helpful you want to go round there especially to slap them. Our GP has been besieged by anxious parents demanding antibiotics just in case. Kate says she and Sally are both on standby, and I'm to call them as soon as I think of anything I need. I really don't know how I'd have got through this without so much support from so many people. I feel myself about to launch into an Oscar-type thank-you speech, so I say good-bye and promise to give Charlie a kiss and tell him it's from James and Phoebe, even though we both know this will annoy him intensely.

There's a loud knock on the door, and I swear silently and hope it won't wake Charlie up. I go over and open the door and come face to face with Mack, who's standing there looking exhausted, carrying his luggage from his trip and an enormous British Airways bag full of toy aeroplanes and a huge teddy in a pilot's uniform. I burst into tears and become incoherent and have to close the door and stand in the corridor. Mack explains that he simply couldn't sit in Tokyo and do nothing, so he managed to get on to the first flight home by telling them it was an emergency, and when the woman on the desk heard his story she put him in first class and informed the entire crew, who kept coming up and giving him items of British Airways merchandise to bring to the hospital. Even the pilot had a word, which Mack says was a bit scary even though you know there's another one actually flying the plane.

Apparently this pilot had a friend whose sister had meningitis years ago, and he just wanted to say she made a full recovery, after terrifying her parents half out of their wits, and is now married with three children and lives in Hastings. Mack says he realises he is babbling, and I am to kick him if I want him to shut up, but he's just so pleased to see me and the nurse says Charlie's doing very well. He holds me very tight for a very long time, and then we go and sit by Charlie and wait for him to wake up. We check with a doctor who says that there's no risk of infection at this stage because Charlie has had so many drugs over the past twenty-four hours he probably couldn't infect a newborn baby, but if Mack's worried he can give him a short course of the mega-antibiotics. I've been given the same tablets, and so have Mum and Dad and Lizzie and Matt, because we had contact with Charlie when he was first ill, and I insist Mack takes them too, just in case, so he accepts and the doctor says he'll get them sent up from the pharmacy. I remember to tell him just after he's taken the first tablet that the nurse warned me they sometimes have the interesting side-effect of turning 'your water' orange, and contact lenses can be permanently dyed a new colour. Mack says he doesn't care what colour he goes as long as nobody else gets ill, and Charlie will wake up and play with his new aeroplane.

Charlie does wake up, and likes all the new toys, but soon falls asleep again. I want to lie down with him and give him a cuddle, and maybe have a quick sleep myself, but don't want to abandon Mack. Somehow he senses this and says he'll go home and get some rest and will come and see us tomorrow. Just as he's leaving Lizzie turns up, and says she's very pleased to finally get to meet him, and gives him a big hug, which he seems to like. Then she gets embarrassed and says sorry about that, but isn't it brilliant how well Charlie's doing, and if you'd seen him last night you wouldn't believe it, and then she tails off and looks close to tears. Mack says he's sure they'll meet again when things are less traumatic, and wanders off the wrong way down the corridor looking like jet lag has just hit him and he's entered the twilight zone. We steer him in the right direction, and then Lizzie sits with Charlie while I doze in the chair. Charlie wakes me up by squirting his water pistol in my face and shouting, 'Wake up, Mummy, wake up.'

He's much stronger now, and sits up for much longer, bossing everyone about. The hospital food is cold and disgusting, so Mum is kept busy rushing backwards and forwards like a contestant on *Ready Steady Cook*. Watching him take his first steps again on wobbly little legs is almost unbearable, but luckily I walk into the bedside cabinet and bang my knee which diverts my attention.

'Mummy, you said a swear word.'

'No I didn't, darling. Do you want me to help you walk?'

'Of course not, I can walk all by myself. I'm not a baby, you know.'

'Yes I know, darling, but you've been ill and you might be feeling a bit weak.'

'Yes, I have been ill. But now I'm better, and I'm a bit bored now, Mummy. Can I have a new Power Rangers Turbo Zord? That would cheer me up.'

He can have the entire bloody Power Rangers collection as far as I'm concerned, but I realise this is a dangerous precedent and so we negotiate for hours about exactly how many toys he can buy when we go home. Leila turns up straight from the airport, and is very good and manages to be very jolly with Charlie. Mack arrives in the afternoon and says Laura has got some special potion for shock, and is making some up for me right now and sends her love, both to me and Charlie. Which is sweet of her, though I'm not sure about the potion as all I need now is an allergic reaction to some weird plant. Apparently Alfie and Daisy wanted to know if Charlie had to have lots of injections, and when Mack said yes they became deeply sympathetic. Mack then comes up with the inspired suggestion of trying to get a video sorted out for the room so Charlie can watch films. He manages to arrange this in under an hour, which I suspect is a record in any hospital, let alone one as busy as this, and then he makes a call and twenty minutes later a messenger arrives carrying a huge parcel of Disney tapes. Charlie is very impressed, and settles down to watch *Peter Pan*.

Dr Johnson announces that we can go back to the local hospital to finish off Charlie's drugs, as they need the beds and Charlie is now completely out of danger. I get very tearful, and he gets all gruff and says, 'Oh well, it's our job, you know. Good job he got that penicillin so early, that really is vital, well done.' The awful thing is I didn't know it was vital to get antibiotics – I just knew it was vital to get the bloody GP to turn up – and I feel a fraud when they keep telling me how well I've done.

Mack offers to drive us down to the local hospital, but apparently we have to use transport arranged by them, and travel with a nurse. Anyway he's due to have Alfie and Daisy for the weekend and I persuade him to stick to the plan because I know he's missed them, and they will have missed him, and anyway I want to have some time alone with Charlie. Mum and Dad and Lizzie will be around, and Leila is on standby to come down if I need anything.

The move back to the local hospital descends into farce when it turns out in the morning that there's no transport available, as Guy's don't want to pay for the ambulance and the local hospital is not keen either. I finally call a cab and say I will pay, which annoys everyone and an ambulance miraculously appears. We arrive back at the local hospital and I get flashbacks to when we were here last, which reduce me to a mute wreck. We're taken to the general children's ward: the noise is phenomenal and there appear to be hundreds of children running around shouting. A nurse is sitting behind a desk, but she's drinking tea and ignores us. The nurse who's come with us from Guy's is having none of this. She marches up and thrusts a folder of papers at her, and then kisses Charlie goodbye and rushes off back down to the ambulance before it decides to go back to Guy's without her.

A very officious-looking ward sister wearing a facemask suddenly appears out of a side room and announces that they are going to do barrier nursing, and we must not hang about in the corridor. She also says we must not leave the side room under any circumstances because it is vital we do not infect the other children. The entire ward looks at us with horror as if we have some sort of plague, and Charlie begins to cry. This is the last straw. I tell her that Guy's have said he is not infectious and have not done any barrier nursing at all. She gives me that look medical people give you which tells you that they have no interest whatsoever in your totally uninformed opinions, and you will do as you are told in their hospital.

I get Charlie settled into our new room, and I've just started reading him a story when the sister sweeps in, still wearing her gown and mask, and says will I wait outside please while she takes Charlie's temperature. I tell her I won't. Charlie looks very frightened and holds my hand really tight. I tell her I think her behaviour is totally unacceptable, she's scaring Charlie, and demand she gets the consultant immediately. She looks like she is about to mount a counter-offensive so I stand up, and luckily it turns out I am about a foot taller than her. I walk over to the door in silence and hold it open until she has left. She is shaking with fury. So am I. She goes straight over to the desk and picks up the phone. I assume she's calling security and will have us thrown out. In fact she must have called Mr O'Brien because he suddenly appears looking thunderous, hurls the door open and strides into the room, obviously expecting some sort of riot. He takes one look at Charlie and says, 'Why wasn't I told this patient had arrived? I expressly asked to be informed.' The sister mutters something, and then launches into a speech about the necessity for barrier nursing. He stares at her, says there is absolutely no need for barrier nursing, and insists she takes her gown and mask off immediately. Then he sits on the bed and strokes Charlie's foot while chatting to him about Power Rangers and how vital it is to have a really good water pistol. This man clearly has a way with children.

The sister meanwhile is standing in the corner of the room looking livid, and I can tell she's longing for Mr O'Brien to leave so she can start her campaign for revenge. I feel close to tears and then Lizzie turns up, and somehow works out without being told what is going on. She glares at the sister and says we will ring if we need anything. Yet again the ward sister finds herself being thrown out of the side room. I cannot believe my little sister is being so bossy. Mr O'Brien looks at her admiringly, and she sits down and begins chatting to Charlie as if nothing had happened.

Mr O'Brien seems reluctant to leave, and is obviously enjoying seeing Charlie looking so well. He says we can give him his drugs in medicine form now, and arranges for the hospital pharmacy to send up a bottle. We give Charlie the first dose together, and Charlie says it tastes like sick but is better than the injections. Mr O'Brien very gently removes the drip from Charlie's hand, and gives him a special smiley-face sticking plaster to put over the spot where the needle went in. Charlie's poor little hand is all red and swollen, but having the drip out seems very symbolic and I have to go and wash my hands at the sink in the corner so nobody will notice that I'm crying. Mr O'Brien strokes Charlie's hair, and says he'll come and check on us in the morning, but sees no reason why we can't go home tomorrow if all is well.

I actually kiss him, which embarrasses us both hugely. Charlie is now dancing on his bed, and despite Lizzie's best efforts he manages to bounce off it straight on to the floor so we all make a huge fuss and the moment passes. Charlie calms down when Lizzie promises to see if she can track down a television, and Mr O'Brien leaves with a smile on his face. A young nurse brings in supper, not wearing a mask, and is extremely friendly. I have a sneaking suspicion that the sister may not be popular and they all relished seeing her being told off. She spends ages fiddling with the blankets on Charlie's bed, and promises to get him ice-cream and find a television on a trolley for us.

We have a celebration supper provided by Mum. The poor woman is turning into Meals on Wheels. I can't really believe we can go home tomorrow, and I lie on the camp bed, which is much more comfortable than the other one, and try to sleep but I can't. I watch the dawn come up, and feel totally drained of any emotion other than relief. Mr O'Brien turns up very early, and says we can definitely go home. I ring Mum and Dad and Lizzie and tell them the good news. Lizzie says she'll ring everyone else and let them know, so no one turns up here to visit. Mum and Dad arrive, and they've filled the car with balloons, which Charlie thinks is marvellous. We get home to discover that Kate and Sally have cleaned the entire house from top to bottom, Mum has filled the fridge with food, and Dad has lit the fire and chopped tons of logs which are now piled up outside the back door. It's lovely to be home, and apart from a couple of shaky moments we all cope and nobody cries. Mum and Dad finally leave; it takes me ages to persuade them that I'll be fine on my own with Charlie. As soon as they've gone I feel a bit wobbly and wish I'd asked them to stay. Charlie is very happy, and wanders from room to room as if he can't quite believe we are home. He's soon exhausted, and after another dose of medicine he falls asleep in my bed – 'Because I've been ill, you know, and I need to be in your bed in case it comes back.' I sit by the fire and try to make some sort of sense of the last few days, but I can't.

Loads of cards have arrived from what seems like the entire village, and lots of drawings from school. Kate brought all the cards round with flowers and a large bottle of gin during the afternoon. She gave me a very emotional hug, and tried to hug Charlie but he wasn't keen so she had to settle for a lot of patting. I pour myself a large gin from Kate's new supply, and start to sob for what seems like hours. I feel sure I'll go blind if I cry any more, the fire goes out, and finally I crawl into bed freezing cold. Charlie stirs, looks at me and says, 'Oh, it's you. Good, I thought it was one of those horrible nurses.'

'No, darling, no more nurses,' I snivel, trying not to launch into another round of sobbing.

'Are you alright, Mummy? Your voice sounds funny.'

'Yes, I'm fine, darling.'

'Good. Mummy, you know the Power Rangers?'

'Sort of.'

'Yes, well, wouldn't it be lovely to have them all?'

'Yes. Now go back to sleep.'

He sits bolt upright. 'Really, Mummy, we can buy them all? That's brilliant, James has only got four. Oh I love you, Mummy.'

'I love you too, darling.' Sniff, snivel.

He snuggles down and is back asleep again in minutes. He's taking up most of the bed, the entire duvet, and three of the pillows. But he has the trace of a smile on his face, and is breathing slowly and deeply. I lie watching him and finally drift off to sleep.

Chapter Ten

Picking up the Pieces

W E GRADUALLY GET USED to being back at home. I spend the entire week trying to cope with a whirlwind of visits from villagers and bad behaviour from Charlie. He has furious temper tantrums over the slightest thing, hurling toys about and swearing, and constantly tells me how ill he's been. The old lady from three doors down comes round with a very oddly shaped sloping cake she's made, with Charlie's name on it in blue icing. This reduces me to tears, and she holds my hand for a very long time saying how sorry she was, is, and will be for ever that such a horrible thing could happen to such a lovely little lad. The lovely little lad is throwing a complete fit because he does not want cake, but she kindly ignores this. Then he manages to fall flat on his face, tripping over the rug in the hall, and screams so loudly that the windows rattle. She smiles and wanders off slowly back up the lane.

Mum and Dad finally relax and stop visiting daily, which is a bit of a relief as Mum kept bringing round huge quantities of food and got very thin-lipped if it was not all eaten before she went home. It was very nice food, but of the build-you-up variety. If I build up any more I won't fit into my black velvet dress ever again. Mack drives down via

215

a major spending spree in Hamleys, but luckily I spot his arrival before Charlie does, and make him hold on to some of the presents or Charlie will go into orbit and I may never get him down again. Part of me wants to give him every single thing he asks for, but apart from the potential for financial ruin I also know that in a weird way what he really needs is to get back to normal as quickly as possible. I check this out with Kate and Sally. Sally comes up with a very interesting theory about how buying too many presents for children is actually hugely threatening for them, and it's far better to give them a bit of string, and lots of attention, than tons of toys and their own televisions. When I point out that William has his own television she says yes, but it was either that or kill him, and she did refuse to buy him a new Lego set last weekend, and he sulked for two days. I sympathise and say yesterday Charlie threw a total screaming fit that lasted for nearly an hour because I refused to buy him a shotgun.

Mack has also brought food with him, and it feels churlish to tell him that Mum has already popped round with a three-course meal. He's got to be in the office tomorrow and plans to leave at the crack of dawn, so we try to get Charlie settled early which backfires badly and he's still running around singing and telling jokes at half past ten. Mack is great about this, and says he'll read him a story and calm him down. I don't think he stands a chance, but gladly accept. He comes back downstairs half an hour later and says very smugly, 'Well, that didn't take long. He's fast asleep, and he looks like he'll stay that way for at least a couple of hours.'

'Good. Are you sure he wasn't faking it? He did that last night and I was just about to creep out when he sat up and said, "Only joking." I nearly had a heart attack.'

'No, I checked.'

'Brilliant.'

'Yes, and cheap at half the price.'

'What do you mean?'

'Oh bugger. I didn't mean to say that. Um, well, we've got a deal. He goes to sleep and I slip him a fiver the next time I see him.'

'Mack, that's awful.'

'No it's not. I'll save it for emergencies, like I do with Alfie and Daisy. Actually Daisy is really getting the hang of it; she asks for the cash up-front now.'

'Well, more fool you; you'll end up shelling out a fortune.'

'Quite possibly. Speaking of which, I brought you a present too. It's in the car.'

He opens the kitchen door to the garden, peers out into the night and then says, 'Christ, someone's stolen the car.'

'What?'

'Look, it's gone.'

I look down the drive and can see nothing, but then you never can because when it's dark in the country it really is dark. I switch on the outside lights, and the car is revealed.

'Oh, right, thanks.'

He comes back in with a very expensive-looking box, and inside it are a pair of beautiful earrings, a bit like the ones Kate lent me, but nicer. Plain silver crosses, with green stones.

'Mack, they're beautiful. Thank you.'

'Well, I thought you should have your own.'

He looks a bit embarrassed, and I put them on and twirl about and say they are the nicest present I've ever been given, and he seems pleased, and then I give him a kiss which starts out as a thank-you kiss but rapidly turns into something quite different. The combination of lust and exhaustion somehow makes things even more perfect than usual. I feel oddly tearful, and then Mack very gently asks me to tell him the whole story of what happened right from the beginning, and I do, and end up sobbing in his arms. Eventually I calm down and we go up to bed, and then I get woken what seems like minutes later by Charlie who's crying and says he's had a horrible dream about injections. I comfort him, and then Mack wakes up and does the same, and starts telling him a very boring story about boats which is perfect because we all fall asleep and the next thing I know it's five thirty and Mack is trying to get dressed quietly without waking anybody up.

I go downstairs and make coffee.

'Excellent boat story last night.'

'Yes, it's one of my specials. Guaranteed to bore the little buggers back to sleep; I've never had to do more than ten minutes.'

'I can imagine. Do you want toast?'

'No thanks, we'd better not risk the smoke alarm.'

'Very funny.'

I wave him off to work and for a moment have a fantasy of being a corporate wife seeing my breadwinner off for a day at the office. But I get over it very quickly, as apart from anything else I'm not wearing the right kind of slippers; in fact I'm not wearing slippers at all but horrible old gardening shoes which were by the door and are caked in mud. I go back to bed and am just dropping off again when Charlie wakes up.

'Where's Mack gone?'

'To work.'

'Bugger.'

'Charlie, please stop saying that silly word.'

'I didn't get my money, and now he'll forget.'

I don't want to get involved in Mack's bribery deal, because if I do Charlie will insist I do the same tonight. But I also don't want him to think Mack is unreliable.

'Oh, he said something about tell Charlie I haven't forgotten the deal and we'll sort it out next time I see him, whatever that means.'

Charlie gives a huge sigh of relief and says, 'Oh, that's alright then. Mummy, what's for breakfast? I'm starving. I need to eat lots, you know; I've been very ill.'

I'm chatting to Leila, and trying to get her to stop sending presents by special courier delivery because apart from anything else the garage is now full of the small white polystyrene pellet things that seem to come in every parcel. Every time I get them rounded up in bin bags Charlie rushes in and liberates them. The garage is now like a giant version of those little plastic things you shake and snow whirls about. Leila says she understands completely, and she's found a marvellous book on post-traumatic stress, and apparently it's vital to get back to normal routines as quickly as possible. She's shopping as much as she can, and suggests I do the same, because it really takes your mind off things. I agree with her, but point out the difference in my case is that if I do indulge in any major shopping sprees, I'll have the added bonus of having my mind taken off things twice: once when I do the shopping and then all over again when the bank manager writes one of his special rude letters.

Charlie is getting slightly calmer, and his tantrums are now less frequent, though still blistering when he does launch into one. There are lots of unbearable moments when he's sitting having a cuddle or I'm reading a story to him, and he suddenly asks why he got ill: did he do something wrong, and can I promise it won't come back? We have long discussions about germs and how it was just bad luck, and he seems to accept this but I'm left shattered. I can't bear seeing him so anxious and afraid. Sally has talked to her friend Mel, a child psychologist, who says it's very common for children recovering from a serious illness to come up with all sorts of behaviour problems, and the only thing to do is just hang on in there. I can't imagine how parents cope with long-term serious illness: it must be crucifying. I feel very lucky, but I also feel traumatised, and there is simply no space for this. I feel guilty that I let him down, and wasn't able to protect him, and guilty that I keep thinking about how I feel instead of concentrating on him. I know this is going to be a long haul, and it seems awful to mind about his furious temper tantrums and anxiety attacks compared to what might have happened. But I do mind, more for him than for me, and seeing him raging away makes me feel like I'm letting him down all over again. I feel somehow things will never be quite the same: once your worst nightmares have started to come true you realise just how fragile everything really is. I'm going to have to work really hard not to be too over-protective. I'd like to wrap him up in blankets and keep him indoors for the next ten years, but realise this is not sensible, and anyway it's probably illegal.

The GP, Dr Bennett, arrives to check Charlie over, and is very friendly once it becomes clear that I'm not going to sue him for failing to come up with the right diagnosis during our first two appointments. Charlie is horrified that a doctor has turned up at the house, and throws Lego at him, and then insists the poor man empties out his bag and puts all the needles and syringes back into his car. Once he's reassured that he's not going to be given any injections, he calms down, a bit, but he's still wary and clings to me and holds my hand very tight. The poor doctor tries his best to be friendly, and even attempts a little joke, but Charlie is having none of it, and narrows his eyes and watches his every move intently. He gives Charlie the all-clear to go back to school, and has a stab at another little joke, and then says he'd better be off.

As I'm showing him out, he says, 'Of course it's a notoriously tricky thing to spot, and we do rely on parents to call us in before things go too far.' I think this is unfair and tell him so.

'So if something terrible had happened, it would have been my fault?'

'No, no, of course not, that's not what I meant at all.'

'I know. But that's how it feels.'

'Oh, well, I really didn't mean it like that. Actually I still feel pretty awful about it. I really am very sorry, you know.' And he looks totally wretched.

'Yes, well, it's over now, and he's fine.'

'Fighting fit with the old Lego anyway.'

'Yes, sorry about that.'

'Oh not at all, not at all; I've had much worse, believe me. I once got a very nasty bite from a toddler, and he was only in with his mum to get a repeat prescription. Really, I can't tell you how pleased I am to see him so well.'

He walks off down the drive, and I return to the living room to find Charlie crouched by the window pretending to shoot the doctor in the back as he gets into his car.

Charlie's first day back at school turns out to be much harder than I'd expected. Loads of parents come over at the school gates to say hello and generally welcome him back. Miss Pike appears and doesn't seem to mind that Charlie nearly knocks her over with a hug. Suddenly Mrs Harrison-Black looms into view and shouts, 'Oh there you are, young man. Honestly, you gave us all such a fright. Poor Dr Bennett was besieged with panicking parents. I told them not to be so silly, but you know what people are like. And here you are looking as fit as a fiddle.'

Charlie shrinks behind me and looks nervous, as if he's being accused of frightening the whole school on purpose. I'm on the verge of telling her to fuck off, despite the long-term consequences of swearing in front of Mixed Infants, when Miss Pike says in her special loud voice, 'Thank you, Betty. What an unfortunate way to put things. I think what Mrs Harrison-Black is trying to say, Charlie, is that it's very nice to have you back at school, and we all missed your lovely smile. Now, dear, do you think you could ring the bell for me and be my special helper today?'

There's a gasp from all the parents standing nearby, as Mrs Harrison-Black is revealed as a Betty. She always signs her PTA letters Mrs Robert Harrison-Black, which is ludicrous, and we always wondered why. Betty is just not the kind of name she would feel was appropriate. I always knew Miss Pike could be lethal when she needed to, but this is a triumph. Mrs Harrison-Black goes bright red and rushes off to her car, and Kate says, 'Goodbye, Betty,' to her as she runs past. Marvellous, marvellous.

Charlie bolts off to get the bell, which is normally strictly out of bounds to the under-tens. I'm not sure Miss Pike meant him to ring it for quite so long, or quite so loudly, but she's smiling as she wrestles it back off him. Everyone smiles indulgently, and lots of parents give their children an extra cuddle before they leave. It's a bit like that film *Truly Madly*

Deeply where Alan Rickman talks about a little girl who has died. Her parents have put a bench in her favourite playground with a plaque on it which says 'For Rosie, who used to like to play here'. And every parent who reads it flinches and goes over to their child and holds them very tight for a moment. I'd like to hold Charlie very tight for a moment but he's off running around in circles. Then he trots into his classroom quite happily, holding Miss Pike's hand and occasionally hopping.

We've agreed that I'll pick him up at lunchtime because Miss Pike thinks that a full day might be too much for him on his first day back. I find myself close to tears, and Kate puts her arm round me. I can't quite believe I'm finally back on my own again, without a small child watching my every move. We decide to go back to my house rather than Kate's, just in case the school rings, so we drive off in convoy and a very emotional hour or so follows while I recount the full saga. But thankfully we soon grow tired of talking about what might have happened and how lucky we all are to have healthy children, and move on to better things: gossip and scandal. We agree we will call Mrs Harrison-Black Betty at every opportunity from now on, and Kate tells me that there was almost a fight at ballet last week when Mrs Bates found that her daughter Sophie had not been picked for a role in the forthcoming show. Sophie dances like a small elephant, and was not deemed suitable for the part of a gladioli. Phoebe is to be a daffodil, but is refusing to wear yellow.

We hate Mrs Bates because she's bossy, a terrible snob, and sometimes wears a leotard to pick up Sophie, and doesn't look fat in it. But more importantly she once disparaged a salad Sally made for the school picnic. There have also been dramas at the recent PTA meeting on literacy, when someone pointed out that there were two spelling mistakes on the information leaflet. And the fire drill didn't go well, as Miss Pike forgot it was a drill and had to have a lie-down in the staff room. And then three boys from Year 6 went missing, and were discovered in the school office trying to ring an Adults Only chatline. Suddenly it's time to pick up Charlie, and I rush off feeling much happier.

Charlie is furious.

'Mummy, Miss Pike said I had to do some reading even though I've been ill, because my reading is so nice she wanted to hear it.'

'Well, that's nice, isn't it, darling, you love reading.'

'Yes, but I was playing and I was busy.'

'Well, never mind, you'll need to get used to being back at school and I'm sure Miss Pike will help you.'

'Miss Pike is a bugger.'

'Charlie, you love Miss Pike.'

'I used to love her, but now I think she's a bugger.'

'Stop being silly. Let's talk about something else. What do you want for lunch? You can have anything you like.'

'Lobster.'

'Charlie, stop being silly.'

'I'm not being silly. I think it will be lovely and just what I need to build up my strength. I feel as weak as a kitten.'

I cannot imagine where he picks these phrases up from. He eventually agrees to cheese and crackers, with butter on but not too thick, and peaches for pudding and we spend the afternoon in a haze of jigsaws and Lego. I opt for an early supper and bath; the pasta is described as disgusting muck but turns out to be edible if there is chocolate cake for pudding. I made the cake during the afternoon, to get away from all the Lego. Actually I think I'm developing an allergy to Lego: every time I see piles of it all over the floor I feel an overwhelming desire to tip it all into the bin. The cake has turned out, as usual, rather flat and not at all like the picture in the book. Maybe Delia is less tense than I am, and does not have to dodge quite so much Lego. Charlie eats it, but asks if we can have a proper cake next time, from a shop.

I finally get him into bed at seven thirty, although it feels like midnight, and I read bloody annoying baby books for the umpteenth time. He's rediscovered them all and wants them read to him again and again. He pretends to snort with derision at the baby-style plots and the endless repetition of phrases like 'I love you, Little Bear', but actually he adores them. He falls asleep and I lie watching him. I realise that I really do love him more than life itself, and never really understood what that phrase meant before. It's all very gratifying, but I also realise I'm on the verge of getting cramp, have to face the supermarket tomorrow and must see about getting some work soon or my bank manager will have a heart attack.

Barney rings, and announces that it looks like the job with the flying piano might be happening, and if I feel up to it he'd like me to come in on Friday and run through it with him. He doesn't want Lawrence to do the job because he's bound to panic.

'I mean, you know what he's like. I think the combination of the piano and the pool is just going to be too much for him.'

'What pool?'

'Well, I've worked on the script a bit. Now the piano comes down the stairs chasing the waiter and then they both end up in a swimming pool.'

'Barney, you've got to be kidding. It'll be a nightmare.'

'Yes, very probably. But great fun, and I think I've worked out a way to do it. Well, almost, and I'll make up the rest as we go along.'

'Oh, so that'll be a nice change then.'

Friday morning, and Edna arrives to look after Charlie. She's been itching to get her hands on Charlie and start feeding him up, and has come round every day to see her boy. In fact she and Mum have developed a sort of vaguely competitive home-baking routine. I get into the office and realise that this job is going to be horrendous. But it will also involve at least three days in the studio, which will cheer up the bank manager enormously. Lawrence tries to be nice and asks about Charlie, but soon reverts to his normal behaviour and gets very snippy when I turn my desk round so it's no longer facing the wall in the darkest corner. He says this ruins his entire redesign of the office and is getting very agitated, when Barney comes downstairs and stands behind him making faces. Lawrence finally works out what's going on, and goes off in a huff for lunch and doesn't come back until five. Barney has another meeting tomorrow with the agency for the piano job and says he'll let me know if we get the go-ahead so I can start booking everything. He reckons we're sure to get it because he's heard no one else is up for it, as they all think it's impossible. This has naturally encouraged Barney no end, and he keeps doing drawings of the set which no one can understand. He is interviewing stuntmen, who are all mad, and has asked me twice if I know how to scuba dive.

Mack comes down for tea on Sunday, which goes fairly well, although hideous tension mounts over the fate of the

226

last KitKat. I must try to remember to never ever buy a pack of six of anything when there are five people for tea, and three of them are children. I try to make out that I don't want my KitKat, but this is overruled as an obvious lie and anyway Mack has already eaten his so that still leaves one child KitKat free. Mack suggests Charlie should have it because he's not been very well. Charlie thinks this is an excellent plan, but Alfie looks close to tears so I come up with a compromise and cut it up into three pieces, with the children watching very, very closely to see each bit is the same size. The result is declared acceptable by the panel and peace is restored. I attempt a bit of bonding with Daisy and tell her that I think her pink shirt is very pretty. She's pleased and says her mummy has got one too, just the same. But then she adds that she doesn't think they do them big enough for me, just in case I was wondering.

The children watch a video after tea, and Mack and I try to work out when we can meet next.

'I don't suppose there's any chance you could get up to town, is there?'

'No, sorry.'

'I'm sure he'd be OK, you know.'

'Yes, so am I. But I wouldn't. I'm sorry, Mack, but I'm just not up to leaving him at the moment. Maybe in a few more weeks. I mean, I'm going to be working and everything; I'll be away enough as it is.'

'I know. I just want a bit of time with you on our own. Maybe we could get a weekend away before Christmas?'

'Maybe. Let's see how it goes.'

I can tell he's not very happy about this, and thinks I might be being just a little bit too fussy. But he's trying really hard not to show it.

'I know this isn't ideal, Mack. But I'm going to need time to get over this, and so is Charlie.'

'Of course you are, don't be daft. Look, forget I said anything, it's fine. I'll come down here, there's no problem.' He puts his arms round me and we are just about to kiss when Daisy thunders in. She's furious because Alfie has said that he'll be sitting in the front of the car on the way home, because Daddy has promised he can, even though it's her turn.

Mack looks panic-stricken and it appears he has indeed promised both children that they can sit in the front on the journey home. Daft bugger. A small riot erupts and Charlie joins in with great gusto, saying he wants to sit in the front, even though he's not actually going in the car. I suggest that they stop halfway and swap over; eventually they accept this and Mack looks eternally grateful as he drives off. Charlie promptly bursts into tears and says he wanted to go too, and sit in the front all the way, and he wants another KitKat. It takes me half an hour to calm him down, two satsumas and lots of back-stroking. He falls asleep in my arms, and I am pinned to the sofa and can't move. I finally struggle to my feet and get him upstairs and into bed. I'm so exhausted I go straight to bed myself, and then get woken up by Mack ringing. He tells me that the seat-swapping plan was not entirely successful, because Alfie refused to swap and clung on to the car door and had to be dragged out. Daisy was furious and wanted Alfie to be made to spend the rest of the journey in the boot. But they're now both asleep in his bed, looking angelic.

'The only problem is I'm far too knackered to go to bed and wrestle with them both for a bit of duvet.'

'What about going in the spare bed?'

'I tried that last time. The little bastards climbed in during the night, and it's half the size of my bed. Actually I was thinking about the top bunk. I reckon that'd fool them.'

'Good plan. But be careful. Last time I slept in a top bunk I nearly killed myself falling out in the middle of the night. Kate and I took the kids on a narrow boat for the weekend. It was hell.'

'I bet. What on earth possessed you to do that?'

'Well, it looked like fun in the brochure, and Kate loves boats. Or at least she thought she did before we went. But it rained, the kids all got diarrhoea and there were millions of midges. The only thing we could find to stop them biting us was Phoebe's face paints. We all looked like something out of *Apocalypse Now*. All we needed was old Marlon saying "The horror, the horror" every twenty minutes.'

'Sounds unforgettable.'

'Oh it was magic, believe me. Now if you don't mind I'd like to get back to sleep. Off you go and clamber into your bunk, tie yourself to the rail by your socks and lift up the ladder. You can ring me tomorrow and tell me if it works.'

Charlie is not keen on going to school in the morning, and it takes breakfast with Buzz and Woody, and the promise of a special cake for tea – a 'proper' shop one – to get him into the car. Then Ted turns up on his milk-float and blocks the drive, and Charlie bolts out of the car and begs for a lift to school on the back of his float. Ted looks like he might agree, so I have to swiftly intervene and claim it is illegal. This prompts a long complicated conversation about whether it might be possible to report the Government to the United Nations, or failing that *Blue Peter*, for its flagrant breach of human rights in banning children from riding on milk-floats.

I spend the entire day trying to book people and equipment for the piano job, but only provisionally because we still don't have a firm date. I pick up Charlie from school and drive home via the local petrol station. It's a tiny little place with only two pumps, which I usually avoid as the old lady on the till is not keen on credit cards because she can't work the machine. I pull the lever inside the car to release the petrol flap, and it flies open rather more energetically than usual. In fact it flies right off its hinges. I finally get it back on, but it will not shut, and hangs off the hinges looking pathetic, and makes a terrible grinding noise when I try to shut it. The old lady comes out to help, and gives it a terrific whack which forces it closed. But I feel certain this is only temporary. I wonder if the AA would come out for a recalcitrant petrol flap. But I reckon this is probably not what they had in mind when they decided to call themselves the fourth emergency service. Although from Kate's recent experiences with them, where they took two hours to arrive and tell her they don't fix punctures before driving off and leaving her stranded in torrential rain, I'm not quite sure what they do mean.

I decide I'd better go to the garage which services the car, and drive along with visions of the petrol cap flying off and injuring a passing motorcyclist, who then crashes into the back of the car and ignites the petrol tank, which turns us all into toast. Charlie senses all is not well.

'Is this an emergency, Mummy?'

'No.'

'Well, why can't we go home then?'

'Look, it's not an emergency but we need to get it fixed.'

'So it is a sort of emergency then. Good. Bugger, fuck, bastard, sod. You said you could only say swear words in an emergency, so I've said them. I've got a new word too – do you want to hear it?'

'No.'

'Twat.'

'Charlie!'

'That's my new word. I think it's a sort of twit mixed in with bottom.'

'Right. Now, don't say it again. It's not that sort of emergency. In fact it's not an emergency at all. You're being very silly.'

He glares at me, and refuses to get out of the car when we arrive at the garage. I run into the service department and shout, 'My flap won't shut,' while looking over my shoulder to make sure Charlie has not got out of the car and sneaked off to play in the car wash. I realise with hindsight that yelling 'My flap won't shut' to a room full of bored motor mechanics was not a very good idea. Once they stop laughing they all wander out and tut and shake their heads, and say the entire car will have to be resprayed, and the job will take months and cost a fortune. I tell them to stop buggering about or I will let Charlie out of the car, and he's tired and hungry and due a major tantrum at any moment. Miraculously they decide that one man with a small screwdriver should be able to manage, and the flap is rehoused on its hinges, squirted with oil, and pops open and shut again as if nothing had happened. I thank them profusely and get my purse out to pay them, but they say, 'Oh no need for that, it's all part of the service,' whilst giving Charlie doubtful looks as he's opened his door and is yelling, 'I am hungry, I am hungry,' at the top of his voice. I tell him to shut up, thank the mechanics and get back into the car.

Charlie and I scream at each other for ten minutes, and then move on to an endless debate as to what might be available for tea. We finally get home and I park the car, and Charlie gets out and slams his door very hard. The petrol flap shoots open, hovers for a moment, and then falls into the flowerbed. I ring the garage and speak to one of the mechanics we met earlier and book the car in for tomorrow morning. Make supper in a very bad temper, and manage to burn my hand draining the pasta. I sulk for a bit, but Charlie doesn't notice, so I end up whining about my sore hand until he makes a fuss and then I feel guilty for being so pathetic. Bathtime goes on for ever but I finally get him into bed and settle down with a gin and tonic, and promptly fall asleep. The phone wakes me up at around midnight, and the sound of an animal in distress on the other end of the line makes me sit bolt upright and wonder if it's some sort of weird agricultural crank caller. Eventually Leila emerges from the wailing and says she and James have split up, and she wants to die. Or kill James and then die. It takes me about twenty minutes to get her to stop sobbing, and then a more or less coherent story begins to unravel.

Apparently James had asked her out to dinner, and made a big show of it being an important occasion. Leila had vaguely imagined a velvet box containing an enormous diamond ring. Instead he said he thought he might be ready to move into her house. He'd rent out his flat for six months to see how things went, and suggested they set up a joint account, although he would keep the rent from his flat, as he was the one facing the upheaval of moving. He also suggested Leila might benefit from a fixed amount of money to spend on clothes each month, and then mentioned a sum Leila says wouldn't even cover her dry-cleaning bills. Leila told him she would spend her money on what she bloody well liked, and he told her she was out of control and needed someone like him to impose a bit of order in her life.

Then things got really nasty and she ended up throwing her dinner at him and walking out. Apparently she was having risotto, so her last sight of James was one of him picking rice out of his hair. But not the kind of rice she'd originally had in mind. Whereupon she goes off into sobs again. She finally rallies and says she was getting bored of him anyway, but really what a cheek and men are hopeless and she's going to become a lesbian because women are so much nicer.

'I think it's the perfect solution, except I don't really want to have to cut my hair. I mean, it's taken me nearly a year to grow out those bloody layers, and I've finally got it how I want it. And actually I don't really fancy women – maybe I could just become a lesbian who has sex with men. Do you think that would work?'

I tell her I think this describes most women perfectly, and she cheers up a bit and says anyway, she's going to treat herself and go off somewhere very expensive for a week and would I like to come? I say I would love to, but I have to work, and anyway Charlie might prove a bit of a liability in a posh hotel. She seems much happier by the end of the conversation, but I know she's really upset and I feel wretched for her. I wish I knew where he worked so I could turn up unexpectedly and slap him. I confide this to her and she says she's already thought of that, and there's this brilliant company who send revenge-type gifts like bunches of dead roses and gift-wrapped offal and she's going to call them first thing tomorrow morning. I think James might be in for a bumpy few days.

Chapter Eleven

After the Ball is Over

I T LOOKS LIKE THE piano job is on. I spend hours on the phone with Barney, the studio, the stuntman and the carpenter who's making the special piano. I also arrange childcare with a complicated combination of Edna and Mum, and plan to travel home each night despite the three-hour drive. Or four if there are police cars about. The job should be great if it works, but I have grave doubts, and don't really feel ready to be so far away from Charlie even though I know he'll be fine. But I haven't really got a choice if I want to pay the mortgage this month. Mack is off to New York on business and has been so frantic in the last few weeks he's only managed a couple of overnight stays – which have been lovely, especially last week when Charlie stayed asleep in his own bed all night and we got to wake up together without a small boy stuck firmly between us.

We've promised ourselves a weekend away before Christmas, and Mack is talking about Venice though I'm holding out for the Lake District because I can't face being out of the country without Charlie. Mack calls from the airport which makes me late for collecting Charlie from school. I rush out of the house grabbing my new smart coat, and arrive at school with two minutes to spare. I spot Kate and we stand near the bushes trying to avoid the PTA woman who's organising an auction of promises. So far there are tons of cakes, hours of gardening and offers of babysitting. But the committee is looking for something more exciting to attract higher bids. Kate says we should promise to give them fifty pounds if they'll leave us alone, but I don't think this is quite what they have in mind. The children start coming out of their classrooms and Phoebe marches over and says, 'I hate Natalie and that's final.' She looks close to tears so Kate takes her off to the car for a debrief and a cuddle out of sight of the other children. I promise to walk James to the car when he emerges with Charlie.

They've been doing PE in the hall, and are consequently still in the classroom trying to find their socks. It starts to pour. My new coat turns out not to be waterproof; in fact it's the exact opposite of waterproof and absorbs water like a sponge. The special detachable hood unexpectedly detaches itself and blows across the playground. I'm in hot pursuit when Charlie and James emerge half dressed from their classroom and join in the chase. Finally Charlie manages to capture it by jumping on it, in a huge puddle. He is very pleased with himself and thrusts the soaking-wet muddy hood into my hands.

'Look, Mummy, I've got it.'

'Thank you, Charlie.'

He's hopping with excitement now, and says, 'Is there going to be a prize? Can we go to the shop on the way home and get sweets? Can we, can we?' I'm too soaked to argue, and also want to avoid a scene in front of James, so I agree to a detour via the village shop. I park as close to the shop as I can, and open the car door to discover we're in the middle of a small lake. I try to get out of the car by a weird sort of leaping combined with limbo-type movements, and end up standing in four inches of muddy water. Charlie is delighted.

We squelch into the shop and find it's full of people with soaking-wet trouser legs, so at least we're not the only ones. A small crowd of children surrounds the sweet shelves, and the noise is indescribable. One boy is firmly clutching an enormous bag of toffees but his mum is holding out for a small packet of Refreshers. Another woman has three children with her, and a toddler who's lying on the floor screaming because he wants a family-size tub of vanilla ice-cream from the freezer. I quickly offer Charlie a small bar of chocolate if we can leave the shop before the slapping starts. Thankfully he agrees, and we rush back to the car in torrential rain. The lake now entirely surrounds the car and Charlie drops his chocolate into the water, twice. Apparently it's fine, it only got a bit wet and the silver paper has saved the day. He's eaten the whole bar before I've got my seatbelt on.

When we get home I put Charlie straight into the bath, and then get waylaid with a stream of phone calls about work. Charlie takes the opportunity to have a really good splash, and we spend ages mopping up the bathroom floor. I end up going to bed at eight thirty and plan to get up and tidy up after a quick nap, but somehow manage to bypass this and wake up just in time to hear Edna arrive. She's very chirpy and makes tea and wipes surfaces while I run about getting dressed. I charge out of the house and I'm on the motorway before I realise I've left half the pieces of paper I need at home. Barney rings on the mobile and starts fussing but thankfully his car enters a tunnel or something and the call is suddenly cut off. I decide to switch my phone off to get a bit of peace, and claim the signal went dead.

I get to the studio to find the set isn't ready. Barney

marches over and says, 'What's the matter with your fucking phone? I've been trying to call you. This set is a disaster, and that staircase is in totally the wrong place. Christ, can't these people get anything right?' I calm him down, and then discover the staircase is in the exact position specified on the plans, but Barney changed his mind and forgot to tell anybody. Finally I get things sorted, and Barney wanders off mumbling about laying a track. He always lays a track when he can't think of anything else to do, and the crew know this. So they all start milling about saying this will never work. The grand piano arrives, and looks enormous. It's reinforced with metal and then covered in wood to look like an ordinary one, so when it flies down the stairs the legs won't snap off. It takes four men to wheel it into the studio on a special trolley. The crew all look at it and start shaking their heads. Barney has gone very pale and is muttering to himself.

The idea is for a new brand of fizzy orange drink. A couple are sitting in a restaurant overlooking a terrace with stairs down to a huge swimming pool. The woman orders a drink, and the waiter starts shaking the bottle before opening it. Assuming it will spray everywhere, she ducks under the table and manages to push a chair over, which trips up a passing waiter causing a chain reaction of crashing trolleys and curtains being set on fire, finally culminating in the piano being given a hefty shove. It careers off down the stairs just behind a waiter, who dives into the pool closely followed by the piano. The final shot is the waiter opening the original bottle of drink which gives an elegant little hiss. The voiceover will witter on about how this drink can be shaken and won't explode because it's a special blend of fruit and spring water. Relax. Just shake it and pour.

Wish I could relax, shake it and pour, preferably with

something involving gin, but just to make things completely perfect a very anxious client, called Adrian, has turned up and keeps trying to ask Barney exactly what his plans are. As Barney is still trying to decide, this line of questioning is not entirely welcome. We finally get everything in place and Barney announces he wants to try to get the piano going down the staircase first, so if anything goes wrong we still have the next two days to play with. The crew start shaking their heads and telling me that this is going to be a disaster. Everyone is getting very nervous, and Barney is still wandering around muttering to himself and obsessing about the lighting.

The stuntman dresses up as a waiter and stands at the top of the staircase. We get four men behind the piano waiting to shove it through the doors. We're finally ready and they begin to push. The bloody thing hardly moves and then when it does it bounces off the first stair, drops to the second, does another little bounce and stops. Barney yells at them to push harder. We end up with about twenty people crouched behind the doors, the piano comes out at about ninety miles an hour, bounces much higher but still only makes it to the fifth step before stopping. We break for a coffee and try to work out what to do next. Barney suddenly announces that the staircase must be removed, and a ramp put in, painted to look like the stairs.

'You've got to be kidding, guv, that'll never work.'

'Yes it will.'

'But, guv, it'll just shoot down the ramp, and anyway it won't sound like stairs.'

Barney considers this for a moment. 'Of course it won't, you'll have to nail bits of wood down to make it bounce a bit. Christ, do I have to think of everything?'

The carpenters look at him like he's mad, but remove the

238

staircase and put in a ramp. We have to break for lunch and we still aren't ready to go. At this rate we're going to take the entire three days just to get one shot. The stuntman points out that the ramp may mean the piano actually catches up with him, but Barney says it'll be fine, and anyway we've got a frogman standing by to fish him out if the piano lands on top of him.

The stuntman does not look pleased at this news, and says that really we should have two divers in the pool: one to take care of the piano, and one to drag him out from under it if it all goes pear-shaped. Barney glares at me, as if I should have anticipated this, and mutters something about snorkels. I decide to ignore this, because I have a sneaking suspicion his next idea will be that I spend hours lurking at the bottom of the pool. I'm not sure my snorkelling skills are really up to rescuing drowning stuntmen from underneath grand pianos.

The ramp is finally sorted, and the frogman gets back into the pool. The piano is repositioned behind the doors, and I get practically the entire crew to stand behind it ready to push. The stuntman stands ready and the tension mounts. A junior copywriter from the agency helpfully points out that if the piano really builds up speed it may veer off in an entirely unexpected direction and demolish half the studio. Everyone tells him to shut up, and we start. The piano shoots through the doors and begins bouncing down the ramp in a most convincing fashion. The waiter starts running, and keeps glancing over his shoulder. The piano is definitely gaining on him and he looks absolutely terrified. Finally he dives into the pool about two seconds before the piano hits the little hidden ramp, flies into the air and splashes into the water. The frogman yanks him out of the way just in time. The entire crew applaud and yell, and

Barney is thrilled. It looks like we've got it, and we're busy congratulating ourselves and watching the tape, which looks brilliant, when the client wanders over looking very worried.

'Um, I don't know about this, you know. I mean, I just don't think it's funny.'

Barney looks at him with utter contempt, and says, 'Oh, sorry, Adrian, was it meant to be funny? No one told me it was meant to be funny.'

The crew fall about laughing, and the client looks furious.

'Look, Adrian, why don't you go back to the agency and work out how to make it funny, and then come back and tell us tomorrow? In the meantime I think we should get on, don't you?'

Adrian is whisked off by the agency, and I ask Barney what he thinks he's playing at.

'What exactly are we going to do tomorrow when he comes back with a load of old bollocks he wants us to shoot, and there's nothing in the budget?'

'We're going to ignore him, that's what we're going to do. This film is going to be great, I just know it. Whenever they tell you it's not funny, you know you're on to a winner – you should know that by now. I'd have been really worried if he'd said he loved it.'

'Yes, but –'

'Don't "yes but" me. We'll tell him we don't have time tomorrow and then on the last day we'll just ignore him, and then we can all bugger off and if he doesn't like it he can stuff it. Now, let's get set up for the next shot, shall we? It's getting late.'

I get home in the middle of the night, totally exhausted. I barely manage to fall asleep before it's time to wake up and head back to the studio, but at least I get to see Charlie, who

240

comes into my bed at some point during the night and has a quick cuddle before going back to sleep.

The second day goes well, apart from the bit with the curtains which catch fire very easily but won't go out again, and threaten to burn down the entire studio before we get the blaze under control. The client turns up with a contingent from the agency who have come up with a couple of really crap ideas, and Barney says we'll see what we can do, and then completely ignores them for the rest of the day.

I make vague noises about our plans being pretty much set for today, but talk about the possibility of having a bit of time tomorrow, and then try to corner Barney and persuade him to at least pretend to listen to them. He points out that he didn't get to where he is today by listening to clients, and anyway can I please shut up because he's trying to work out the next shot. I get away at a reasonable hour, but the client is clearly furious and I anticipate ructions tomorrow.

I know we're in for a hard day when I spot Lawrence arriving early the next morning. The crew start muttering as soon as they see him as they know this means trouble, and sure enough the client asks for a quick meeting before we start and says that Lawrence has told him this will be fine. Barney sits through the entire meeting in silence, and then says, 'Thanks, Adrian, that was very interesting,' and wanders off to chat to the lighting man. The client seems happy with this, and the agency people look very relieved. They take him off for coffee, and the minute they've disappeared Barney marches back over and starts shouting at Lawrence.

'You little fucker. Get back to the office right now. If I want any more meetings fixed up, I'll let you know.'

Lawrence looks like he's about to say something, but then

thinks better of it and storms off. And then Barney turns on me.

'And as for you. What the fuck were you doing when he was fixing up meetings with the fucking client?'

I use my special reassuring tone of voice which I usually save for crisis moments with Charlie.

'Now look, Barney. I know you're tired, but don't start yelling at me or I'll go home. Let's get a coffee and you can tell me what you want to do next.'

I almost take his hand as I would Charlie's but stop myself just in time. Barney looks at me with a horrible sneer on his face and I know he's tempted to continue yelling. But last time we played Call My Bluff I did actually walk out, admittedly only to sit trembling in my car trying to work out how I was going to find another job. But then Barney came and sat in the back of the car and said I'd better not think I was walking off his set. Which was Barney-speak for an apology, so we both went back and finished the job. He finally says, 'Don't treat me like a three year old. I'm fucking annoyed.'

'All right then, let's go for the old-fashioned approach. If you speak to me like that again I shall slap you hard, and then you'll be sorry. Just tell me what you want to do next, or shall I get them to build a nice big track while you have a little think?'

I realise I am pushing it, but am too tired to care and anyway Barney is delighted and starts laughing. The rest of the day goes fairly smoothly, and the client gets bored and leaves early. He's so stupid he actually thinks Barney has taken some of his ideas 'on board', whereas in reality he's ignored them completely.

In fact we all get away pretty early, and I'm in serious danger of arriving home just in time to catch Charlie's bedtime, which I cannot quite face, so I loiter in McDonald's drive-in drinking coffee. I notice a couple of other women apparently doing the same, and realise there must be working mothers all over the place wasting an extra half-hour rather than walk in slap in the middle of bedtime. We could start a whole new trend in bars and cafés. Not so much Happy Hour as Don't Get Home Before Bedtime Is Over Hour. The coast is clear when I get home, and Mum has made supper which is keeping warm in the oven: shepherd's pie. Bliss. Mack rings up and says he's back, the trip was totally exhausting but interesting and can he come down at the weekend? Yes please. Leila is due down on Sunday, so I arrange for Mack to come down on Saturday and push off shortly after Leila arrives, which suits him because he has to go back to the States on Monday. I have a long chat with Mum about plans for Christmas, which gets rather fraught, but we end up agreeing that everyone will come to me on Christmas Day. I'm still not sure quite how this happened because my secret plan was that we would all go to Mum.

I wake next morning to find Charlie is already up and has made me breakfast in bed. Five digestive biscuits covered in honey, which he's managed to spread over the entire kitchen, and a tea bag in a cup of cold water. Yum. I go down to the kitchen to make tea and find the soles of my feet stick to the kitchen floor. Try to be grateful but fail, and Charlie sulks.

'Honey is very difficult to spread, you know, Mummy. Lots of biscuits cracked into bits before I got the hang of it.'

The kitchen bin is indeed full of bits of broken biscuits, and what seems like ten gallons of honey. I try to gently suggest that next time plain biscuits would be fine, but Charlie says I'm being horrible and he will never make me breakfast again. I end up feeling mean and eat the biscuits, which are revolting. Charlie cheers up and wanders off to watch cartoons. I spend so long trying to wash honey off the kitchen surfaces that we're late leaving for school.

We arrive just as the bell rings, and I'm cornered by a pincer movement from the PTA women on the auction committee. I wave Charlie goodbye with a very fixed smile on my face, and am then cross-examined for ten minutes as to why I cannot come up with a truly startling promise which will raise hundreds of pounds for school funds. Aren't I something to do with films? Couldn't I arrange for a day watching a film being made? People would love that. I point out that actually it's very boring, with lots of sitting about, and directors aren't really very keen on strangers turning up to watch. I can just imagine Barney's face when I tell him I've put him up as a star lot in the PTA auction. I end up agreeing to see what I can do, which will turn out to be absolutely nothing but naturally I do not tell them this.

Saturday afternoon, and Charlie has a birthday party to go to. A small boy called Justin from his class, with rather nervous parents who for some reason have gone for the traditional approach and are having fifteen children to their house for tea and party games. Daft buggers. I'm almost tempted to offer to try and track down some Valium when I drop Charlie off. I pick him up at five and he's almost hysterical with the combination of sugar and a rather disastrous game of Musical Chairs. Apparently Justin's daddy got the music wrong, so Justin was out first and spent the rest of the game trying to push everyone else off their chairs, until he was finally sent upstairs in disgrace.

'Oh, poor Justin.'

244

'Serves him right. He pushed James really hard. He could have broken his leg. James had to do hopping for a bit, and I helped him get a chair. That was nice of me, wasn't it, Mummy?'

'Yes, darling. That was very kind. Well done.'

'Oh yes. I know all about being kind. We did it at school yesterday. Kind hands and kind feet, Miss Pike says. Me and James think it's really boring. And then Miss Pike said we were being silly and made us tidy up the home corner. That wasn't very kind, was it, Mummy? You should tell her, you know.'

I decide to ignore this and try to change the subject.

'So did poor old Justin get to come back downstairs and enjoy the rest of his party?'

'Yes. We did Pass the Parcel after that, and Justin got the prize.'

I bet he did. His father was probably instructed on pain of death to get the music right this time, or spend the rest of the afternoon upstairs with a hysterical birthday boy.

'And was the tea nice?'

'Yes. Quite. There was little sausages. But the jelly was horrible; it was green.'

He pauses for the full ghastliness of green jelly to register.

'Justin threw his on the carpet.'

I must remember never to invite Justin to tea.

Mack turns up later on, and Charlie is already in bed. We go up to say goodnight and get involved in a marathon Random-Chatting Routine about electricity, and how telephones work. It turns out Mack doesn't really know either, but he promises to look it up properly tomorrow and eventually Charlie relents and gets back into bed. We go back downstairs and start making supper.

'So how was the trip?'

245

'Oh, well, great really. But I've got some news.'

'Oh yes?'

I look up and notice that he seems rather nervous. My mind races through various scenarios involving supermodels, and I'm in the midst of imagining a four-page spread in *Hello!* featuring Mack and his new wife when he says, 'Yes. We've bought an American agency, it's a huge deal. I'm sorry I couldn't say anything about it sooner but I really didn't know if we'd pull it off. Anyway we have, and they want me to run the whole thing. It's a huge job, and I think it'll be great. But, um, well, the thing is I'll have to live in New York. I mean, I'll travel a lot, they've got offices all over the place, but mainly I'll be in the States. So I was wondering, would you come with me – I mean you and Charlie obviously. Come to New York with me, and we'll get a big apartment and all that.'

'Christ, Mack, this is all a bit sudden, isn't it?'

'Yes, well, it all happened a bit quicker than I thought. What do you think, though? Fancy living it up in New York for a while?'

'Mack, you can't be serious. I can't just drop everything and come to New York. What about Charlie and his school? He's really not up to any huge changes at the moment. And what about Daisy and Alfie?'

'I know, the timing's not great, but it never is, is it? I've talked to Laura and I reckon I'll see the kids more than I do now. They'll come out for the holidays, and I can still call them every night. Look, this is a lot to take in. Take your time; you don't have to decide now.'

'Right.'

There's a long silence while we both look at the kitchen floor, which is filthy.

'Mack, there's just no way I can see me moving to the

246

other side of the world and putting Charlie through all that upheaval. It's just not fair, and anyway we aren't ready.'

'What do you mean, we aren't ready? I think we are. I mean, I am. Look, if it would make any difference we could get married if you like.'

'Mack, stop it, you're being ridiculous. You don't get married just because one of you gets a new job. And anyway I don't want to get married. I mean, if I did it would be to you, but we've only known each other a few months. I like my life here. Charlie loves his school. You can't seriously expect me to give all that up just because your bloody agency has gone all multinational and you want to go and play with the big boys in New York. It's ridiculous.'

'I love you. Did I say that bit?'

There's another long silence while we both stare at the floor. I'm tempted to get the mop out, but I know this is classic displacement activity, and anyway it's broken since Charlie used it as a sword last week and snapped the top off. It feels like I've suddenly inexplicably found myself sitting in the front carriage on the top of a rollercoaster. One minute I was making supper and the next I'm in the middle of a terrifying major conversation.

'I love you too. Why don't you turn the job down and come and live with me in rural bliss? You can learn to relax more.'

'That's not what I want, Annie.'

'I know. And I don't want to move to New York. I hate New York. Well, I've only actually been once, but I hated it.'

'You could have another baby.'

'You bastard. You don't want another baby; you just said that because you think it'll make me change my mind.'

'Well, a bit, I suppose. But if you did want one I wouldn't mind.'

247

'Oh great. So we move to New York. You have a transatlantic relationship with your two kids, Charlie loses all his friends and his family, and then to cap it all I get pregnant with a baby you don't mind having if it keeps me quiet. Perfect recipe for a stable family life. Not quite *The Waltons*, though, is it?'

'Look, you can't live your whole life for Charlie, you know.'

'I know that. But I can't ignore him either. Three months ago he nearly died in my arms. It kind of makes you focus. He needs peace and security, not total bloody upheaval. And anyway it's not just Charlie. I like my life here, and I like my work. What am I supposed to do in New York? I don't want to be stuck in some flash apartment all day long. What would I do – master the art of making the perfect martini, or get heavily into flower arranging or something? I'd turn into one of those daft women you meet at parties who go on and on about winter foliage. And anyway you might hate the job. They might fire you after six weeks.'

'Hardly, darling. I own half the agency now. I've got money coming out of my ears. Wouldn't you like to help me spend it?'

'No. I hate shopping. I'd have to keep getting Leila over. Look, let's stop this. You go to New York and we can meet up whenever we can. It's only a plane ride. Then we can see how it goes, and look at moving and everything in a few months' time.'

'I'm sorry, Annie. But I don't want to do that. This job's going to be huge. I can't be flying backwards and forwards all the time. I've thought a lot about this. I don't mind if you need time to think, but it's got to be all or nothing. Either come with me, or we'll have to call it a day. I miss you too much as it is when you're not around. The fucking journey is killing me already. I want you with me all the time. I know Charlie will always come first, and I accept that – in fact it's one of the things I love most about you. But I want to come a close second. I'll settle for that. But not from the other side of the Atlantic.'

'I can't do that, Mack. Not now.'

Tears are rolling down my cheeks now, and I notice that Mack looks pretty close to tears himself. We stand there in silence.

'I guess I should go now.'

'I suppose so.'

And then I really start to sob and he puts his arms around me and we stand in the kitchen for what seems like an eternity. Slowly he pulls away.

'Look, I'll call you. You can always change your mind. I'm not leaving for a couple of weeks. We can talk some more.'

And then he walks out of the door and sits in his car. I stand watching him, but finally he drives off, very, very slowly.

I ring Leila in hysterics. She's on her way to a dinner party but abandons it and says she will drive down immediately. Thank God for Leila. Just when I thought nothing else could reduce me to a snivelling wreck, this comes along. I rage and sob in the kitchen until she arrives. She takes one look at me and throws her arms around me, and we both end up in tears.

'I don't understand. It's just like one of those awful Swedish films where it's all perfect and then suddenly there's a blizzard, someone commits suicide and the boiler blows up. Why don't you go to New York? Mack's perfect for you. What are you going to do when Charlie grows up anyway – join a convent?'

'No, but this isn't just about Charlie. I like my life, I don't live here for a joke, you know; I like living in the country.'

'Oh stop it. What about pesticides and rural poverty, and all that inbreeding? What's Charlie going to do when he grows up – drink cider and drive tractors? He's going to bugger off to London as soon as he can. This isn't *Little House on the Prairie*, you know. If Pa is moving to New York, then you're supposed to go with him.'

'Yes I know. But he's not, is he? I mean, Mack's not really Mr Fatherhood, is he? He loves his kids, sure, but he's perfectly happy to live on another continent to them, and only see them in the holidays. He says he loves the fact that I put Charlie first, but I don't think he really gets it. His work is what he loves, and it comes a long way second for me. Charlie deserves one hundred per cent and so does Mack. But that makes two hundred per cent and I just can't do it, and anyway what does that leave for me?'

'I know, I know. You're just not cut out for "Stand By Your Man", are you? Quite right too. He's got a bloody cheek, actually, expecting you to just drop everything. But I guess that's not really the point, is it? Oh bugger it, you were so good together.'

'I know. Christ, I'm going to miss him. I don't know how I'm going to get through this.' I start to cry again.

'Oh you will, somehow. You know you will. I'll help. We can go shopping next week. And I'll bike some offal round to his office first thing on Monday.'

'Leila. Mack hasn't done anything wrong, you know.'

'I know. But he's upset you, so I hate him. Fair enough?'

'Fair enough. Talking of men we hate, is there any news of James?'

'Yes. Stupid fucker sent me an email saying he hoped that we could remain friends, and that I'd stop sending him things at the office.'

'Leila. I thought you *had* stopped.'

'Yes, well, I had. But after his email I just had to come up with one last gift from the heart. So I got a pig's head from the local butcher and biked it round.'

'Leila, you didn't?'

'I did. Serve him right. Anyway I'm over him now; I really can't work out what I saw in him. I hope you get like that about Mack but I have a sneaking feeling you won't. Mainly because Mack is not a total fuckwit. Anyway, I met a rather fascinating new man at a drinks party last week. A Dutch architect called Frank. Lizzie might know him – he works over here in some trendy firm in Islington. I'm thinking of having the house totally redesigned. It's early days, but it's looking promising.'

'Oh good.'

'Yes. But never mind that, back to you. How are you feeling?'

'A bit shaky, actually. Would you mind if I went to bed now? You'll stay the night, won't you?'

'Yes please. Then I can see my best boy in the morning. I'm pretty knackered too – let's get an early night and then we can plan something splendid for tomorrow. I'll take you out for lunch, if you like.'

'Thanks, Leila.'

I get into bed and lie weeping quietly, feeling over-whelmed by sadness. I'm debating whether to get up and make some tea and biscuits when the door opens and Charlie staggers in. He climbs into bed half asleep, and snuggles in for a hug. I'm very, very pleased he's chosen this

251

precise moment to wake up, and as I lie there cuddling him back to sleep I get the first faint glimmers of hope that life will go on, somehow, despite the feeling I've been run over by a truck.

Chapter Twelve

We Wish You a Merry Christmas

I HAVE A SERIES of agonising conversations with Mack where he continues to insist that I should come with him to New York, and I continue to insist that I can't. We have a blazing row on the night before he leaves where I accuse him of being selfish and he accuses me of being a martyr, culminating in him slamming the phone down. I want to ring him straight back but know deep down it will be pointless. Even though we're still talking, it already feels like he's left. I go to bed hoping he'll call, but he doesn't. I wake up early the next morning and realise he's probably already on his way to Heathrow. Lurk by the phone hoping he'll have a change of heart, and Charlie is thrilled when I agree to crisps and biscuits for breakfast. I drop him off at school and race back to see if there are any messages. There aren't.

I can't believe this is really it. Surely there should be something major going on, an announcement on the breakfast news at least. But apparently there will just be silence. Bastard. I ring up Leila who agrees that it's awful, but then she spoils it by saying she rather admires him really, because at least he's not prolonging the agony: he's made up his mind and is sticking to it. I know what she means: one of the

253

things I really love about him is how determined he is. It's a bit ironic really, as the thing he seems most determined about at the moment is leaving me and getting on with his new life.

Kate comes round to commiserate, and says I'm doing absolutely the right thing and if he really loved me he would realise that. This makes me cry. I become addicted to soppy love songs, and sit in the car after the school run singing along to Whitney Houston's 'I Will Always Love You'. I nearly jump out of my skin when a woman delivering the parish newsletter knocks on the car window and asks me if I'm alright. I've explained to Charlie that we won't be seeing Mack again for a while, because he's gone to work in New York, and Charlie has accepted this without a murmur. In fact he doesn't seem to have noticed that his mother is distraught, except that he's started refusing to get into the car unless I agree not to play any music.

I'm tucking him up in bed a few days later when he says, 'Mummy, why are you so sad? Is it because I was ill? You don't think I'm going to get ill again, do you?'

He looks very anxiously at me. Oh God. I've been indulging myself by wallowing in misery, and he's been half terrified that the hospital has called to give me early warning of a relapse.

'No, of course not, darling. I don't think you'll get ill again, I promise. I'm just a bit sad about Mack. I miss him, that's all. I'm sorry if I've upset you, sweetheart.'

'Oh that's OK. I miss him too. Shall we get a dog? That would cheer us up, you know, Mummy, and it would be a friend for you when I'm at school. And if Mack comes back one day it could bite him, and serve him right for going to America. What do you think, Mummy, can we, can we?'

I spend the next half-hour trying to convince him that

owning a Great Dane would not cheer me up and finally come up with what I consider to be an excellent argument: 'Anyway, Buzz and Woody would be frightened by a great big dog charging round the garden. That wouldn't be fair.'

'Don't be stupid, Mummy. It would be a tiny little puppy when we got it, and they could all play together and everything. Then when it got big they would be used to it. It might let them ride on its back. They'd love that.'

I try to persuade him that rabbits do not like riding round gardens balanced on the backs of huge dogs, but he's not convinced. In the end I give up and bring the conversation to a close by simply walking out of the bedroom and switching off the light. Charlie promptly bursts into tears, and I feel guilty. I stand outside the bedroom door for a bit trying to decide what to do, and then go back in and we have a cuddle with me kneeling by the side of his bed and getting a severe crick in my neck. Eventually I get him off to sleep, and decide that I've got to pull myself together or Charlie is going to get really worried. I try to distract myself from thinking about Mack by writing my Christmas shopping list, but this is so depressing I end up watching *The Bodyguard* on video. Again. It looks like my new-found Whitney habit is going to be a hard one to break.

The end of term is looming, and the PTA has gone into overdrive. The auction is next week, and then the Nativity play. Miss Pike is desperately trying to give everyone a part, and not offend any parents. But there are only so many donkeys and sheep you can fit on a tiny stage at once, and the role of Mary is being hotly contested. Mrs Bates is lobbying hard, and keeps sending in bunches of flowers and cakes for Sophie to share with Miss Pike. But Miss Pike is wise to this, and finally selects a very sweet girl called Ellie.

Charlie has refused point blank to be a sheep and decided instead that he'll be a pheasant, and Miss Pike agrees because she thinks it will be fun. So could I just make a pheasant costume, please?

No would be the honest answer, but I somehow find myself saying yes, and spend hours sticking feathers on to a pair of tights and a long-sleeved vest, and making wings from an old velvet dressing-up cloak. I use the feathers from an old pillow, but these are tiny and look pathetic, so I supplement them with special decorative feathers, which are bright blue, purple and red, and cost a fortune. When Charlie tries it on I'm overcome with laugher. He sulks and refuses to wear the costume. I finally persuade him he looks marvellous; Miss Pike agrees and Charlie relents and says he'll wear it if he can have a special beak. I make a special beak out of tinfoil. Now he looks like a cross between a mad emu and an illustration of what will happen if you try to pluck your Christmas turkey yourself. He adores the beak.

I have a night out at the pub with Kate and Sally, leaving Roger at home to babysit all the kids. The children are all clamouring for pizza and a game of hide-and-seek as we leave. Roger is wearing his whistle on a string round his neck. It makes him look a bit like a PE teacher, and he says he bought it specially for evenings with under-twelves. The sound of a whistle being blown repeatedly accompanies us as we drive down the lane. We get to our favourite pub, which is in a nearby village, and discover there's a quiz night on, with Our Vicar leading one team, and the chairman of the local Tories heading up the other. Deadly. We hide in the back room, and compete to see who's going to have the most draining Christmas. Kate wins, as usual, because she has to go to her mother's. We've agreed not to talk about men or children, or we'll get depressed. So we talk about clothes, and what we'd do if we won a million quid. Kate reveals a passion for villas in Barbados, and Sally says she would never cook again, ever. Kate is doing the driving tonight, so Sally and I get rather drunk. The quiz finishes and the vicar's team wins, and then we organise an impromptu karaoke session. I find myself standing up with Kate and Sally belting out 'I Will Survive' at the top of my voice. We stagger back outside into the pitch blackness, and Sally falls down a hole in the car park and says fuck just as Our Vicar walks past. He pretends not to have heard, and we spend the entire journey home debating whether he could have identified exactly who was spreadeagled on the tarmac swearing. We decide he couldn't, but Sally makes us promise not to tell Roger, because he is thinking of standing as a school governor and the vicar is on the selection committee.

When we get home we cross-examine Roger as to why on earth he wants to be a school governor, and he goes all coy and says, 'Oh well, just a thought.' And then Sally explains that he read an article in the paper about how vital it is to have school governors who are not just local busybodies. Apparently schools now manage entire budgets on their own and cannot rely on those whose only real qualification for the job is a strong desire to read the confidential school records of other people's children. We all agree with this, especially given Mrs Harrison-Black's recent comments to a mother of a slow reader, and elect Roger as our number-one choice.

My Christmas shopping list is now getting so long I need two separate sheets of paper. I decide to drive up to town early and get a couple of hours of shopping in before wandering into the office. Barney is taking everyone out for a Christmas lunch, which last year went on until midnight. I park in the usual car park and manage to find a space without having to drive up the bouncing metal ramp. Then I spend a fraught couple of hours dashing between Liberty's, Hamleys and HMV.

The prices in Hamleys are extortionate, so I only buy the things not readily available in local toyshops. I finally get into the office at around eleven, desperate for a coffee and a nice little lie-down. I'm trying to work out if it's too risky to have a nap on the sofa in Barney's room, as he's not turned up yet, when Lawrence comes upstairs and says he's sorry to hear things didn't work out with Mack MacDonald. And did I know he's the toast of New York, and has been seen with a succession of beautiful young women on his arm? I'm just about to punch him when Barney arrives, and has clearly overheard the last bit of Lawrence's little heart-to-heart.

'Hello, darling. You look gorgeous, as ever. What's old Lawrence wittering on about now? Telling you all about his latest plans for the office furniture, is he? He's going to sit on the door with a special little peaked cap on, so he can keep an eye on everyone and not miss out on any of the gossip. Aren't you, Lawrence?'

Lawrence tries to laugh, but Barney isn't finished.

'Oh and by the way. If he's telling you about Mack MacDonald, don't believe a word of it. I bet he's hating it. All those hideous American piranha women scenting fresh blood – he's probably gone into shock. Anyway, Lawrence, if you wouldn't mind, I'd like a word with Annie.'

Lawrence goes back downstairs devastated to be excluded from the conversation.

'Thanks, Barney. But I bet he's having a ball.'

'More like having his balls off. That job won't be easy, you know. And if he does end up with some New York princess, then good luck to him. He's going to need it. What happened with you two, anyway?'

'Oh nothing really. He wanted me to jack it all in and follow him to New York, and I didn't want to.'

'Quite right too. What would you want to live there for? And anyway, I need you here. Shame, though, you seemed really happy.'

'I was. Now can we stop talking about this or I'll end up in tears.'

'Been a bit of a rough year for you, really, hasn't it, darling?'

'Well, yes and no. I mean, Charlie got well again, and I had some good times with Mack. Don't look at me like that; I'm trying to be positive.'

'That's the spirit. Look on the bright side. You might meet another little fucker who'll totally bugger you about next year – think what fun that'll be.'

'Thanks, Barney, that really helps. I can't tell you how much I count on you to cheer me up.'

'Don't mention it. Anytime. Now, before we go off to lunch I've got you this. I don't want Lawrence to see you open it or he'll sulk all afternoon. Anyway, it's just to say thanks, it's been a great year and all that bollocks.'

He goes bright red and gives me a Liberty's bag, containing the most beautiful velvet scarf I've ever seen, in a mixture of blacks and purples. I saw something similar this morning and was tempted to get it for Lizzie, until I saw the price and decided I'd better go for something that wouldn't require a bank loan.

'Oh thank you, Barney, it's beautiful.'

259

When I lift it up to try it on, a piece of paper falls out and flutters to the floor. I pick it up and realise it's a cheque, for a thousand pounds.

'Just a little bonus. To say thanks for all your hard work.'

'Oh, Barney, I don't know what to say. Thank you.'

I give him a hug and a kiss, and he goes rigid with embarrassment and says, 'Right. Glad you're pleased. Now for God's sake get off. You're squashing my jacket.'

The office lunch goes very well, but everyone gets very drunk and as I'm driving I can't join them, so I end up creeping off at around five and meeting Leila for a cup of tea.

Leila is thrilled with Barney's present, and wants to help me spend it immediately. I eventually manage to persuade her that I would rather lie down in the middle of Oxford Circus and get flattened by a bus than go shopping again today.

'Anyway, you haven't told me, how's the Flying Dutchman?'

'Oh, shaping up very nicely, thanks. I'm trying to pace myself a bit this time. Bloody difficult, though, he's gorgeous. I'm seeing him tomorrow, actually, to look at his plans for the house. In fact I'm almost as excited about the plans as I am about seeing him again – do you think that's a bad sign?'

'No, don't be daft. It's probably all mixed in together. And even if he turns out to be a pillock, the house will look great. So you can't lose really, can you? Anyway, never mind about that. When are you coming down to see me and Charlie? We've got presents for you.'

This is guaranteed to send Leila into a frenzy, as she adores being given presents. She's incredibly hard to buy for, since her idea of deferred gratification is to wait until

260

after lunch before she gets out the credit cards, so this year I've gone for the basket-of-goodies approach. I've bought her loads of little sparkly things and Charlie has made her a picture frame using about half a ton of glitter and four yards of tinsel. He has put in it a photograph of Leila holding him when he was about an hour old, and done her a special picture with the words 'I love Leila' on it. Pink features heavily in his colour scheme, along with a great deal of silver and gold. She'll love it. I tell her about Lawrence's helpful news about Mack, and she says she is sure it's bollocks and that Barney is far more likely to be right. She offers to ring her friends in New York and find out, but I tell her I don't really care. We both know this is a huge lie but pretend it isn't, and move on to talking about designs for her new bathroom.

The night of the Nativity play arrives, and I take Charlie to the village hall. We are greeted by a very odd procession of small children trooping in dressed as assorted farmyard animals. It's freezing, and I sit in the audience with Kate for hours before the performance actually begins, hearing lots of muffled thuds and bumps from behind the curtain. Sally and Roger creep in very late and sit in the seats we've saved for them. Apparently William had a last-minute crisis with his sheep costume. The tension in the audience has built almost to breaking point when the curtain finally opens and the show begins. I'm in tears almost immediately: a very tiny boy in a donkey costume falls off the stage, and a small sheep stands up and waves to his mum. Mary is quite overcome and cannot speak until jabbed in the ribs very sharply by one of the angels. Probably Sophie Bates, but it's hard to tell under all that tinsel.

I've forgotten to bring tissues, so I'm reduced to sniffing

quite a lot, but luckily half the audience is doing the same. The school has very sensibly banned people from taking pictures or using home video recorders, because last year there was almost a fight as two dads jostled each other for the perfect spot at the back of the hall. This year Mr Jenkins is making a video which the PTA will sell to boost funds. I'm not sure he's quite got the hang of the automatic zoom button, as he keeps rushing forwards and then walking backwards very slowly. But I'm keeping a low profile because Mrs Harrison-Black suggested I should get one of my 'director chaps' to turn up and do the video, and I refused. I explained that all the directors I know would rather stab themselves repeatedly with forks than be involved in anything amateur, but she wasn't convinced. Then I said that they'd need a full crew and would want to remove at least one wall of the village hall to get the lighting right. Mrs Harrison-Black thought Our Vicar would not like the hall being dismantled, and thankfully the subject was dropped. But I could tell she thought I was being unnecessarily artistic.

Charlie enters the stage with James and William dressed as sheep for 'While Shepherds Watched Their Flocks By Night'. He flaps his wings enthusiastically, and half the audience begin to laugh, and then try valiantly to smother this with lots of coughing. Their song is completed, and the audience claps. Charlie does more flapping of wings, and the audience claps louder. I can tell Charlie is delighted and is about to launch into an encore when Miss Pike's arm appears from behind the curtain and he is removed, apart from a few feathers which linger centre stage.

The play rolls on, the baby is born, and the top class attempt a rock-and-roll version of 'Away in a Manger' which is a huge mistake, although the boy on drums is very enthusiastic. Then it's the final song, and everyone troops back on stage for 'We Wish You a Merry Christmas'. Mrs Taylor appears and makes a speech thanking everyone for coming, and says we must all stay inside the hall and buy tea and mince pies from the PTA while the teachers get the children off the stage and out of their costumes. I know without a shadow of a doubt that their chances of getting Charlie out of his costume are nil. Charlie continues flapping throughout her speech, and lots of people give me amused glances. Then there's lots of applause, and the children all bow and look pleased. The curtain shuts and the lights go back on, and everyone surges forwards towards the tea trolley.

Kate thinks Charlie's costume is a triumph, and wants to know if she can borrow it for her loathsome nephew, Liam, so he can wear it to her father's traditional Boxing Day shoot. She says getting Liam shot would do them all a huge favour, and her Uncle Geoffrey always gets so drunk he shoots at anything that moves. Last year he narrowly missed Polly, the family Labrador. Miss Pike finally appears with the children, who run around yelling with relief now that their ordeal's over. As predicted, Charlie is still in his costume, flapping his arms and pecking people with his beak. Miss Pike comes over to say hello, but a fracas is developing in the corner of the room involving lots of small boys and mince pies so she rushes off to sort things out.

Charlie is now showing people how he can fly by jumping off a chair, so I feel it might be time for us to leave. It's snowing outside, not actually settling on the ground but with lots of snowflakes whirling about which looks magical. Charlie is thrilled and runs round trying to collect snow in his outstretched wings. A passing van nearly drives into a wall as the driver spots a giant bird-like creature hopping about while a frantic-looking woman tries to shove it into a car. I have a hell of a job persuading Charlie he can't sleep in his pheasant costume.

'I need to keep it on, in case a werewolf comes. Then it will get a surprise and I can peck it.'

'Charlie, there are no werewolves. And all your feathers will fall off if you sleep in your costume all night. Now stop being silly and put your pyjamas on.'

'I hate you, Mummy. I really do.'

'I thought you were brilliant in the play; I can't wait to buy the video and show everybody.'

'Will you show people at your work?'

'Oh yes.'

The sad truth is I probably will, and Barney will have a lovely time saying he can't believe the poor quality of the video, and was the man blind? Just like he does whenever I take photos of Charlie into the office and he insists on seeing my 'snaps', and then goes into fits of laughter and mutters about being astonished that I have picked up nothing after being around experts for so long.

'If people see them at your work they might want me to be in a film.'

Over my dead body. I cannot begin to imagine the combination of Charlie and a film crew, but I know it would end in tears. Mostly mine.

'Hurry up and put your pyjamas on, and maybe we'll have a story.'

'OK, Mummy, but I'm keeping my beak on.'

It feels very odd reading a book about penguins to a small boy wearing a large tinfoil beak. I go up to check on him later and he's fast asleep, with his beak still attached, making amplified snoring noises and clutching a small handful of feathers. I can't wait to get a copy of the video, which I shall treasure. It will also be a useful bargaining tool for when he's a teenager and has girls to impress.

The last day of term arrives, and I still have a long list of things to do before Christmas. I'm really getting desperate now, and have taken to muttering about satsumas and cranberry jelly as I drive, in between singing along to a new Whitney cassette, which I felt compelled to purchase when I should have been buying a gift for Auntie Joan. But I'm no longer reduced to a snivelling wreck by 'I Will Always Love You', and in fact I'm starting to get rather irritated by it, so progress of some sort is being made. Today is party day at school, and all the children are allowed to take a toy in. Charlie wants to take his Lego castle, complete with knights, cannon and assorted animals including a dragon. I tell him that he's only allowed to take one small toy, but he will have none of it. In the end I rely on an old trick of Kate's by pretending to ring up Miss Pike and seek guidance. Charlie hops up and down in the kitchen waiting to hear what Miss Pike says, and when I finish my pretend conversation I confirm that only one small toy is allowed. He accepts this without a murmur. I cannot explain why this is so annoying, but it is.

He finally selects a hideous robot thing that turns into a gorilla and then back into a robot, and shoots small plastic missiles out of the top of its head. I feel sure Miss Pike will not approve, but am not up to another round of pretend telephone calls so we set off for school. There's no school uniform today, and it's odd seeing all the children in normal clothes: they look so much more relaxed and unruly. I can see why schools go in for uniforms with quite so much vigour: it seems to break their spirits before they even get in the door.

Kate and I have volunteered to help at the tea party. Mrs Harrison-Black had a clipboard at the school gates, and there was no escape. It was either party helping or carol singing. Last year two boys from the carol-singing group went missing halfway round the village, and the parent helpers spent ages retracing their steps in pitch darkness trying to find them. They were on the point of calling the police when they found them, watching unsuitable videos at a friend's house. So we feel sure party helping is the soft option. We turn up at two to help set the tables, and realise we have made a tragic mistake. Some mad woman has made enough jelly to feed the entire county. Every single item of food either contains levels of sugar guaranteed to send the average five year old into orbit, or enough additives to bring on epilepsy in those unaccustomed to children's party food. And some bastard has put us down to help with the reception class, most of whom can barely cope with the excitement of eating a normal packed lunch, let alone party food with jelly.

Kate suggests one of us pretends to faint, and then the other one can drive her home, but we can't work out who should faint and anyway we suspect someone is bound to be a Red Cross first-aider and will force the fainter to sit with her head stuck in a bucket for hours. So we set the tables, and try to hide the jelly. The party-goers troop in, and the next hour passes in a horrible blur of screaming children, lots of wet crêpe paper, food flying about, and very loud music. Miss Pike keeps smiling, but I think she's gone into a trance. Our Vicar has dressed up as Father Christmas, and is rugby-tackled by a mob of screaming children as soon as he enters the room. He tries to walk around with a small boy attached to each leg, but fails, and then Mrs Taylor restores order by blowing on her whistle repeatedly and demanding 'Fingers on lips, every-body, now'.

Kate and I stand with our fingers on our lips, and Miss Pike finally gets the message and does the same. The rest of the staff reappear from the kitchen where they have been hiding, Father Christmas shakes off his hitch-hikers and gradually the riot calms down. He then gives each child a handful of sweets, just to keep the sugar levels at optimum, and they all begin swapping them and throwing wrappers on the floor. Just when it looks like we might actually get out of there in one piece, Mrs Taylor announces we have just enough time for a little bit of dancing before the mummies and daddies start arriving. Is she mad?

Apparently she is. The music is turned back on and we are all doing the hokey-cokey like our lives depended on it. It turns out to be very revealing: some children are quite able to put their left leg in and left leg out as many times as you like, while others have to concentrate very hard indeed to get their left leg in at all. And just when they've got that bit sorted, everybody else has moved on to shaking it all about. Charlie and James are doing their own version, which seems to involve sticking out your bottom as far as you can without actually falling over, and Phoebe is doing hopping, without seeming to be aware of the music at all. As Kate says, all those ballet classes have really paid off. There's so much jelly on the floor children are going down like ninepins, and most of them just stay down and wave their legs in time to the music while eating bits of food they've found under the tables.

Parents finally start turning up to take their children home. One very smart dad is clearly horrified to find his two little daughters covered in jelly and crisps, and makes them sit on sheets of newspaper in the back of the car.

Another rota has been organised for clearing up after the party, and we are not on it, thank God. So we all go back to Kate's house, along with a huge collection of bags full of PE kit, artwork and God knows what else. Charlie appears to only have one plimsoll, but has gained a pair of shorts, and James has no shorts but two PE shirts. The children watch television, and Kate and I hide in the kitchen smoking and drinking gin.

I get so drunk we have to walk home, with a huge torch Kate has lent us that lights up the whole lane, and weighs a ton. It's very dark and cold, and it feels like it may snow again. Charlie is thrilled to be out at night. He begs me to turn off the torch so we can have an adventure. I'm too drunk to argue, so I switch off the torch and promptly fall into a vast crater which has appeared out of nowhere. I end up landing on a small tree which turns out, naturally, to be a holly bush. Charlie's delighted, especially as he thinks he heard me say the F-word. We tiptoe forwards and stumble about until I can bear it no longer and put the torch back on, promising to switch it off again when we get near the house, so he can walk the last bit in the dark.

When the house is in sight, I keep my promise and turn off the torch, plunging us back into darkness. We know this bit of the lane really well so we walk along fairly steadily. I look up and see millions of stars, and Charlie pretends he knows all their names and points out the Bear to me, and the Giraffe and the Lion. We finally get back inside, and the fire is still alight, just. Charlie is exhausted and practically falls asleep standing up while I help him into his pyjamas. We're getting the Christmas tree tomorrow, and I still have a list of things to buy that makes me feel faint every time I think about it. But I'm still drunk so I don't care. 'Tis the season to be jolly and I feel very jolly indeed.

Next morning I have a desperate hangover, and Charlie is annoyingly loud and excited about getting the tree. I have Panadol and black coffee for breakfast, and Charlie has Shreddies. Finally I can't put it off any longer and we drive to the local nursery, choose an enormous tree and then realise I can't get it into the car unless Charlie sits on the roof. After much shoving and pushing I manage to wedge it in without snapping the top off, and Charlie crouches on the back seat behind me, with his seatbelt on because I insist. He moans that he can't breathe, and keeps saying he's swallowed pine needles, but we finally make it home and get the bloody thing out of the car. Each year I buy one of those special tree stands, as I can't find the one from last year. I'm determined that this year will be different, and begin hunting. I discover all sorts of things I'd completely given up hope of ever seeing again and eventually find it on the top shelf of the airing cupboard, behind piles of old towels and beach mats, which I'd spent hours searching for in the summer. I put the tree in its stand, nearly poking my eye out in the process, and finally manage to get it almost straight. The smell is wonderful. Charlie claps, and does a dance in celebration.

Things then get very fraught as Charlie's idea of decorating involves shoving everything on the lowest branches, and I want to space things out. He disappears off to get more things to hang up, and returns with various plastic birds to go with the robin we bought last year. The robin is lightweight, feathery and has a ribbon. The plastic eagle weighs a ton and looks as if it is about to swoop down and eat the robin for lunch. The flamingo also looks odd, as does the large black rubber spider, but Charlie is very pleased with the effect so I let him leave them on, and then cover them up with lots of tinsel when he's not looking. The lights still work, which is a miracle because Charlie has sat on the box. He sits and stares at the lights for ages, and goes into a sort of trance, and then rushes off to find more plastic animals to put on, so that the birds won't be lonely.

I spend the last few days before Christmas doing non-stop shopping. The office has closed for the duration, and I manage to survive an endless round of Christmas drinks parties in the village without getting too drunk, or doing anything too embarrassing, though I did manage to introduce myself to the same person twice in the space of five minutes, and could see she thought I was either very drunk or very stupid. Or possibly both. Edna has spent the morning with Charlie, and I've got the last-minute food shopping done by the simple process of going into Marks and Spencer's and buying one of everything still on the shelves. I'm sure tinned kiwi fruit will come in handy one day.

I had to reserve the turkey in June, and cannot remember what I ordered. The butcher's van turns up late in the afternoon on Christmas Eve, and two men stagger up the drive with what appears to be a dead ostrich. I can't remember why I ordered such a huge turkey, nor can I work out how it will fit in the oven, but a large gin and tonic takes the edge off my panic and I decide to seek help from Mum when she arrives.

Charlie is writing last-minute instructions to Father Christmas. He's decided he's going to be a spy when he grows up, and I now have to preface every request with the words 'Your mission, should you choose to accept it'. He wants a special wristwatch that can fire bullets, and a pen that squirts poison ink, but I've told him Father Christmas doesn't bring presents that you can kill people with, unless you count roller-skates. I'm getting fed up with this spy business. It was bloody annoying in Safeway's yesterday: 'Your mission, should you choose to accept it, is to get some Flora and put it in the trolley.' I announce his new mission, whether he chooses to accept it or not, is to go to bed and get to sleep as fast as possible or Father Christmas won't come at all. I wrap presents like a demented person, lose the scissors and feel sure I've wrapped them up but can't face opening all the parcels, so end up using nail scissors instead which takes ages. I just hope Charlie doesn't get the real scissors in one of his parcels, or he'll insist on keeping them and cutting things up.

I get rather drunk by mistake, since I have a swig of wine each time I wrap a present. As a result I can't really walk when I try to stand up and stagger around piling up presents on the sofa and under the tree. Getting upstairs with Charlie's stocking proves very tricky, but I finally manage it and collapse into bed. What seems like minutes later I'm woken up by Charlie yelling, 'He's been, Mummy, he's been,' and playing a small trumpet, which I do not remember buying. I certainly will never buy one again, except for children whose parents I hate. My bed is soon full of pieces of paper, Charlie is eating chocolate coins and playing his trumpet with all his might, and it takes all my negotiating skills to get him to agree to stay in bed for another hour and play with small stocking toys. I hide the trumpet under my pillow. Apart from the trumpet I also wish I hadn't bought a balloon shaped like a chicken which deflates with a rude noise, a small flexible torch that can shine right in your ear, and a book of rude poems.

Finally I can stand it no longer and we get up. Charlie finds the huge pile of presents downstairs and goes into a frenzy of ripping up wrapping paper and screaming with delight. He wants to start playing his new board game, build his new Lego spaceship and watch his new video simultaneously, and refuses to eat any breakfast except chocolate. I start peeling sprouts and Charlie 'helps' by chopping up carrots with a small blunt knife, so that each one takes about ten minutes. Then he spends hours feeding all the peelings to Buzz and Woody for their Christmas lunch. We've put tinsel on their hutch, and they look very festive. The cavalry arrive in the form of Mum and Dad. Dad takes Charlie off to do Lego, and Mum finally stops laughing at the size of the turkey and works out how long it will take to cook the bloody thing. She says it will have to 'rest' for half an hour after being cooked so there's space in the oven for the potatoes. I quite fancy the idea of half an hour's rest, preferably right now, but Mum rather pointedly remarks that parsnips do not peel themselves, and could she please have a sherry.

Auntie Joan and Uncle Bob turn up. I'm not entirely clear why Auntie Joan thought I would like an apron with 'Cooks Do It Standing Up' written on it, but I thank her all the same. Mum and Dad seem pleased with their present from Charlie: a rather flat nest with baby birds in it, made out of modelling clay which we baked in the oven. I think I might have got the temperature wrong because it took days to go solid. The baby birds are very comic, especially as Charlie insisted on painting them bright orange. Auntie Joan has knitted a jumper for Charlie, which is about six sizes too big and has a Postman Pat motif on the front. Charlie looks horrified but thanks her nicely, and we have a whispered conversation in the kitchen where I promise he will never ever have to wear it, ever.

Lunch is finally ready at teatime, but everyone declares the food delicious and Auntie Joan begins a long story, which she tells us every year, about the time she had ten people to Christmas lunch and there was a power cut. Charlie gets very excited about the crackers, and insists everyone wears paper hats. He also thinks the jokes are excellent. He appropriates the presents from all the crackers, and the wheels fall off the small plastic car he's liberated from Uncle Bob.

'Mummy, these crackers are a swiss. My car just broke for no reason.'

'Well, never mind, darling, eat your lunch.'

'Yes, but it's a swiss, Mummy. You should go back to the shop and get your money back.'

'It's not a swiss, Charlie, it's a swizz.'

'No it's not. James says it and it's swiss.'

Dad helpfully joins in and says he think swiss is the perfect word for something that looks exciting but turns out to be very boring, like fondue. Charlie says he wants fondue, and what is it? Auntie Joan says she loves Switzerland and can't imagine what Dad means. Uncle Bob says he hates Switzerland and is not going again, ever, and that's final. It looks like a heated discussion is imminent so I decide to open the bottle of champagne which Uncle Bob brought. This is an excellent diversionary tactic, as everyone has to put their heads under the table in case I hit them with the cork. I've never quite mastered the technique of opening champagne without the cork ricocheting around the room, and everyone knows this.

Calm is restored, and lunch continues. I've cooked and peeled chestnuts to chop up and put in with the sprouts. It took bloody hours, and just as I finished Mum helpfully pointed out that you can buy them ready-chopped. Charlie peers at his sprouts with suspicion and begins picking out all the nuts, and I tell him he's being silly. It seems daft to make such a fuss about this, but I end up getting more and more annoyed, and Mum starts to laugh. Dad explains that I once did something similar with almonds in a trifle, and it's very nice to see Charlie carrying on the family tradition of annoying your mother at mealtimes. I gradually calm down, although setting fire to the Christmas pudding proves harder than I thought, and in the end I use so much brandy it looks like the flames will never go out. I eat too much brandy butter and feel sick, but everyone else seems happy and Charlie finds a pound coin in his pudding and is thrilled.

Finally lunch is finished. There is intense lobbying from Charlie for us all to play Snap, but we hold firm and then Lizzie and Matt arrive. They've been to Matt's parents for lunch: not a huge success as Matt's grandmother is not getting any better and hardly recognises anybody now. This time she decided Matt was a burglar and kept throwing brazil nuts at him. More presents are exchanged, and they've brought Charlie a sword that extends to about ten foot long so we all have to keep ducking. It also makes a piercing whistling noise. Lizzie apologises but says Matt was adamant Charlie would adore it. I point out to Matt that if he doesn't find a way to stop the noise he will have his tea in the garden, with Charlie and his new sword. Matt enters into long negotiations with Charlie, and I escape to the kitchen to prepare tea.

The Christmas cake is greeted with much hilarity because Charlie and I decorated it ourselves. I still think my reindeer were very sweet. Charlie insists we have candles, because then it will be like a proper party. Leila rings up and wishes us all Happy Christmas; the Flying Dutchman has flown home to Amsterdam for the holidays so she's staying with friends in a castle in Scotland. She says this sounds a lot more glamorous than it really is, and it's absolutely freezing and she has to wear three pairs of socks and a woolly hat in bed, but apart from that she's having a brilliant time.

Kate also rings, but she's not having such a brilliant time. Lunch was a disaster as her mother insisted that the children should be forced to eat sprouts, which they both hate, and should not be allowed to leave the table until they'd eaten everything on their plates. Kate finally cracked and told her she was a fascist, and took the children off to watch television. Her mother is still sulking, and Kate has been reduced to sucking out the contents of liqueur chocolates.

With a slight shock I realise that I haven't thought about Mack at all today. I've had a lovely time, and feel very happy with life, even without Mack in it. I hope he's enjoying himself – unless he's with a new woman in which case I hope it's a nightmare. I still want it to be him every time the phone rings, and haven't completely overcome my new-found Whitney habit, nor can I listen to Frank Sinatra, especially 'New York, New York'. But there is definitely light at the end of the tunnel. Sort of.

Mum and Dad are staying the night, and are downstairs making supper while I try to get Charlie to go to sleep.

'I think Nana and Grandad really loved my nest, don't you, Mummy?'

'Yes, darling.'

'And do you really love your slippers?'

'Oh yes, they're very lovely.'

Actually this is a downright lie. They're revolting and I can't think what possessed Mum to go for gigantic bunny-rabbit slippers in white fleecy material with tartan-ribbon bows on the ears.

'Yes, I did very clever choosing, didn't I? Nana helped a bit, but I saw them first.'

'Yes, darling, now snuggle down and go to sleep. It's very late.'

'Mummy, I love turkey, don't you? Can we have it tomorrow as well?'

'Yes, Charlie, and the next day too probably.'

'Brilliant. I love you, Mummy. To infinity. How much do you love me?'

'To infinity and beyond.'

'Yes, to infinity and beyond. Now you have to say "And back again".'

'Alright, darling. And back again. Twice. Now shut up and go to sleep.'

A NOTE ON THE AUTHOR

Gil McNeil has worked in advertising, the film business and publishing and is now a director of Hobsbawm Macaulay Communications. She lives in Kent with her son.

A NOTE ON THE TYPE

The text of this book is set in Linotype Sabon, named after the type founder, Jacques Sabon. It was designed by Jan Tschichold and jointly developed by Linotype, Monotype and Stempel, in response to a need for a typeface to be available in identical form for mechanical hot metal composition and hand composition using foundry type.

Tschichold based his design for Sabon roman on a fount engraved by Garamond, and Sabon italic on a fount by Granjon. It was first used in 1966 and has proved an enduring modern classic.